Geoffrey Norman ... *Esquire*, *Forbes*, *Spo* ... *American Way*. He is the Edgar A ... ining author of three previous thrillers, SWEETWATER RANCH, BLUE CHIPPER (published in the UK as BLUE STREAK) and DEEP PURSUIT, all featuring Morgan Hunt. Married, with two children, he divides his time between Vermont and the Gulf Coast.

Blue Light

Geoffrey Norman

First published in Great Britain in 1995
by HEADLINE BOOK PUBLISHING

First published in Great Britain in paperback in 1996
by HEADLINE BOOK PUBLISHING

A HEADLINE FEATURE paperback

10 9 8 7 6 5 4 3 2 1

ISBN 0 7472 4712 9

Typeset by Keyboard Services, Luton, Beds

Printed and bound in Great Britain by
Mackays of Chatham PLC, Chatham, Kent

HEADLINE BOOK PUBLISHING
A division of Hodder Headline PLC
338 Euston Road
London NW1 3BH

For Marsha

One

The senator looked good. His tanned, angular face was framed perfectly by the television screen and he seemed to bask in the kind of harsh light that would have made me wilt like a gardenia in August. He had straight white teeth, a strong chin, level eyes, and one of those haircuts that is supposed to look like you did it yourself, with nail clippers, but is actually the work of a stylist who is knocking down about a hundred dollars an hour.

He was answering questions at a press conference having to do with the budget or something equally large and incomprehensible. But to hear the senator tell it, everything was under control and the situation was not just hopeful but absolutely sunny. It was the dawn of a new age. A time of free beer and wide roads.

'What do you think of him?' Semmes said.

'He's kind of cute,' I said.

'How much do you know about him?'

'I don't pay real close attention to politicians, Nat. Seems like there are short ones and tall ones. Also, fat ones and skinny ones.'

Semmes used the mute button on the remote so that we

could still watch the senator but did not have to listen to him. It was an improvement.

'This one is a rising star, Morgan,' Semmes said. 'One of those people who have the glow. Comes off of him like X-rays. He is the youngest senator ever elected from the State of Florida. Undergraduate at Vanderbilt; *cum laude*. Yale Law where he finished first in his class. He could have waltzed into any of the big firms in the state and started making the kind of obscene money people are willing to pay lawyers these days. Instead, he took a job as a prosecutor with one of the State Attorney's offices where you work long hours for low pay, putting away people the state does not have room enough to keep.'

'Sounds like somebody I should vote for,' I said.

'He was a good prosecutor,' Semmes said firmly. 'No question about it. Real good. Very smart and very tough. These days, in Florida, when a tourist can't get his rental car out of the Miami airport without getting shot, that counts for a lot. The papers loved him. One of those TV news shows – not *60 Minutes* but one of the knock-offs – did a segment on him, playing him up as the two-fisted, crime-fighting DA. You know the script. But it wasn't all that far-fetched. Like I say, he *was* good.'

'And then he moved on to bigger things?' I said.

Semmes nodded, rocked back in his chair, and looked through his office window at the view of the bay. The water was the color of primer paint and broken by whitecaps. A cold front was moving through. The sky was gray and thick and the wind was blowing strong and steady out of the north. The worst kind of Gulf weather in February. It felt good to be inside.

'A senate seat opened up,' Semmes went on. 'He won a tough primary and then an even tougher general election. He was able to run as every liberal's favorite conservative and every conservative's favorite liberal. Nobody could call him "soft-on-crime", so he mixed his reputation as a fighting DA in with a lot of stuff about "compassion" and the "social compact" which translated into more money for the social security people along with fewer muggers to take it away from them. He also ran on making government work for the people instead of the insiders – which is a fairly safe and conventional formula. But he had actual experience, getting convictions against a man who was making a fortune off nursing homes where the help all had phoney credentials and the old ladies sat around in wet pants watching television all day. In other words, he ran a good, tough campaign and, best of all, he didn't have to play a lot of ads attacking his opponents. After he'd won, he was still respected. No easy trick, these days.'

Semmes was still staring at the bay. I recognized the look on his face. Ten per cent of his brain, maybe, was on the conversation he was having with me. The rest was off somewhere else, wrestling with the real problem. He would explain it to me in his own good time.

'How did he do in Washington?' I said, just to keep the conversation going. As wonderful as Semmes had made him sound, the senator was just another cheap politician to me.

'He did fine,' Semmes said. 'He seems to have a feeling for how these things work. He wasn't the brash new kid. The smartest little boy in school, you know, and wasn't it good luck for the nation that he'd gotten there when he did, before things got so screwed up that even he couldn't fix them. The old bulls up there have seen that one over and over again. They would have cut his balls off with a rusty ax.

'So he was cautious and respectful. He kept his mouth shut and he listened. But he was nobody's sycophant. When he voted, he didn't just do what he was told. He made it count. If he sold his vote, then he – by God – ran a hard auction and sold to the high bidder.'

I nodded and remembered what some wise soul once said. *If something sounds too good to be true, then it probably is*. The way Semmes was describing him the senator sounded way too good to be true.

Without turning away from the window and his view of the lead-colored water of the bay, Semmes caught my mood.

'You are skeptical,' he said, 'right, Morgan?'

'Yes,' I said.

'One of those cynics who thinks that politics is hopelessly corrupt. So you don't keep up and you don't vote, right?'

'What can I say, Nat? I don't go to malls and I don't drink Coca-Cola, either. I guess I'm just not a good American.'

'Do you like baseball?'

'Not much.'

'Why not?'

'Too slow,' I said.

'You ever play?'

'A little. But I quit for football.'

'More action, right.'

'That's right,' I said. My lifelong weakness is for action. That's why I do jobs for Nathaniel P. Semmes and was

4

hoping he'd have one for me on this stormy Sunday morning. I needed the action.

'You and the senator have that much in common, anyway,' Semmes said. 'He is a man who doesn't let any grass grow. Even when he was in his period of self-imposed apprenticeship, keeping his mouth shut and generally minding his manners, he was busy. He got on committees that were concerned with things he actually knew about – crime and drugs, social security, agriculture. And he did his homework on the things he didn't know about – foreign policy, defense, and such. He was a busy boy, his first couple of years, but he didn't scream and wave his arms and bite people on the ankle to get attention. So what he got, instead, was respect.'

Semmes paused again and I said something obvious, just to plug the gap.

'Sounds like a shrewd man.'

'That doesn't necessarily make him sinister.' The tone of his voice was the one he uses when he is cautioning someone.

'I know,' I said. 'You're right.' Semmes' mind is a lot more supple than mine. Where I am generally just a wise-ass, he is truly wise. Or something pretty close. I try to learn from him.

'He is ambitious and he has a formidable ego,' Semmes said. 'Otherwise, you don't go into that line of work. If you are going to be a football player, you have to enjoy hitting people. Comes with the territory.'

I nodded.

'But while the senator seemed to have all the usual politician's corpuscles, he did *not* appear to be one of those repulsive narcissists who have bred like goddamned rats the last few years. Not at first, anyway. And that is what I liked about him.'

Past tense, I noticed, but did not say anything and Semmes went on talking. He likes to talk. In some ways, I think, talk is a lubricant for his thinking.

'After a couple of years in Washington, the senator started making himself more and more visible. He gave the occasional tough speech and he tacked a couple of serious amendments on some legislation. People noticed. There were some newspaper stories. He got himself invited to some of those Sunday morning shows where everybody sits around being serious. He made a couple of speeches that people said were "thoughtful". Then, the *Washington Post* published a long, adoring article about him. He got himself re-elected without breaking a sweat and that started talk about how, with a little more seasoning, he might be presidential material. But according to the experts, the first thing he needed to do was either come back here and run for governor or get himself nominated for vice-president so he could get some national recognition.'

'So I'm looking at an American prince,' I said and nodded at the image on the television screen.

Semmes picked up the remote and turned off the VCR. We'd been watching a tape.

'Yes,' Semmes sighed. 'Yes, sir. Daniel Vincent is either a prince of the realm or . . . he's a rapist. You'd be doing me a favor, Morgan, if you'd find out which it is.'

Two

It was a four hour drive from Nat Semmes' office to Tallahassee and it rained the whole way. I had the highway pretty much to myself and I played the Stanley Brothers on the machine in my truck. *Saturday Night & Sunday Morning* was the name of the two-disc set. The Saturday Night part was secular blue grass. Sunday Morning was the gospel stuff. The mournful mountain music seemed right for a cold and rainy Sunday afternoon.

The rain blackened the trunks of the pine trees growing on the low sandy ridges of Panhandle Florida and made their green crowns glisten. A kind of fine gray mist hung in the gaps between the trees so the woods looked like they were smoking, as though the rain might have put out a fire.

In the low ground, between the ridges, the little black-water rivers and the cypress swamps soaked up the rainwater and carried it, like nature's own storm drains, down to the Gulf. With the sun not shining, the swamps looked especially gloomy and forbidding. I consider myself something of a swamp rat; have loved the river bottoms all my life. But today, the swamps looked more haunted than enchanted.

Altogether, it was a nice quiet drive. Good for thinking.

So I thought about the job Semmes had asked me to do. Semmes never *tells* me to do anything. He is a gentleman, the kind who is good at more than wearing properly tailored suits, although he can handle that too. Semmes is invariably correct in his dealings with other people. He despises informality and easy intimacy. But on a job, he had always treated me as an equal. He didn't tell me what he thought I needed to know; he told me everything. In his mind, I was not merely his employee, but his associate.

But he was holding back on me this time and I didn't know why. I didn't know who his client was. Couldn't even say for sure that he had a client. I was driving to Tallahassee to look into a rape charge against Senator Daniel Vincent but Semmes hadn't said he was representing the senator. And it would have been a little out of character if he had been.

No US senator would have any trouble finding a gold-plated lawyer to rescue him from a sea of trouble and Semmes wasn't one of those. I didn't think so, anyway.

I worried over it all the way to the Apalachicola River, where I changed my watch over to Eastern and decided that Semmes would tell me in his own good time. So I thought about other things and listened to the sound of the rubber on the pavement and to Ralph Stanley picking banjo for the ages.

I checked in at one of the chains. Got a second story non-smoker and unpacked. I washed my face then walked outside, in the rain, across the parking lot to a Waffle House. If the American Heart Association runs a 'Ten Most Wanted' list, then the Waffle House chain has got to be right up near the top. They serve things like pork chops and eggs, with grits and buttered toast on the side. You can use up a year's cholesterol ration in one Waffle House meal.

I ordered a large coffee to go. The kid behind the counter carefully secured the lid on the styrofoam cup, then put it into a paper bag along with a paper napkin and a couple of those little envelopes of sugar. By the time I got back to the room, the cup had leaked all over the napkin and the little envelopes of sugar. The bottom of the bag was coated with a kind of coffee-flavored syrup. All styrofoam cups always leak. It is a hard and fast rule.

While I drank my coffee I went through my notebook, looking over some of the things Nat Semmes had told me. I found the name I was looking for. The name of a place, actually, not a person. The Gator Pit Lounge.

I looked up the number in the phone book and dialed it.

'Gator Pit,' the voice said, 'he ain't here.'

'You open?' I said.

'Till dawn,' the voice said, 'if the Sheriff don't close us down.'

'And you're on Moccasin Gap Road, right.'

'One mile east of the Church of the Redeemer,' the voice said.

'Thanks,' I said and hung up.

I opened my book of county maps. It covered every county in western Florida. I had another for southern Alabama. I like spending time in the woods and the maps show all the little section roads and aimless red clay farm roads that you can follow to get back in deep enough to find some woods to yourself.

I ran my finger down the list of road names until I came to Moccasin Gap, then I read off the coordinates. I found them on the map and traced my route back to the interstate. I wrote the directions to the Gator Pit down in my notebook. Also the phone number. Then I finished my coffee. Put on my parka. Turned out the lights. And went back out into the rain.

Moccasin Gap was a narrow two lane that ran like a tunnel through the live oaks and old, straight pines. I didn't have any trouble finding it or the Church of the Redeemer, an austere little clapboard building with a fresh coat of white paint, some carefully pruned azalea bushes out front, and a tidy little graveyard surrounded by a wrought-iron fence in the back. It was modest, I thought, but it was also, no doubt, the absolute center of a few dozen lives.

Probably the Gator Pit was, too. It was a large, ugly building made of cinder block. There were no windows and the parking lot was unpaved and littered with broken glass and flattened beer cans. A half dozen pickups stood near the front door, all of them with gunracks, enough dents and scratched paint to show they had been used hard, and the usual bumper stickers for the Seminoles or the Gators. A weary looking redbone hound sat in the passenger seat of one truck, his mournful, liver-colored eyes fixed on the front door of the roadhouse like he knew it would be a long time before he got home for supper.

The dog watched, with no interest, as I opened the door and went inside.

The place smelled of old, trapped cigarette smoke and sour beer. Except for a fluorescent light over a pool table and a few promotional beer signs behind the bar, it was

10

dark and empty, with unoccupied tables covering half of a floor big enough to be a basketball court. The other half, I guessed, was for dancing. Two men were playing pool at the table and another five or six sat listlessly at the bar, watching television and drinking beer. But it was early, yet. Not even five o'clock.

I took a stool at the bar and waited for service and for my eyes to adjust to the gloom of the place.

'What'll it be?' The bartender was tall and lean, with an angular, bony Panhandle face.

'Beer.'

'Any particular flavor?'

'Whatever is cold.'

He brought me a Budweiser, which is the generic in most honky-tonks. I took a sip from the bottle and looked around the room. It surely did not look like the sort of place where a US senator should be spending his Saturday nights. First, on grounds of propriety, although that doesn't count for much these days, especially among US senators. And second, on grounds of prudence. You'll find North Florida boys in places like this who would fight their mothers on Saturday night. And if she wasn't around, a senator would be even better.

'What time do things get started?' I said to the bartender.

'Depends,' he shrugged. 'Band starts at nine. By ten, it'll be going pretty good. But this is Sunday. Likely to be pretty slow.'

His eyes were narrow and full of natural suspicion. I wanted to get on his good side.

'Your dog out front?' I said. 'The big redbone?'

'Nah. Belongs to Lonnie over there shooting pool.'

11

'Much dog?'

'Lonnie thinks so. According to him, Pete – that's the dog's name – runs bigger than any dog in the county. I don't know if he's that good. Close though.'

'He looks plenty strong.'

'Run all night,' the man said. 'Seen him do it. Or *heard* him do it, anyway.'

'Good mouth?'

'The dog will purely *sing*,' the man said. 'Make the hairs on your neck stand up, just to listen to him. Makes all the other dogs on a race sound like they are just backing him up.'

'I've heard a couple like that,' I said. 'Not many. But a couple.'

And we talked like that for another ten minutes, the bartender and I. About coon dogs and coon hunting. I felt a little shameful, like I was conning him, which I suppose I was. But I did know something about coon hunting. I'd grown up with it and spent enough nights out in the swamps following a pack of hounds that I remembered listening to the wild music of animals going for the kill the way some people remember a Rolling Stones concert.

It was about as incorrect as anything could be, these days, using animals to run down and kill other animals and taking pleasure in the sounds of the chase. You were supposed to be repelled by the whole idea of it and if you weren't, that made you into some kind of monster. I have some of the monster in me, I suppose. I'll take the coon hunters of the world over a lot of their enemies.

So I enjoyed talking with the bartender about dogs we had known and races we had listened to while standing around a fire and passing a jug. But I was looking for a way to change the subject.

I got my chance when he left to serve another customer. When he came back, he asked if I wanted another beer. I shook my head and said, 'I suppose Saturday is the time to be here?'

'That's right. Them concrete walls are bulging. Feels like the place is about to explode.'

'Were you here last Saturday night?'

He gave me a look, then nodded.

'You mind if I ask you a couple of questions?'

'You ain't with the law, are you?'

'No.'

He thought for a moment and said, 'How come you're asking questions about last Saturday night?'

'I'm an investigator.' I always hated saying that. When people used to ask me if I was a 'Green Beret', I'd say no, I wasn't, but my hat was.

'An investigator,' he said. 'Who you working for? Somebody I know, or can you even tell me?'

'A lawyer,' I said.

'Would I know the name?' he said.

'Nathaniel Semmes,' I said, making it sound like a question.

He stared at me for a moment, to see if I was bluffing, then said, 'No shit.'

I shrugged.

'You work for Semmes?'

'Yes.'

'Well,' the bartender said, 'he is a good man and you can't say that about many lawyers.'

'No.'

'I've read about him a lot in the papers.' Which wasn't surprising. Semmes is probably the closest thing to a celebrity lawyer in the Panhandle. He'd handled a number of high-profile cases; not all of them local. Semmes usually won and he took no prisoners.

'He's one tough sumbitch,' the bartender said, admiringly.

'He's that,' I said, 'for sure.'

'So what does he care what went on in some piney woods honky-tonk last Saturday night?'

He thought about his own question, then said, 'It's about Senator Hotrocks, ain't it?'

I nodded.

'Stepped in some shit, did he?'

'I don't know,' I said. 'Semmes told me to come over here and find out what the senator was doing Saturday night.'

'He was doing what everybody else was doing. He was drinking beer and hustling some skirt. Actually, the truth is, *she* was hustling him.'

'Do you know the woman?'

'Comes here every Saturday night,' he said, 'so I can tell you what she drinks. Never caught her name, though.'

'How about the senator?' I said. 'He ever been here before?'

'No. Not that I recall.'

'Surprise you to see him in here?'

'Nah. Not really. He was staying at one of those bird-hunting plantations, on the way up to Thomasville. There's a lot of hot shots pass through those places. General Schwartzkopf was visiting one of them, last year. Jerry

Jones, fellow who owns the Dallas Cowboys. The governor gets invited to one of those places. Shit, Ted Turner *owns* one of them. Jane Fonda invites people in.'

'You ever see her?'

He shook his head. Emphatically. 'Not my kind,' he said. 'But I've seen some of the others. They come in here because this is the rockingest place around and even though it looks like you'd have to check your straight razor at the door, we don't have a lot of trouble. We get a good mix of people. There's FSU, so we get a lot of college kids. Tallahassee is the capital so there's a bunch of Yuppies working for the government or trying to get something out of it. Then, there are a lot of north Florida shitkickers who just like to come in and dance and listen to country music. It's probably the hottest honky-tonk in five counties and if the senator was looking for a place to party after a hard day of bird shooting, then this would be it.'

He paused and smiled.

'That's the long way of telling you I wasn't surprised to see him walk in here.'

'And the woman you were talking about,' I said, 'he meet her right away?'

He smiled, slightly, with one corner of his mouth. 'He didn't *meet* her at all. She took one look at him, recognized who he was, and was on him like a cheap suit.'

'You remember the time?'

He cocked his head, slightly, to think, and said, 'Not exactly. But it was late. Near midnight.'

'And the woman,' I said, 'was she drunk?'

'Not knee walking, no. But she'd had a couple.'

'What about the senator?'

15

He shook his head. 'Nursed one beer. I suspect he gets high on other things.'

'How long were they here together?'

'Every bit of one hour,' he said. 'Not as long as two. Band plays one-hour sets. That's how I keep track of time.'

'Did they dance together?'

'A little. He didn't seem to like dancing. But he got out there a couple of times. Mostly, they stood at the bar and she stayed real close to him and kept looking into his eyes and reaching out to touch his arm when she laughed at something he said.'

'Did they leave together?'

'Nope. He came in with two other men – from the plantation, I suppose – and that's who he left with. Gave me a big tip and thanked me like I'd saved his life or he needed my vote, one or the other. Then he left.

'She stayed around, for about fifteen minutes, looking at her watch. And then she left, too.'

'Alone.'

'Looked like it to me. She came with a girlfriend. Most of them do. I suppose they don't want to look too much like targets. But the girlfriend was still here after the other one had left.'

I took a swallow of beer and thought about what he'd told me.

'I ain't no investigator,' the bartender said, before I could think of another question to ask him, 'but I believe I have figured something out, all by myself.'

'What's that?'

'I believe the senator has himself a small pussy problem.'

16

Which was one way of putting it.

'And I will tell you something else. I don't believe the problem is that he went out one Saturday night and found himself some strange.'

'Why not?' I played along. 'It could hurt him with the voters. Some of them, anyway.'

Like the people whose lives orbited around the Church of the Redeemer, back down the road a mile, I thought.

'Maybe,' the bartender said. 'But I don't think you could find a newspaper or a television show that would pay it any attention. It ain't news any more. Bigger dogs than the senator have done it – done worse – and it didn't hurt them. So it just ain't a big deal any more.'

Sounded right to me. And not a bad thing, either. Of all the methods for deciding how to vote, evaluating the candidates' carnal habits had to be among the worst. Might as well study chicken guts.

'And another thing,' the bartender said, getting into it now, 'if it was about fooling around, I don't believe Nathaniel Semmes would be involved. Way too small.'

I nodded. Right again.

'I believe that before Semmes would get his hands dirty, it would have to be the kind of thing that would purely ruin Senator Hotrocks. Even send him to jail. Murder, maybe. Or rape, most likely.'

'That,' I said, 'would make the papers.'

'Which is it?'

'I didn't say it was either one.'

'No. But you didn't say it wasn't either. If it was murder, then there would have already been stories. And I haven't seen anything. So it has got to be rape.'

'You're making a lot of assumptions,' I said.

Now he shrugged. 'Something to do on a rainy Sunday night,' he said. 'But I'll bet I'm right even if you can't say so. And I'll tell you something else...' He paused and seemed to be thinking deeply on what he would say next.

I waited.

'You ought to get on your horse, ride back home, and tell Semmes to drop this one like a bad habit.'

'Why's that?'

'*Rape*? Shit, you tell me what rape is anymore.' The amiable, half-bored tone was suddenly gone and there was an edge to the bartender's voice and look of real malice on his face.

'She was coming on to him, strong. If I could feel it, then you know the senator damn sure could too. Say she followed him out of here and met him at some motel. And then ... something happens that she doesn't like. He's too fast for her. Or too rough. Or she's drunk and when she wakes up she remembers that she used to be a good little Baptist girl and sing in the choir and now here she is in bed with this man she don't hardly even know. Well, it couldn't be because she's bad. The only way it could have happened is if he forced her. So she says *rape*.'

He shook his head.

'And now what he's got to do is say "No, it was love."'

I didn't say anything. I had been feeling a kind of heavy reluctance about the whole thing and this had to be a part of it. I'd never had anything to do with a rape case and I considered that my good luck. Murder seemed straightforward and clean by comparison.

'You aren't going to find out what the truth is, you know

that,' the bartender said. 'I mean, what it is going to come down to is – he's going to say she wanted it and she's going to say he forced it.

'And you know something else,' there was an acid of righteous anger in his voice now, 'no matter what you find out, the women aren't going to listen. Because according to them, if she said it was rape, then that's all there is to it. End of story. She said it was rape so it was rape.

'The senator would be a lot better off if he'd just gone ahead and killed her.'

Three

I drove back into town. It was still raining. And dark, now. The Church of the Redeemer looked empty and forlorn when I went by.

I was hungry but I didn't feel much like looking around for a good restaurant and then eating alone. So when I saw a Popeye's, in one of those ugly little strip shopping centers, I stopped and ordered a couple of chicken wings, a plate of dirty rice, and a cup of black coffee. I ate at a little plastic table in the flickering light of a fluorescent bulb that had a weak transformer and popped like hot grease. There were some loud kids at one of the other tables. I ate too fast to enjoy the meal.

The motel parking lot had filled up considerably and I had to park a long way from my room. I walked along a bank of rooms to get to the stairway. Some of the occupants had not bothered to pull the curtains and I could see them through the glass, stretched out on the bed, watching television. One of them was a very big man who had stripped down to his boxer shorts and T-shirt. He had turned off all the lights, so the only illumination in the room came from the television. He looked like a corpse, stretched out for viewing in some sad little basement morgue.

I turned on the lights in my room and did not turn on the television. Then I sat at the table and wrote down everything the bartender at the Gator Pit had told me. When I finished with my notes, I picked up the phone and dialed a number I knew from memory. It was long distance. The voice at the other end made the word 'hello' sound cheerful and melodic.

'Hello, Phyllis,' I said. 'This is Morgan.'

'Well how *are* you?' she said.

'Fine,' I said. 'How are you?'

'I'm good, Morgan. But you need to come around sometime and see for yourself. We've been missing you.'

'How're the babies?'

'Getting bigger. They aren't hardly babies anymore, Morgan. It just goes so fast.'

'Give them a hug for me,' I said.

'I will. Now I *know* you didn't call me to talk about babies.'

'Is he there?'

'Out in his shop. Hang on and I'll get him.'

I waited for a few seconds and then heard the sound of Tom Pine's voice, like it was coming from a mine shaft.

'How yew doing, Morgan.'

'Good, Tom. You?'

'Not bad. Tired of this rain. My knees start feeling like they need a shot of WD-40.'

Tom had been an All American and the Packers loved him. But before he could play pro-ball, he ruined his knee. He didn't do it playing football, though. The knee collapsed when he jumped out of a chopper on a hot LZ.

'What can I do for you?' Pine said, before I could tell him

22

I was sorry about the knee. Probably he didn't want to hear it, even conversationally.

I told him I was in Tallahassee.

'Everybody has got to be somewhere,' he said. It was one of the old, standby lines in Vietnam.

'And I'm here,' I said.

'So what can I do for you,' Tom said, 'you being in Tallahassee and all?'

'I need someone to talk to,' I said. 'You got any friends in the department over here?' Tom was a lieutenant in the Escambia Country Sheriff's Department, the highest-ranking black on the force, and a man who people liked to know, or say they knew. There were people he could call, all over the state.

'Are you working?' he said.

'Yes,' I said. 'But I can't tell you much because Semmes isn't telling me anything at all.'

'I see. Well, I do know somebody over there. Frank Swearingen. Used to be a detective in Jacksonville. A real good one.'

'*Used to be?*'

'Well, he came down with a drinking problem.'

'Oh.'

'He wouldn't admit it and he wouldn't quit. "Denial," I believe they call it. Finally got him bounced from his job. Worked as a private investigator for a while until he finally just decided one day that he'd had enough. Quit drinking. Moved. Got a new job. He's the chief investigator for the Public Defender over there. He's well wired, Morgan. Can't help himself; he just likes to know things. I'm all the time calling him on stuff.'

'He sounds perfect,' I said.

'Want me to talk to him?'

'You mind?'

'Give me a number. I'll tell him to call you tonight.'

'I appreciate it, Tom.'

'Call me when you get back,' he said. 'We'll clean some ribs and you can tell me how it worked out.'

I hung up. Watched the rain ticking against the window glass. After five minutes the phone rang.

'Hunt?' a sandpapered voice said.

'Speaking.'

'This is Frank Swearingen. Tom Pine told me to call you, and I do everything Tom tells me to do.'

'I appreciate the call.'

'What can I do for you?' he said. 'You want to get together?'

'Yes.'

'Tonight?'

'If it isn't inconvenient...' I started but he shut me off.

'It's just me and the television and the dog. Everything on television is dumb and the dog doesn't do anything but sleep. I could be at your motel in fifteen minutes.'

'I'll be here,' I said. Then I hung up and went back to watching the rain as it pelted the window like spent birdshot.

Swearingen was a fairly short man with a thick body and face that looked like it had been soaked in brine. He had thin, greasy hair and yellow, smoker's teeth. He was wearing khakis, Nikes, and a plastic raincoat; and he carried a paper bag with a Dunkin Donuts logo.

'Pleased to meet you,' he said. 'Nathaniel Semmes has always been kind of a hero of mine.'

We shook and I offered him a chair. There were only two.

'I ought to hang this up,' he said, meaning the coat. I pointed to the little alcove, off the bathroom, with the aluminum bar and the hangers that you could not remove.

He put the paper bag on the table and hung up his coat.

'I forgot to ask if you wanted coffee,' he said. 'So I got you a cup anyway. You don't want it,' he shrugged, 'you can throw it out.'

The authentic Brooklyn accent sounded almost alien after the bartender at the Gator Pit, who was pure piney woods. The bartender let his words linger, almost lovingly, on his lips; Swearingen bit them off, like a dog crushing bone.

'Coffee sounds good,' I said.

He sat at the table, fished around in the bag, and brought out two large styrofoam cups. Both were leaking around the tops. Swearingen lifted the top on his cup, took a sip, and made a contented sound.

'If it wasn't for coffee,' he said, 'an old alkie like me wouldn't have a chance.'

That didn't seem to call for a response, so I merely nodded.

'Coffee and cigarettes,' he went on. 'Fucking lifesavers. But don't worry. I won't smoke.'

Swearingen had unusual ideas about small talk. I nodded again.

'Tom Pine didn't tell me what, exactly, you wanted. But since he told me who you work for, it doesn't take a fucking rocket scientist to figure it out.'

He sipped more coffee and drummed his yellowed fingers on the table.

'Only thing is,' he went on, 'I can't feature Semmes taking the job.'

'Why not?'

'Same reason you don't find Barbra Streisand dancing in some topless joint,' Swearingen said. 'It's not Semmes' style.'

'That bad?'

'You got your basic male type of human being, accused of rape. So your sympathy level is starting out at about zero. He's white, so you take away some points for that and you're in minus country. Then, make him a United States senator ... now you are down deeper than whale turds.'

'What if he is innocent? He might be, you know.'

'That,' Swearingen said sourly, 'is a minor, trivial, insignificant detail. Nobody gives a shit about that.'

'What do you mean?'

There was a look of exasperation on his rough, pitted face. I suspect he still thought of people like me as dumb hicks. People like Swearingen believe real smarts comes strictly from the streets.

'If they were together – the senator and this babe – and it looks like they were, then people are going to believe what they want to believe, no matter what the jury says. Some people are going to think that she is a trashy, hot pants, little slut. And some people are going to believe that he is a randy, evil bastard who ought to have his nuts cut off.'

'There's a jury,' I said. 'It has a say.'

Swearingen waved a hand, like he was shooing a fly. 'In something like this,' he said, 'nobody except the defendant gives a cold crap what the jury says. For your man Semmes, it is a no-win deal. If the jury comes back with an acquittal, the people who think the senator ought to have his nuts chopped, they'll just say that Semmes got him off. If the jury votes to convict, they'll say "Good deal and how about that sleazebag Semmes, defending a guilty rapist and coming down so hard on that poor woman." Because he will have to come down hard on her. That's what you do when you defend a client in a rape trial. The woman who is saying she was raped . . . you try to make her look like a slut or a liar or both. Win or lose, people hate you. Semmes doesn't need the grief.'

I couldn't argue with him so I didn't try. I sipped coffee and waited for him to go on.

'The only way Semmes could come out shining is to plead the senator guilty and then get him to say how sorry he is and that he wouldn't have ever done it if his mother hadn't been so cold and his father hadn't regularly beat the shit out him. But now that he's remembered all that, and come to terms with it, he's going to be a good citizen, get some counseling, and stop raping women. After that, the senator and Semmes could do the TV shows until it was time for the senator to go off to the jailhouse for a few years.'

'I don't think that's what Semmes has in mind.'

'I'm not surprised,' Swearingen said. 'Question is, what *does* he have in mind? Do you know?'

'Nope.'

'What about you, then? What do you have in mind?'

'I'm trying to find out what happened. See what kind of case there is.'

Swearingen nodded and seemed to be thinking. So far, he hadn't done much thinking. Just talking.

'How much do you know?'

I told him about my talk with the bartender at the Gator Pit.

'Okay,' Swearingen said when I'd finished. 'Now you want me to pick it up for you, later that night, early Sunday morning, to be precise?'

I nodded.

'Well,' he said, trying – without much success – to settle himself in the cheap motel chair, 'about six in the morning, a local rape crisis center gets a call from a woman. Hysterical. They get her calmed down, give her directions to the emergency room, and the woman who runs the center goes over there to meet her.'

Swearingen drained his coffee cup and looked into it like he wished he hadn't. Now he would have to get through the next few minutes without coffee or cigarettes. Not to mention whiskey. It was hard.

'The woman who runs the place is named Dixie Price,' he said dreamily. 'Never could figure why somebody would name a kid "Dixie".'

'Better than "Yankee",' I said.

He gave me a tired look.

'Yeah, well ... Dixie Price is stronger than onions. She has been running that center for about five years now. She is there every Saturday night, all night, because that's when business is strongest. She went over to the hospital and met the woman and when she saw that there weren't any broken bones or missing teeth, she took the woman back to the center with her and listened to her story. That's one of the things she does,' Swearingen said, 'she gets the victims to talk about it.'

I nodded.

'This one said she had met the senator at the Gator Pit and that they had talked and danced and had a couple of drinks together and that she thought he was "nice". After a while, she said, they both felt like going somewhere a little quieter. They were having such a nice time talking, don't you see.'

Swearingen sighed and shifted his bulk in the little, uncomfortable chair.

'The senator said it probably wasn't a good idea for them to leave together and she said she could understand that. But he was staying at one of those rich folks' hunting plantations a few miles up the road and he had the guest house all to himself. Maybe he could leave and then, a few minutes later, she could follow him there. She said that sounded like a nice idea.

'The directions were complicated and she nearly got lost a couple of times, trying to follow those little dirt roads, out in the woods. But she found the place. And the senator was still up, waiting for her. He'd even chilled the wine.

'But he got ugly, according to the woman, and when she tried to hold him off, he got mean. She was afraid that if she tried to fight him, he would hurt her bad. Maybe kill her. So...'

Swearingen shrugged and raised his hands, palms up.

'When he was finished, he threw her out. She was a mess. Crying and hyperventilating so she couldn't remember where she was or how she got there. This time she did get lost. By the time she made it back to town and found a phone, it was nearly dawn.'

Swearingen stopped talking, sighed, and looked out at the fat raindrops hitting the window glass.

'Was she hurt bad?' I said.

'Some bruises,' he shrugged. 'Could have been from a struggle.'

'What else could it have been from?'

'Somebody who likes it a little rough.'

'Did they do any tests?'

He nodded. 'She'd had intercourse recently. But that's no big deal.'

'Why not?'

He shrugged. 'Senator could say, "Yeah, we did and we both thought it seemed like a good idea at the time." No law against a quick, loveless fuck on a Saturday night.'

I stood up and stretched and thought, for a moment, about what Swearingen had told me.

'Did she ever report it to the law?'

'Nope.'

'So there aren't any charges?'

'None so far.'

'Then I wonder what I'm doing here.'

'Ask me another one,' he said and stood up to get his raincoat.

Four

I was up early. The cold front had moved east and the hard
rain had eased to a cold drizzle. The clouds were still too
heavy for the sun to break through, so dawn came in as gray
and thick as laundry lint. In the weak light, I ran a path
around the campus of Florida State, dodging the puddles
and wiping the mix of cold rainwater and warm sweat from
my face and eyes.

The red brick dormitories and classroom buildings
looked depressingly modern and institutional. But that
could have been the weather. Or my mood. Or both. Still,
it seemed like a place of learning ought not to look like an
industrial park where they assembled wiring harnesses or
solenoids. There ought to be vast old spreading trees and
aging stone buildings with tall windows and slate roofs and
a little ivy growing on the shady surfaces.

But, then, this was Florida. And most things in Florida
are built to look like they could fit right in at any strip
shopping center. Schools. Churches. Even the jails.

I did five miles, then went back to my room for a shower,
dressed, and left again for breakfast. It was a quarter to
seven when I parked at a place called 'The Coffee Cup', on
a side road leading into the old part of town. I bought a

31

newspaper before I went in and was checking the front page when the waitress arrived at my table.

'Coffee for you this morning?'

'Please.'

She left and was back in a few seconds with the pot and an empty mug which she filled. The coffee steamed in a satisfying way.

'Thanks,' I said.

'You're welcome, hon. Now do you know what you want, or should I bring you a menu?'

I asked for eggs, over easy, sausage, and grits. I like breakfast.

There was nothing in the paper about Senator Vincent. Strange they hadn't picked up on it yet. When they did, it would be feeding time at the zoo. I wondered, again, why Semmes wanted any part of it.

These days, courtroom trials and rock concerts do what the circus did for the Romans. They entertain a bored, ignorant, and slightly bloodthirsty citizenry. But Semmes had always thought of himself as a good country lawyer; not a gladiator. Much as I like the action, I sort of hoped that in this case there wouldn't be any.

'Here you go hon,' the waitress said and put the eggs in front of me. I put the paper away, put a little tabasco on the eggs and a pat of butter on the grits, then went to work. It was a good, country breakfast and I enjoyed every bite. I gave the waitress a generous tip and left 'The Coffee Cup' feeling like I was right with God.

The day started with Dixie Price. Her office was in a little stucco house on a street that might have once been prosperous and busy but was now just old and faintly shabby. The stucco on her house was flaking and the front door was warped so she had to force it open with her shoulder. The flowerbeds were grown up with weeds and the shrubbery needed trimming. A few bruised camellias bloomed on one bush. Otherwise, the yard looked derelict.

'Frank Swearingen told me about you,' she said, looking at me as though I were the enemy of all things decent. 'Come on in.'

I stepped into a small, dark room and said, 'I appreciate your seeing me.'

'I don't know how much help I'll be,' she said, standing with her arms folded, as though to stop me from coming any further inside. 'Until now, I've always admired your Mr Semmes. I can't believe he's going to defend that creep.'

She looked strong and defiant with a wide face and light brown, almost red, hair, cut very close and parted low so that it ran across her head and covered one ear. There was a small, gold loop in the other ear. She wore a very faint shade of lipstick and no eye makeup. There was a lot of conviction in that face. Righteous conviction. It was the face of a prosecutor who never doubts.

'I don't know for sure that he is,' I said.

'Then why are you here?'

Good question, I thought.

'He asked me to come over and see what I could find,' I said. 'And that's what I'm doing.'

'What's to investigate if he isn't representing that *man*?' She made the word sound like it described something unclean.

'I don't know,' I said. 'I just do what he tells me.'

'Like a good soldier, right?' She wasn't smiling.

'I suppose so,' I said.

'Well, you're wasting your time. There probably won't be any need for Mr Semmes' talents.'

'Why not?'

'Because, right now, the victim is afraid to press charges.'

'Why?'

'Oh come on. You're not really that stupid, are you?'

'I can be pretty stupid,' I said. 'Is she afraid someone will hurt her?'

Her eyes narrowed a little. 'Well, now, that is always a possibility in a rape case. If you've already done that to a woman, then just beating her up a little doesn't seem like such a big deal. Women have to learn when to keep their mouths shut, right?'

I didn't argue with her. No point in it.

'But senators don't have to resort to physical threats, do they? Prominent men, rich men, they don't threaten to beat you up if you go to court; they threaten to beat you up when you get there. Actually, they won't do it themselves; their lawyers will do it for them. First you get raped; then you go to court where you are violated again. Is that a great system, or what?'

It made no difference to her whether I agreed or not. So I nodded.

'Well,' she said, 'if we're going to talk, you might as well come in and sit down. We'll talk in my office.' She made it sound like a concession.

I followed her through a small room with two couches, a television, and a coffee table littered with magazines. It looked like the waiting room of some third-rate lawyer, except for the posters on the walls. One was a photograph of a woman being forced on to a couch by a man. The print above the picture read, 'A date is not an invitation to rape.' Another showed a cartoon figure of a woman putting her knee into a cartoon man's crotch. The caption read, 'When he won't take *no* for an answer, make sure he gets the point.'

There was another small room off this one. It held a wooden desk, covered with papers, files, and message slips. There was a computer on a small table next to the desk. A phone and answering machine next to the computer. More posters on the wall. A small window with no curtains. She pointed to a chair with faded upholstery and said, 'Have a seat.'

I did.

She sat behind the desk and looked at me; her eyes full of hostility, bordering on loathing. The light was better in here. I could see that she had fair, smooth skin and straight white teeth. I was careful not to look too close.

'Now, then,' she said, 'you're looking for evidence, right?'

I nodded.

'Have you ever investigated a rape before?'

'No.'

'Ever been involved in one?' she said. It was like being slapped.

'No.'

'Are you sure?'

I could have told her that I'd been pretty close to a couple but those had been men raping men. But this wasn't *Crossfire* and I wasn't here to make cheap debating points. If I had to listen to a little sermon before she would tell me what I'd come to learn ... well, small price. I'd put up with worse. Anyway, not my fault I was born male.

'Maybe you haven't,' she said, after the silence had hung there between us for a while. 'But you need to know that we don't take that on faith, around here, anymore. When we have to work with men who are investigating a rape, we don't just assume that they're our natural allies. They could just as easily be the enemy.'

'Okay.'

'You're probably feeling angry,' she said.

Actually I was feeling more bored than anything else. But I didn't say so. I didn't say anything, which was all right, since she had a speech to make and was getting on with it.

'You're wondering what gives me the right to ask you that kind of question and make you defend yourself when you haven't done anything wrong. Well, think about the woman who came in here after she was raped by that great statesman. She'll go through exactly the same thing, only worse, because it will be in court, under oath, and she'll have to answer some four-hundred-dollar-an-hour lawyer's insinuating questions about how many men she's slept with and what color panties she wears. That's the way it works and we don't like it.'

We? I guess she was speaking for her organization. Or maybe for all women.

'Do you understand that? Can you *try* to understand it?'

'Yes.'

She gave me another of her hard, suspicious looks. 'I'd like to believe that,' she said.

I nodded. It was hard, I'm sure.

'So what do you want to know?'

'If there is evidence of rape, I'd like to hear about it.'

She shook her head. 'There is no "smoking gun" in a case like this. The rapist puts it back in his pants.'

I nodded again.

'It would be nice if the weapon could be tagged and bagged. Checked for fingerprints and test-fired to get a match. But there isn't any hard evidence ...'

She stopped and smiled and said, 'Pardon the expression.'

'Sure,' I said. 'But you'll need something that will stand up in court.'

She looked puzzled at first, then she smiled. And then she put her head back and laughed.

'"Stand up in court,"' she said, still smiling. 'That's pretty good.'

'Thank you.'

'Did I come on too strong? I did, didn't I?'

'I don't know.'

'Well, look, I know it isn't your fault, personally, but I've been doing this for a long time now and I say a plague on all the goddamned lawyers who defend rapists by violating the victims. And a plague on all the goddamned investigators who work for them. Sorry, but that's the way I feel. It's a war and we're on different sides.'

'Fair enough.'

'What I just don't understand is how Semmes could do it. Why does he want to take this case, can you tell me that?'

'He hasn't told me. Like I say, he hasn't even told me for sure that he is taking the case. I don't know for a fact that Vincent is Semmes' client.'

'All right, then, tell you what. Go back and tell your Mr Semmes that you and I have talked and that I am not some crazy, hysterical witch and that I know my business. I know there are women who will cry *rape* when there was consent and plenty of it. It happens. Not as often as men like to think; but it happens. I've seen it a couple of times.

'But this is *not* one of them. No way, shape, or form. This woman is not lying. Not in a million years. I was with her that morning, and what I saw can't be faked. She was traumatized. Still is. That's why she hasn't gone to the police.'

'Do you want her to go to the police?' I said.

'You bet. Even though it is hard on the woman. Hard and degrading, I want the men to know that they are going to have to stand up in court and, just maybe, go to prison, even if it isn't anywhere near long enough, if they rape a woman. I want to lock those bastards up; fill up the prisons with them. Maybe while they're inside, they'll get a taste of their own medicine. Wouldn't *that* be nice for Vincent?

'So, yes, I try to get every woman who comes in here to press charges and tell her story in court. Of course, I also tell all of them what a tough road it is. Sometimes I'll talk a woman out of pressing charges, but I have to be honest with them. The next time I talk to this woman, I'll have to tell her that it looks like Vincent has hired one of the best lawyers in the state and she can expect a hard goddamned time on the witness stand and in the newspapers. She's afraid, already, so this will probably finish it. Wouldn't that be nice for Vincent? He gets off just by waving his lawyer at the woman he raped. No publicity. No bad press for him or for Semmes. Costs him a few thousand, I imagine, but he can afford it. And his political career just keeps rolling along. This doesn't amount to a pothole on his road to glory. Like I told you, it's a great system we've got here. Really great.'

Five

Dixie Price probably wasn't any happier about our talk than I was. Before I left her office, I'd asked her for the name of the woman. She laughed.

Actually, I was just going through the motions. I don't know what I would have asked the woman if Dixie Price had given me her name. I knew what her story was and it seemed likely that she would stick to it. Semmes might break her down on the witness stand – which wasn't a very pretty picture in my mind – but I wasn't likely to do it in an off-the-record interview.

I drove out of the fading neighborhood where Dixie Price worked, wondering what I should do next. It was way too early for lunch and I didn't have any other good ideas. Ordinarily, when I work for Semmes, there are more things to do than there is time for doing them. Seems like there is always one more lead to follow up or one more person to talk to. But in this case, there weren't any witnesses to what had – or hadn't – happened. You could talk to the woman and you could talk to the man and then you could decide whose story you believed. Which is, I suppose, what most rape trials come down to.

Before I'd left his office, Semmes had told me to forget

about the senator. That left the woman. I was telling myself that there wasn't any point in talking to her but I knew that was horseshit. I was just stalling.

So I decided to drive out north of town, into the country, to take a look at the hunting plantation where the rape was supposed to have occurred. I might get an idea.

I took a narrow, winding two lane that took me out of town, past the usual car lots flying plastic pennants, the strip malls, and the restaurants selling franchised fast foods. Then it was the suburbs, looking newer and rawer and more expensive the further you got from town. I knew I had reached the perimeter when I passed a D-9 cat methodically knocking down the stumps of freshly cut pines and pushing them into a pile where they would be burned.

Then, very quickly, the suburbs became the country. The houses weren't brick split-levels any longer, with central heat and air and lots of glass. Out here, the houses were made of rough-cut pine boards and a lot of them were so rundown that the satellite dish out back, next to the chinaberry tree, was worth more than the house.

This was the old south, not that far removed from the days when families farmed on shares, nobody had any money, and all the kids had hookworm. I passed an old store, which hadn't been painted since Kennedy was president, with rusting Nehi and Dr Pepper signs nailed on the walls. It took me back to a world before WalMart.

I followed the highway to an unmarked crossroads and turned. After a mile or so, I was no longer on pavement, but a hard-packed, red clay road that ran through the tall, somber pines. There was a wire fence on either side of the road and every few feet, on one of the fence posts, there was a square steel sign, neatly lettered. The signs prohibited trespassing and stated that the property was patrolled by Plantation Security Systems.

I didn't see any plantations but, then, you wouldn't build one that people could see from the road.

I crossed a sagging old wooden bridge over a swollen slough, then went around a wide, slow curve in the road. Where it straightened out, there was a gate with a small, discreet sign that read 'Ewell' in an ornate script. A larger sign, in block lettering, said it was a private drive. Furthermore, it added, 'Keep Out'. I turned up the drive.

For a mile or so, it led through more of the same kind of country – tall, straight pines that were widely spaced with live oaks and dogwood growing here and there, in the gaps. Various grasses covered the ground and, in some places, the broomweed was so thick and tall it looked almost like western grainfields.

Then the ground rose gradually and when the road took a turn I could look up ahead and see a large white house at the top of a hill. It was built in the Greek Revival style, just like the authentic plantation houses which some people seem to think were as common in the old south as double wide trailers are today. If there had been as many plantations of that sort as there are people who claim their ancestors owned one, then the Yankees would never have been able to burn them all down. Sherman would still be stalled somewhere between Atlanta and Savannah, setting fire to plantations.

Still . . . just looking at this replica, built on the top of this insignificant Panhandle hill, you could see why the style has such appeal. It was a striking house. Both formidable and restrained. It had dignity and gravity and it seemed to require a lot of land around it. The house would look absurd on a five-acre lot. It needed an uncluttered vista.

I was trying to watch the house and the road when I realized something had pulled up next to me. I looked over my shoulder and saw a man riding one of those little buggies with the big tires. All Terrain Vehicles, I believe they are called. It was on my rear fender and the driver was racing to catch up with me. He was wearing a cowboy hat. When he saw me looking at him, he motioned for me to pull over.

I did.

He went on by me and stopped the little buggy in the middle of the road, got off and started walking back my way. He wore cowboy boots and levis and walked with his legs bowed and his weight forward like he'd spent the day on a horse. He had a large bushy moustache and one cheek bulged with tobacco.

'There's a sign,' he said, around the chew, 'I don't believe it would be possible to miss it.'

I was standing next to the truck. He was less than two feet from me when he stopped. Too close. He was in my space and that was the point.

'I'm here to see Mr Ewell.'

'That a fact?' he said. Still close. He was shorter than I am. By half a foot. But he didn't mind getting close and looking straight into my eyes. I felt like one of the boxers at a weigh-in, where they pretend to stare each other down for the excitement of the crowd.

'You got an appointment?' he said.

'No.'

'He expecting you?'

'No.'

'Then why don't you make like horseshit and hit the trail?'

One of those.

'You do some kind of work around here?' I said.

'I am the manager,' he said, making it sound very important.

'Then maybe you could tell Mr Ewell that I'm working on an investigation for Mr Semmes and that I'd like to talk to him.'

'Like I told you,' he said, 'I am the manager. I am *not* the secretary. You want an appointment, you make it yourself. I got better things to do. The rain is letting up and I believe that some of the gentlemen here will be wanting to go out and do a little hunting. So you run along. You want to talk to Mr Ewell, then call first and set it up. Maybe he'll see you and maybe he won't.'

'It's about Vincent,' I said. 'Daniel Vincent. The senator.'

'I know him,' the man said. 'He stayed here last week.' That was a big source of his strutting pride. He worked at a place where senators came to play.

'You remember what he was doing last Saturday night?'

'Hey,' the man said, switching the chew to his other cheek, 'it wasn't my turn to watch him.'

He stepped even closer and put his hand out and let his finger tips touch my chest, without much pressure.

'Now you'd better run along,' he said.

'And you'd better take your hand off me.'

We glared at each other. He held the stare for several seconds, long enough that he could take his hand away from my chest without losing face. It was chickenshit stuff, I suppose, that we both carried around in our genes. Wolves threaten each other the same way.

Once his hand was off me, and back at his side, the tension eased and there was less electricity in the air.

'Are you,' he said, very slowly, 'going to leave this property?'

'I'm on my way,' I said.

That satisfied both of us and followed the rules of ritual display. He stepped back, out of my space, and I turned and got back in my truck.

We'd done a good job, I thought, as I got the truck turned around and drove off the Ewell property. We had made it through the crisis with just a little growling and baring of teeth and pissing on each other's ground. No fists, no knives and, best of all, no guns. The wolves have a good system. The big city gang kids could learn a lot from them.

I had been as close to the scene of the crime – assuming that there had been a crime – as I was going to get without an invitation or a warrant. But it probably didn't matter. I wasn't likely to learn anything here. There wouldn't be any physical evidence.

Her word against his. That is what it came down to. Just now, I couldn't talk to him. Semmes had told me Vincent was in Washington, doing the nation's business, and I should leave him alone. So it would have to be the woman. I needed to talk to her.

Which meant I had to learn her name and, probably,

where she lived. Or, even, where she might be hiding. Dixie Price might have her stashed away somewhere.

But first the name. I could worry about finding her safe house after I had the name.

I considered several different plans as I made my way back to the black top and on south to town and my little motel room.

When I got there, I sat on the bed and used the phone. For some reason, motels will not put a long cord on the telephone so you can drag it across the room and make your calls sitting in a chair with your papers spread out in front of you at a table. One of those little aggravations, like leaky coffee cups.

I dialed the county hospital and asked for the Emergency Room.

'This is Steve Hawkins,' a young, but firm voice said. 'How may I help you?'

'This is Lewis Ferguson,' I said. 'I am an investigator with the governor's special task force on sexual crimes.'

'Yes sir.'

'I need to ask you a few quick questions, Steve,' I said, 'and I was hoping this would be a good time. Are things fairly quiet?'

'Real quiet,' he said. 'We haven't had an admission yet this shift.'

'I see. So you can talk? It will only take a minute.'

'Yes sir.'

'Good. Now I need some information about a patient you had there early Sunday morning of last week. About six.'

'I was on duty then.'

'Good,' I said. 'But actually, what I need will come straight off the admissions paperwork. We have been contacted by a woman – and her lawyer – and she claims to have come in to the Emergency Room early Sunday morning after she was raped. She says she was examined and then released. I need to verify that.' I tried to sound slightly impatient; as though this were a minor, clerical nuisance cluttering up my agenda of important duties.

I could hear the sounds of papers being shuffled in the brief pause that followed. Then he said, 'I have the logs right here.'

'Okay,' I said. 'Just read off the name and the times when she was admitted and discharged.'

'Lisa Hutchinson,' he said, without hesitation. Then he read off the times.

'Is that all?' he said.

'Yes,' I said. 'I just needed to verify that information.' I was tempted to ask for an address and phone number but I decided not to press it. I thanked him and hung up. Governor's special task force on sexual crimes, my ass.

I'd written the name in my notebook. Now I moved from the bed to the table to look up the name in the phone book. There was only one Lisa Hutchinson. I dialed the number. It rang twice, then a woman answered. She sounded impatient.

'I need to send a fax,' I said. 'Before the end of the day.'

'What?' the voice said.

'This is Custom Copiers?' I said, trying to sound flustered.

'Not hardly.'

'I'm awful sorry,' I said. 'I must have dialed the wrong number.'

'I guess you did,' the woman said. Then hung up.

Somebody was home and maybe it was Lisa Hutchinson. I copied the number and the address in the book. Then I looked up the street on my map. It was just off the Florida State campus, not far from where I done my running earlier in the morning. I checked my watch. Not quite noon.

I parked on the street where Lisa Hutchinson lived, in one of those apartment buildings that spring up sudden as mushrooms. They are all stick lumber and sheetrock; stapled together instead of nailed; and after a strong wind there is nothing left but the slab.

This one was occupied chiefly by FSU students. It was close to the campus and it had to be relatively cheap. There was no landscaping to speak of. Not even a couple of flowerbeds or a few shrubs. It had been a while since the trash had been picked up.

There were fifteen buildings in the complex and four apartments to each building. I found her building and went inside. Her name was on one of the mailboxes. I pushed the button underneath it and heard a buzzer in one of the second floor apartments. I took the stairs and was waiting on the landing when one of the doors came open a few inches and a voice said, 'Who is it?'

'Miss Hutchinson?' I said.

'Who are you?' She had the south Georgia, wiregrass accent. So softly cadenced that even if she was telling you to pack sand, it would sound like she was apologizing.

'My name is Hunt,' I said. 'Morgan Hunt.'

'So?' She did not open the door. Campuses seem to draw the sick specimens who wash back and forth across Florida, like trash on a tide. They have killed a dozen or more college women in the last few years. Even if she hadn't been raped, Lisa Hutchinson would have been likely to keep the chain on the door.

'I am an investigator,' I said. 'I can show you some identification.'

'Why are you here?'

'I'd like to talk to you about last weekend.'

'Who sent you?' she said. 'Are you from the police? I don't want to talk to no police.'

'I'm not with the police. I work for a lawyer.'

'I don't want to talk to no lawyer, either. I don't want to talk to anybody.'

'Miss Hutchinson,' I said, making my voice as soothing as I knew how, 'I suspect that, sooner or later, you are going to have to talk to somebody about last weekend. Whatever you say to me will be confidential. It can't hurt and it might even help.'

'How?'

'Some people think better when they think out loud,' I said. 'And some people think better when they get good advice.'

'I'm supposed to listen to your advice?'

'Not mine. But the man I work for ... The people who listen to his advice usually aren't sorry.'

I hadn't been, anyway.

'What's his name?'

'Semmes,' I said. 'Nathaniel Semmes.'

'I think I've heard of him.'

'You probably have.'

She didn't say anything for a few seconds. But neither closed the door nor unbolted it.

'Why,' she finally said, in a much softer, almost pleading voice, 'does he want to talk to me?'

I told her, gently, that if she would allow me to come in, I would explain it to her. Which, of course, was a lie. I still didn't understand myself.

Six

She was tall and there was something fleshy and ripe about her, although she was anything but fat. She was dressed in loose jeans and a large sweatshirt, but when you looked at her you thought instantly of the women wearing bikinis in the beer commercials, put there to provide jiggles.

She had blonde hair and lots of it but it was the mass and not the color, a sort of dirty straw tone, that struck you. Her face was a little round but she was still pretty. Not beautiful, but pretty. She looked like a lot of the cheerleaders and baton twirlers and beauty queens who come out of the small towns in Georgia. But she was a little older and a little wiser too, in a certain sense of that word. You could look at her and tell that she knew what she wanted and had learned how to use what assets she had to get it. She had a way of looking at you that made it clear she was evaluating you and deciding just how much effort you were worth.

Once I was inside the apartment, she came around me and I could smell perfume. A lot of perfume. I'm no expert but this did not smell like the vintage stuff.

She sat down on a couch and nodded for me to take the

53

opposite chair. There was not much furniture in the apartment and it all looked like it came from one of the discount places that specialize in dealing with students. There were some posters on the walls. A CD player and a few discs on a stand in the corner. No bookshelves or books. No rugs. It all looked very lonesome and temporary.

She looked at the card I gave her and then read through the 'To Whom It May Concern' that Semmes had given me before I left. It did not say much – 'investigating a confidential legal matter ... any assistance you might provide would be greatly ... etc. etc.' – but it came on imposing looking stationery. She handed it back and said, 'Why is he interested? Does he want to be my lawyer?'

'I don't know,' I said.

'I might need a lawyer, if I decide to press charges on this thing.'

I nodded.

'I don't know if I want to or not, but if I do ... I'll need a lawyer, for sure.'

'Yes,' I said. 'You probably will.'

She looked at me for a long time, then said, 'Why should I talk to you?'

The correct answer to that question was, of course, that there was no reason at all. In fact, she shouldn't talk to me and if another lawyer were here in the spare little apartment with us, he would advise her not to give me the time of day or even tell me where to buy a wristwatch. But there was nobody here to advise her and she wanted a reason. So I gave it my best.

'Like the letter says,' I told her, 'anything you say to me

will be held in strict confidence. That comes from Mr Semmes and you can rely on it. There isn't a lawyer in the state who is more respected.

'If you do decide to hire a lawyer, you couldn't do any better than Mr Semmes. He is honest and he works hard and he wins. There was an article about him, a couple of years ago, in *People*,' I said, although it hadn't been about him, actually, but about a case he'd tried. There was a picture, taken outside the courthouse. And some generic stuff about Semmes. He had politely, but firmly, declined to talk to the reporter.

'I could get you a copy of the story,' I said.

She shook her head.

'In these cases,' I went on, 'where there is a lot of publicity, you'll see all kinds of people involved who are looking out for themselves, trying to cut themselves a piece of the pie. Semmes isn't like that. He doesn't think about anybody but his client. Nothing else matters to him.'

'You'd say that,' she said. 'But you work for him.'

'And before I worked for him,' I said, 'he was my lawyer.'

'Were you in trouble?'

'Worse,' I said, 'I was in prison.'

'What for?' she said and I told her the story. It isn't something I enjoy telling, certainly not to strangers and I didn't like my reasons for deciding to tell it to her. But I did it anyway.

I had beaten a man to death. On the facts, I was unquestionably guilty. The man I killed had been married to my sister. He was a sportsman with a vast trust fund and the kind of languid good looks that can get you a job doing cologne ads. In private, he was an insecure, spoiled, bad-tempered coward who made himself feel better by hitting women. My sister put up with it as long as she could, then left and came to stay with me. He took that as an insult and followed her. When I walked in and saw her bloody face, I lost it. He tried running and he tried begging but neither worked.

My first lawyer, a public defender, tried to get me to take a deal but I played proud. I didn't think – and still don't – that I was guilty of anything. The jury disagreed and took about thirty minutes to do it. They never even sent out for sandwiches.

Semmes read about the case and went to work. My war record, he said later, got his attention. He decided against going for an appeal and a new trial since there hadn't been enough of a trial in the first place to create much opportunity for error. And, anyway, he could see I wasn't interested in whether the system decided I was technically innocent or technically guilty. All I wanted was out.

'I believe we can sell a pardon,' Semmes had said the first day he met me, at Holman prison, in Alabama, where I was stacking time. Very slowly.

'I want to make the governor see that it is an embarrassment for the state to be holding a man with your background in prison when there are so many others – a lot of them with offices just down the hall from his – who are so much more deserving.'

I told him I would take whatever he could get. I wasn't so proud anymore.

So he went to work and since there wasn't a lot I could do to help him, I watched him work and I learned first to

respect him and then to admire him and, finally, to ...
might as well say it, to *love* the man. I would flatly do
anything for him.

While the final negotiations for my pardon were going
on, some advisor to the governor had wondered what I
would do to make myself a useful citizen in the free world.
Most of my work experience, up until then, had been as a
soldier and there was less and less call for them these days,
even though there still seemed to be lots of wars. One of
those mysteries.

Anyway, Semmes told the governor's man that he would
give me work, as an apprentice investigator in his office,
just across the state line, in Florida. I took to the work and
these days, when Semmes says 'frog', I jump.

She listened to the story without interrupting or even
taking her eyes off me. When I finished, she said, 'He
sounds like a good one.'

'He is.'

'If I needed somebody, would he take me?'

'I don't know, for sure,' I said.

'If I tell you what happened, will you tell it to him?'

'Absolutely.'

'All right, then.'

She started her story at the Gator Pit and made it sound
like she had stopped off there, with a friend, after church.
Maybe for a glass of milk. I wanted to ask her if she went
there a lot and what she ordered and what she was wearing
– all the questions any ordinary prosecutor would be
asking, but I decided not to. I didn't want to rattle her. I
was more interested in the sound of the whole story than
the inconsistencies within it.

She told me about meeting Vincent when he came into the Pit, late on Saturday night. She managed to make it sound almost wholesome. They talked. About 'things'. And they danced. He seemed 'real nice'.

But it was loud in the Pit, she said, too loud to talk. She said this almost as though it came as a surprise. They were having a sort of serious conversation. She had told him how her mother had just died and he said he knew what she was going through because his wife had died not long ago. But it was hard to hear anything in the Pit, so he had said they ought to go someplace quieter, where they could talk.

I wondered if he had brought that line out in a wheelchair.

When she agreed that it would be nice to find that quiet place where they could talk, he told her about the guest house where he was staying. It wasn't that far, he'd said, but the directions were kind of complicated.

'He wasn't lying about that, anyway,' she said. 'I made so many turns and got back so deep on those little farm roads that I didn't know *where* I was.'

But she did find the house, I said.

Yes. She found the house.

'I knew it was the right place because of the car. He was driving a rental. From Avis. It had the little red sticker on the back window. They used to have the special plates, you know, but they quit that on account of all the tourists, down in Miami, getting killed. You remember?'

'Yes,' I said.

She parked next to the Avis rental. It was a Buick, she remembered, and went inside where the senator was waiting for her.

'He had this bottle of champagne,' she said, even though they had been drinking beer back at the Pit.

Champagne. This Vincent was some kind of stud. Good to know he was up there in Washington, writing rules for the rest of us.

But right away, she went on, she noticed something different about him. He was in a hurry. Real impatient, you know. She almost expected him to look at his watch. They weren't talking about her dead mother and his dead wife anymore and he didn't have the same sad, faraway look in his eyes anymore, either. He was looking right at her. It was a kind of creepy look, too. Bright and eager. She was raised on a farm and the look made her think of animals. It was like the way one of the pit bulls her daddy kept looked at a chicken.

'I got real nervous,' she said. 'I ... well, I *know* about men. I'm not some kid. But that was kind of scary. And it wasn't just the way he was looking at me, either. A lot of it was how much he'd changed and how sudden it was.'

But she sat in the chair across the room from him, sipping her champagne and trying to make conversation. When she would say something, he wouldn't say much of anything back. A word or two. He might say, 'really', or 'fascinating' and then he would grin and show her a lot of very white teeth.

'Just like a wolf,' she said.

I doubted that she'd ever seen a wolf on her daddy's farm. But I got the picture.

'When I finished the champagne, I put the glass down, real soft, and I said that I thought it was probably time for me to be getting back because my roommate might be getting worried about me. I don't know why I said that, except maybe I wanted him to think there was somebody out there who was thinking about me and would notice if I was gone. I guess I was really scared.'

She stood up and, when she did, he came across the room at her. He moved very fast. Like he was closing in for the kill. She tried to back away from him but he was too fast. When he put his arms around her, she tried to break free and he pushed her hard, so her head hit the wall. It stunned her.

He was on top of her then and he seemed so strong that she didn't know how to fight back. When she screamed, he slapped her. Everything went blurry.

He was very fast. It was almost like there was this terrible thing inside of him that he had to get rid of; not like he enjoyed it at all. It was just an urge, like with the animals back on the farm. Something you had to get done before you exploded.

When he was finished he just got up, off the floor, and without looking at her, said, 'Put your clothes on and get out.' When she hesitated, he shouted, '*Right fucking now.*'

She dressed as fast as she could and went outside and got in her car. Didn't even put her shoes on.

He didn't say anything, didn't even look at her, when she left. She got in her car and drove back out the way she came but she was so rattled she must have made a wrong turn and maybe another, because pretty soon she was lost like she had never been lost before, out on those little farm roads with no signs and no phones. No houses, even, for miles. She was hysterical, crying and trying to get her breath and

60

taking right turns whenever she came to a road junction and then, after a while, taking left turns. Driving and sobbing and pounding the steering wheel until all of a sudden, the dirt road she was on turned to hardtop and then she was at another road junction and there was a sign pointing back to Tallahassee.

She took the turn and drove back into town and went to the hospital.

I didn't interrupt and she went right through the story. But not like it was rehearsed. More like it was something that boiled steadily inside her and that once she opened up, the pressure was just too much. It all came out.

She pulled at her fingers and made fists, then claws, with her hands while she talked and her voice got heavy and strained, her eyes clouded with a thick, pink film and I kept expecting for her to break and start sobbing. She came close to the edge but never quite went over.

Just then, I was inclined to believe her. Or to believe that in her mind, it had happened exactly that way. If she was lying to me, then she was also lying to herself. Which is always possible.

It was also possible, I knew, that I was letting myself be conned. Instinct is fallible, just like everything else that is human. And it wasn't real likely that she'd gone out to that guest house expecting to spend the night talking about her dead mother.

Anyway, I had heard her story and I could play it back to Semmes. I'd done my job.

'I'm sorry,' I said to the woman.

'What for?' she said. 'You didn't do anything. It was that bastard senator.'

61

Better anger than self-pity, I thought, and said, 'No. I'm just sorry it happened to you.'

'Does it make you mad at that sonofabitch who did it?'

'Yes,' I said. 'It does.'

'Yeah. Well it should. And you know what should make you madder than that?'

'What?'

'There ain't no way to get back at him. He's going to get away with it.'

'Why?' I said, stupidly. I knew the answer.

'Shit. Every woman more than sixteen knows the answer to that one,' she said. 'What I'm supposed to do is take it to the law. Go into court and tell my story. But if I do that, then he'll have him some million-dollar lawyer who will make me look like the biggest slut in the universe and that if anything happened it was because I wanted it. And the jury will agree with him.'

'Is that what Dixie Price told you?'

'I talked to her. But nobody had to tell me about that. I been knowing it for a long time.'

She paused for a second and gave me a look.

'How do you know about Dixie?'

'I talked to her earlier. I heard you'd seen her.'

'Yeah. She's on me to testify against that piece-of-shit senator. Easy for her.'

'Maybe she's right.'

'What if she's not?'

I didn't have an answer to that.

'What I want to do is get even with that bastard,' she said, her voice had gone from hot to very cold. 'And that isn't going to happen in no courtroom.'

I just nodded and waited to see where it was going.

'He needs killing,' she said.

I waited.

'Why don't you kill him for me?'

I started to say something but she cut me off.

'You done it for your sister, right?'

'Yes,' I said. My voice sounded a little weak.

'Well?'

I just shook my head.

'Well, all right. I can understand that. You don't have no dog in this fight. But that bastard didn't count on one thing when he ripped my pants off.'

'What's that?' I said.

'I'm somebody's sister, too.'

Seven

It was early afternoon when I left Lisa Hutchinson's little apartment. The front had passed, leaving a clear sky with the sun out and a mild breeze blowing in from the south, off the Gulf. Nice afternoon to be out in the woods, I thought, instead of studying the miseries of life in town.

I was unlocking the door to my truck when I noticed a car parked up the street. It was new and white. The kind of American-made mid-size that the rental companies buy up by the millions. I started my truck and drove slowly away from the curb in the direction of the white car. When I passed it, I could see that there was somebody sitting in the front seat but I couldn't make out the person's features because of the tinted glass. I did see the small Avis sticker on the back window and I wrote the license number in my notebook.

When I was out of the residential neighborhood and back on the highway, I headed for the airport.

There was a young woman working the Avis lot. I waited until she had finished checking in a red Firebird, and then approached her.

'Wonder if I could ask you a favor,' I said.

'Never hurts to ask,' she said, cheerfully.

'It's about a car you rented to someone who was staying at the Plantation where I'm also a guest.'

'Yessir.'

'Well, I left something in the car. A small briefcase. And this other person turned the car back in before I realized he'd left. I was hoping you might have found the briefcase.'

'I haven't seen anything like that. Do you know the name of the person who rented the car?'

'Actually,' I said, 'it was somebody you've probably heard of. Daniel Vincent. The senator.'

'Oh sure. I was here when he came in and rented. Would have been last Thursday. At first, we didn't even know he'd turned the car in. He was supposed to fly out on Sunday afternoon but he must have had to change his plans because that car was in here Sunday morning when we opened. There is one flight out, at six in the morning, and we don't open until eight on Sunday. If someone gets that flight, we just tell them to park the car in a special place and we give them an envelope. They put the keys and the contract in the envelope and put it through a slot in the office door. But we only do that for people who tell us they are going to catch that early flight. So something must have come up sudden for the senator.'

'Yes,' I said. 'That's why my briefcase was still in the car.'

'Well, I haven't seen it. But maybe if you check with the people at the desk, inside, they can help you.'

'Thank you,' I said and went inside.

The terminal was as empty and quiet as an abandoned warehouse. There aren't that many flights in and out of

Tallahassee every day. Even though it is the capital of the fourth largest state in the Union, it is still a small town. It seems improbable, when you think about it, that people pass laws here, in the piney woods, that apply to the people down in Miami which is more and more a South American city. But when it comes to government, there are things a lot more irrational than geography.

I walked along the line of desks where they sell tickets and check your bags. Behind each counter, there was a big board listing all of that airline's flights – arrivals and departures. There was only one 6:00 a.m. departure. A Delta to Atlanta.

I went back outside, to the Avis lot, where the woman I'd talked to earlier was going through some invoices on a clipboard.

'Hello again,' I said.

'Hi,' she said and smiled. Lots of teeth. 'Any luck?'

'Afraid not. Must not have left it in the car. Or maybe Dan ... ah, Senator Vincent, grabbed it and took it to Washington with him.'

'Well, I sure hope you find it.'

'Thank you,' I said and took a step or two in the direction of my truck, then stopped and walked back toward her.

'By the way,' I said, 'do you rent Corsicas?'

'Oh sure. Lots and lots of them. They're a big part of our fleet.'

'White?'

'One of our favorite colors.'

'I thought I saw a friend of mine, Lew King from Atlanta, out near the Plantation where I'm staying, this morning.

He was driving a white Corsica with an Avis sticker on the rear window. If he's in the area, I'd like to give him a call. Could you check your records?'

'We've got a lot of white Corsicas...'

'I saw the license,' I said and got my notebook out of my pocket. I read off the plate number.

'Well,' she said, 'I can check.'

'I'd sure appreciate it. I haven't seen Lew in years.'

She flipped through the invoices and stopped. 'Well, here's the car,' she said. 'But it's checked out to someone named William Longacre from Miami.'

I scanned the sheet, looking for a phone number. And memorized the only one I saw with a 305 area code.

'Too bad,' I said. 'I could have sworn it was Lew. Must have been his double.'

'They say everybody has one,' she agreed sweetly.

'Thanks again.'

'Sure. Just remember us next time you need a car.'

'I will. Strictly Avis from now on.'

I drove to the motel and sat on the freshly made bed to make some calls. The first was to the number I'd memorized from the Avis invoice. I punched in the numbers, then the number of my credit card.

'Longacre Investigations,' a woman said, efficiently, after the second ring.

'William Longacre, please.'

'I'm sorry sir. He's out of town. But he is calling in for messages. May I take your name and number.'

'No. Thanks. I'll try back. Any idea when he'll be back in town?'

'No sir. But he's on a case, so it could be some time.'

'Thank you.'

'You're welcome.'

I hung up and wrote the Longacre number in my book before I forgot it entirely. Then I looked up another number, picked up the phone, tried to find a way to get comfortable on the bed, and started punching buttons. A machine picked up on the third ring.

'Hello. You have reached the office of Randolph Atkins. Leave your message and I will get back to you.' The voice was flat and a little melancholy.

I waited for the beeper, then said, 'Randolph, are you there? It's Hunt.'

'Hello Morgan.' Atkins never picked up the phone and answered it when it rang. He waited and listened to the voice coming through the answering machine. He'd never told me exactly why he was screening his calls like that. Someday, I'd ask him.

'Are you busy?' I said.

'Busy? No. I was just surfing the net.'

'Say again.'

'Fooling around on the Internet. You know.'

'Barely.'

'Come over sometime,' Atkins said. 'I'll show you how it works.'

'I'd like that,' I said. It was the first time he had ever invited me into his house, which he seldom left. The world, for him, was all digital and he lived in front of a computer. Which is why I was calling him.

'Something I can do for you, Morgan?' Atkins likes it when I call. My jobs give him a fingerhold on the real world. Sometimes they involve breaking into computer systems that were meant to be secure. In Atkins' world, that is the highest form of risk and danger, and everybody likes a cheap, adrenaline thrill.

I told Atkins what I needed. It took a little explaining.

'Piece of cake,' he said, when I finished. 'They won't know what hit them. I'll get right on it. Give me a number. I'll call you right back.'

I read the paper while I waited. It was a slow news day. I read a story about a senate debate on a bill that was supposed to fix the welfare system. For the local angle, a reporter had called the two Florida senators for quotes. Daniel Vincent said he was in favor of the bill. He said it was 'a return to individual responsibility. We need to remember that we are all responsible for the consequences of our decisions and the shape of our own lives.'

I'd buy that, I thought. And soon, we might all see just how far the senator was willing to go with it.

Randolph Atkins called back in about half an hour.

'I got what you needed, Morgan,' he said. 'The airlines are easy.'

'Good.'

'Senator Vincent did change his reservation, from Sunday afternoon to Sunday morning. Did it by phone, a couple of hours before the plane left. Flew first class and paid with a credit card. It wasn't a discounted fare so he didn't have to pay any penalty for making the change.'

'I see,' I said.

'I also checked the rental car that went out to the name of Longacre, like you wanted.'

'Good.'

70

'He took the car for a week and his local address is a Ramada.'

Atkins read off the address and the phone number of the motel and I wrote them in my notebook.

'I did a quick search of the Miami papers, like you asked, to see if his name came up in connection with any famous cases or big name lawyers.'

'Uh huh.'

'He was mentioned a lot about six months ago, in that trial of the Palm Beach stud who shot his wife. He was the chief investigator for Lander White, the attorney down there.'

'Never heard of him,' I said.

'He's big. Been in all the magazines. Usually they show him on his boat.'

'Doing what?'

'Fishing, sometimes. For marlin. Or just cruising and drinking. With a "companion". She'll generally be of the blonde persuasion.'

'I see.'

'You really never heard of him?'

'No,' I said. I'd quit following the news regularly. 'What happened with the Palm Beach case?'

'Oh, he won, in a manner of speaking. The prosecutors wanted to send the party boy trust funder to the electric chair but White got it down to manslaughter, so I suppose you'd call that winning.'

'I suppose.'

'Seems like this investigator – Longacre – found a lot of witnesses who could tell stories about the dead wife. She was a trust funder, too. And a nasty piece of work. Screwed around a lot. Kind of a horse lady and a hunter when she wasn't doing the party circle in Palm Beach. She carried a pistol around and had threatened a couple of people with it, including the husband, at least once, when they were having a little public skirmish. White made the jury believe that the husband had reason to fear for his safety. Even after the trial, he was saying it should have been self-defense.'

'And Longacre is his man?'

'That's right.'

'All right, Randolph,' I said. 'Thanks a lot. I have one more thing. It isn't quite so urgent, which is probably a good thing since it might take a little time.'

'Good,' he said. 'I like a challenge. I'm tired of this easy stuff.'

I stood up and paced the room for a minute or two. Then I sat at the desk and made a few notes and thought about what I knew and what I was only guessing. Then I called Semmes.

'Morgan,' he said, after his secretary had put me through. 'How go the wars?'

'I'm learning things,' I said.

'I suspected you would. Anything worth knowing?'

'I'm going to let you be the judge of that,' I said. 'I can tell about it now. Or wait until later, if you are busy.'

'There ain't no time,' he said, almost joyfully, 'like the present time. So go ahead. I'm listening.'

I walked him through it, reading off my notes. He listened without saying anything until I had finished. Then, after a long silence, he said, 'So what do you think?'

'About what?'

'The senator? You think he did it?'

'Be hard to prove,' I said.

'That's not what I asked you, Morgan. Seems like everybody wants to be a lawyer these days. Hell, it's worse than that. Everybody wants to be an *appeals* lawyer. Civilians know as much about the exclusionary rule as your average, working judge. They're more interested in what kind of case the lawyers made than whether or not the defendant is guilty.'

'Okay,' I said.

'Don't tell me whether there is a good case or not,' Semmes went on. 'I'm the lawyer in this team. I'm trained to twist the facts and manipulate the truth and I'm paid well for doing it.'

'Well, I haven't discovered any facts that prove he did it.'

'I know,' Semmes said. 'You told me what facts you found and I'd say that, given the situation, you did about as well as anyone could. So what I'm asking you now is ... what is your feeling?'

'About whether or not he did it?'

'That's what I'm trying to find out and I'll tell you, Morgan, it is like pulling wisdom teeth with a pair of eyebrow tweezers. Just go ahead and spit it out, man. You think he did it? Or is the woman lying?'

I thought a minute. Nothing passed through the phone line between us but soft static.

I finally said, 'I think he probably did it.'

'Okay. Why?'

I thought about that for a while, too.

'Two reasons,' I said. 'First, I don't like the way he left

73

town, early on a Sunday morning when he had a plane reservation for later that evening.'

'Maybe something came up,' Semmes said.

'I'm sure he'll say so. But I don't think he got a call at that honky-tonk. And it was after midnight, on Saturday, when he got back to the guest house where he was staying. That's an unusual time to be hearing from the office, even if you work in Washington.'

'Okay,' Semmes said. 'What's the second thing?'

'It's not as firm.'

'Doesn't have to be,' Semmes said. 'Just give me the benefit of your keen intuition.'

'The woman,' I said, 'I don't see why she would put herself through something like that...'

'It happens,' Semmes said. 'People – even women – will lie about the goddamnedest things. You remember the Medea of South Carolina? Sank her car into the lake with her two little babies strapped inside. Watched 'em drown and then went on television and told the world that some black dude did it. And people believed her.'

'The cops didn't,' I said.

'That's right,' Semmes said. 'They didn't. Something to do with their instincts, I suppose. You spend enough time around people like that and you probably learn to recognize the signs.'

You do, I thought. You do, for sure.

'Your instincts tell you she's not lying, then,' Semmes said.

'About some of the small things, maybe,' I said. 'But I don't think she's lying about the big thing. Dixie Price doesn't either and that counts.'

'Why?'

'She has more experience than I do and I don't think she is a bullshitter.'

'People with her job can turn into advocates. Real zealous advocates. They empathize, which makes them good at their work but unreliable at sorting out a story. They want to believe too much. They *have* to believe.'

'I understand that,' I said.

'And you believe her?'

'She's hard,' I said. 'If she gets fooled, it isn't because she wants to be.'

My hand was wet on the receiver of the phone. The plastic was slick and warm. I was uncomfortable sitting on the bed. My back ached. I stood and walked as far as the telephone cord would stretch and then I walked back the other way. While I paced my little franchised, no-smoking room, Semmes thought over what I had said. The silence lasted a while.

At the end of it, Semmes said, 'Okay, Morgan. I appreciate your input. I always do. Now let me ask you one more question.'

'Sure.'

'How would you feel about my taking this case?'

'You'd win,' I said. 'You'd never break a sweat.'

'Kind of you to say so.'

Semmes has a courtly, old-fashioned way of accepting compliments. He is old school in most things, including manners.

'But, Morgan,' he went on, 'you haven't exactly answered my question. You seem evasive today. Especially for you.'

'What was the question?'

'I asked you how you would feel, if I took the case.'

'How I would *feel*?'

'Yes.'

'What difference does it make?'

'Morgan,' Semmes said, with the first trace of exasperation, 'would you humor me on this one? Please.'

Ordinarily, Semmes did not need advice. Certainly not from me. He knew his own mind and he did not try to argue with himself and talk himself out of something when he already knew the answer. Some dazzling minds are supple and some are hard. Nat Semmes has a dazzling mind that is also diamond hard.

So what was this?

'Like I said, Nat, you'll get him off.'

'But . . .'

'But you'll have to take a long shower afterwards.'

'I see.'

'The senator doesn't need you, Nat,' I said. 'There is talent out there that would crawl over ground glass to take his case.'

'Probably so.'

'And you goddamned sure don't need him.'

Eight

I told Semmes there was one more thing he ought to know.

'What is it?' he said.

I described the Miami investigator who was staking out the apartment where Lisa Hutchinson lived. 'His name is William Longacre,' I said.

'Never heard of the gentleman,' Semmes said.

'He works for Lander White,' I said, 'who is a Miami lawyer.'

'Oh, I know who *he* is,' Semmes said. 'Everybody knows who Lander White is.'

I hadn't, but I didn't say so.

'Good?' I said.

'Well, that's not exactly the word I would use. I'd certainly call Lander White *successful*. Very goddamned successful. He belongs to the new breed. For him, there ain't no such thing as truth. Only verdicts.'

'Then if Vincent has hired him,' I said, 'he probably won't need you. Not unless you and White are going to work in harness.'

'That,' Semmes said, 'will happen when pigs start wearing dresses.' ·

Semmes paused but I knew he was not through.

'Morgan,' he said, in a different tone, 'I appreciate what you've done over there. Now, I wonder if you would do something else. It's a large request.'

'Sure.'

'Don't be too hasty.'

'Okay,' I said. 'I won't. Now what do you need?'

'I already know that Senator Vincent *could* have done it, under the circumstances. Now I want to know now if he is the kind of man who makes a habit of this sort of thing.

'We all know he's never been arrested and charged for doing anything like this. If he had, that would have come out in a hummingbird's heartbeat. What I want to know is ... has he ever *not* been arrested for doing something like this?'

'Check his history, then?'

'Exactly.'

'Where do you want me to start? College? High school?'

'No. I'd start in Washington. If he is the kind of man who'd do that on an average Saturday night, just being in Washington wouldn't have stopped him. And memories will be fresh.'

'Washington?'

'That's right,' Semmes said. 'Go on up there, Morgan, and see what you can find out.'

I had to fly. Driving would have been my first choice. But I didn't have the time. So I checked out of my little motel and drove out to the airport where the travel agent Semmes used had already fixed me up with a reservation.

It was a three-hour flight, counting the plane change in Atlanta. I read a book and survived it.

The plane landed at National Airport. At that time of night, it wasn't too bad. Only moderately dirty and not very crowded. I've come through the place when it was bad enough to make you think you'd been diverted to some third world backwater on the far side of the equator.

I got a car. Called around and found a motel on the Virginia side. I checked in and unpacked. I was in bed by midnight. I had no idea what I would do or where I would get started in the morning. I slept soundly.

In the morning, I ran in one of the green areas along the river, not far from the Jefferson Memorial. It was barely dawn but a few other runners were up and putting in their miles. Washington is full of people who like to get after it.

I showered, dressed – a suit and tie for business – and drove across the Potomac on the 14th Street Bridge. I parked at Union Station. Ate some eggs and drank some coffee for breakfast. Then walked up to the capitol.

There were two kinds of people on the Mall. The people who worked in Washington and carried attaché cases and the people who were there as tourists and carried cameras. The people with the cameras looked happy and the people with the briefcases looked grim. I'd been in Washington a few times and the mood of those people never seemed to change. It made you suspect that governing the rest of us must be a rotten, thankless job.

Senator Daniel Lee Vincent had an office in the Dirkson Building, which was one of several office buildings scattered around the capitol. Compared to the capitol, they were not much to look at. But that is an unfair comparison, I suppose. Like comparing Westminster Abbey to one of those modern red brick churches. The difference, you suspect, is that back when they built Westminster, they genuinely believed in the enterprise. And they probably believed honestly in the nobility of government back when they started on the capitol.

There was a guard at the front door of the Dirkson Building. And a metal detector.

'You have a pass?' the guard asked me. He was a large, but soft, black man.

'No.'

'You got an appointment?'

'No.'

There were impatient people piling up behind me. I was screwing up the system.

'Sorry,' the guard said.

'I'm a constituent,' I said.

'*Jesus*,' somebody behind me muttered.

'Don't make any difference,' the guard said, 'you got to have a pass or an appointment with your name listed on my clipboard here.'

None of this surprised me. I was just getting myself worked up a little. It would have been the same little ritual if I had dropped in at the headquarters of the NRA saying I wanted to talk ballistics with the Executive Director. These were busy, important people and they only had time for other busy, important people.

'So I need an appointment,' I said, pleasantly, 'or a pass. Is that right?'

'That's right.'

'Do you *mind*?' a voice behind me said.

'To go up and see where my own senator works?'

'For Christ's sake,' another voice said.

'That's right,' the guard said. 'Now you're holding these people up so you've got to move on.'

I stepped out of the way. But I had my game face on.

I walked a block or two, until I found a bank of pay phones. Two out of the three were broken – the handset had been yanked off one and the other looked like it had been smashed with a ten-pound maul – but the third one was working and I used it to call, first information and, then, Senator Daniel Vincent's office.

I got one of those machines that gives you a little speech about how to use the system and then tells you which button to push for whatever department or person it is you'd like to talk to. When the voice said, 'Push 8 if you wish to speak to someone in constituent services,' I did exactly what it told me to do.

The phone rang and someone answered.

'Senator Vincent's office, this is Carol in constituent services, how may I help you?'

I told her I was a faithful supporter of the senator and that I was visiting Washington for a couple of days. I understood the senator was a busy man, way too busy to stop and talk to someone like me, but I would like to just see him making a speech or asking a question at one of those committee hearings they had and was there any way she could tell me where and when I should go to do this. I made myself sound as much a simple rube as possible and, in a lot of ways, I wasn't really acting. Except that while I might be dumb, I don't have any interest at all in watching some pol make speeches. I would sooner sit around the barber shop and watch haircuts.

Carol put me on hold for a couple of minutes. When she came back on the line, she told me that she had looked at the senator's schedule for the day and that he would be attending hearings by the sub-committee on marine fisheries which was considering a bill on limiting in-shore netting.

'He should be there all morning,' she said, 'unless he gets called to the floor for a vote.'

She told me the number of the hearing room and how to find it. I thanked her and hung up.

I had a while. So I took my time and strolled the corridors of the capitol, along with the tourists. I was just about the only one without a camera. It made me feel naked.

The capitol is a majestic building, there is no getting around that. The big corridors with marble floors and high ceilings seem hushed and solemn even when they are full of loud-talking people. The scale of the place, and the reverently cast busts of old political warriors, give things a scale and a frame that sort of humbles you and lets you go on for five minutes or so thinking that only work of the gravest importance goes on here. Then you remember that most of the business conducted behind the doors that lead off these halls is just raw horse trading. Special favors for the bean farmers and such. Probably nothing that goes on here, in the average day, has the nobility of a father and mother teaching a kid to ride a bike.

But the building will fool you.

* * *

I got a seat near the front row of the committee room. Which was paneled in oak and had this big raised platform up front, with long tables and high-backed chairs where the senators would be sitting. Off to one side, there was a little stall with chairs that did not look quite so much like leather-covered thrones. This is where the press sat. The rest of us were in ordinary, wooden-backed chairs that were slightly more comfortable than concrete.

A couple of senators were already milling around up in the front of the room. I recognized Kennedy. He looked old and depleted and it was hard not to mourn for all the loss you could read in his face.

But he was laughing, in a robust way, at something the other senator had said. It was a good laugh. Hearty. And the other senator was smiling warmly. They both looked likeable and it occurred to me that this has to be the first secret. They are almost all of them likeable and you tend to let your defenses down around a likeable man. Even those you ought to fear.

Dan Vincent came through a door in the back of the room and joined Kennedy and the other senator. Pretty soon, he was laughing too. They looked like they were sharing a good new dirty joke.

Vincent was younger than the other two. Healthier looking – almost athletic – but with the same kind of agreeable, open, friend-to-man way of carrying himself. He was wearing a subdued, gray suit with a white shirt and a rep tie that had a lot of maroon in it. His hair was plainly styled and he had a fresh, healthy tan. That came from quail hunting in the piney woods, last week.

He had his hands in his pockets and there was something in his posture that was both relaxed and confident; something in his way of standing that made it clear he wouldn't be easy to back down. He did his share of talking until it was time for the hearing to start, then he took a chair, put on a pair of reading glasses, and started looking through a stack of documents on the table in front of him.

The committee chairman was banging his gavel as I slipped out of the room. I'd come to get a look at the senator. I wasn't interested in commercial fishing regulations.

I wondered, as I walked down those big stairs in front of the capitol, what I'd learned, if anything, from my up close inspection of Vincent. He didn't look like a rapist, or any other kind of criminal. He looked like a confident, high-flying young politician. But, then, if you took him out of that suit and put him in baggy orange coveralls and a stocking cap, with a couple of days' beard and the vaguely stunned look of someone who has been sleeping the fitful sleep of an inmate ... then you might think differently.

It was mid-morning and the day had turned cold and gray, poised to rain or snow, but for now it couldn't seem to make up its mind. If you were taking a poll, you would have marked it down as 'undecided, leaning against'.

I felt pretty much the same way. I'd never turned down a job when Semmes offered one. Certainly never asked to be taken off a job. A small part of me was tempted. I didn't need the money and I didn't like the work. But I couldn't quit.

So, now that I had seen the senator up close, I needed

to come up with a plan for snooping into his most personal life. Just thinking about it made me feel like there was something green and scaly growing on the backs of my hands.

Nine

'You look good, considering,' Al Stackhouse said.

'Thanks. You do, too.'

'Bullshit. I'm getting old and I'm already fat. Hard to believe I used to be what I was when you knew me.'

Stackhouse and I went back a long ways. We were sitting in a rundown Thai restaurant in a sad little strip shopping center in Virginia, out past Fairfax, in what used to be horse country. We were drinking Singhai beer. Which didn't taste any better than it had the last time, a million years ago in Bangkok.

'It's living in this town,' Stackhouse said. 'This place is the soul of fat. We've got a man in the White House who jogs every morning and he is *still* fat. This place runs on grease. You want something, you take somebody who can give it to you out and you feed him. You eat an expense account lunch, then you go to some kind of reception in the evening and eat a lot of cheese and sour cream canapés. Drink wine. Then you go to dinner. Everybody's mouth is open half the goddamned time, because they are either eating or talking. And the talk is fat, too.

'One of the things I miss most about the old days,' Stackhouse said, pouring beer from the bottle into what looked like a jelly glass, 'is the way you never thought about food. Remember how we'd go out on one of those five-day trail surveillance deals with nothing to eat but a sockful of rice and a shaker of salt?'

I nodded. I remembered, for sure, but I couldn't honestly say I missed the cold, gluey rice. Some parts, maybe, but not that. But, then, I didn't live in Washington. Stackhouse had been here for a long, long time.

'I'd lose ten pounds on one of those operations,' he said. 'And back then, I didn't have it to lose.'

He drank half a glass of beer and exhaled with a sound of genuine contentment. 'And we couldn't talk on those operations. Five guys, maybe seven, in the jungle for five days and no talk. You might not say ten words, the whole time. You can't believe how far that is from life in this hole.'

'Maybe you ought to leave,' I said.

'And quit show business,' Stackhouse said, grinning. His smile hadn't changed. Still wicked and sinister, like the man behind it.

'I thought about leaving, back when they purged the Agency. Threw all of us old fieldmen and pavement operators out on our asses. Kept the new breed, don't you know? The high tech crowd and the computer commandos. So we get Aldrich Ames who was selling our agents' asses to the KGB for the money to buy himself a red Jaguar. I said, back then, that something like that was going to happen. You show me a technoshit and I'll show you somebody who will sell out for money or sing when somebody puts his nuts in a vice and starts to squeeze.

'They didn't want any of us old rogue cold warriors. We

weren't cool and detached enough for them. I admit I don't test real high on cool and detached. I get my best scores in anger and hate. But I never would have sold out my own guys for a red Jaguar.'

Stackhouse grinned again. 'A Lamborghini, maybe. Or a Ferrari. But a fucking Jaguar? No way. The Limies never learned how to build those things right. Ignition system is strictly number ten. But those techno-weenies at the Agency, they aren't smart enough to know that.'

'What have you been doing since you got out of the Agency?' I said.

'Consulting,' he said, quickly. 'You've heard of Oliver North?'

'Yes. Sure.'

'Well, I did some jobs for him. Through Secord, our old boss man at SOG.'

That was Studies and Observation Group in Vietnam. The blackest unit over there. I did one tour with them. Stackhouse had done several.

'Can you still find work?' I said.

'Not like the good old days,' he said, a little mournfully. 'It'll never be like that again. But I still eat.' He slapped his ample stomach.

'Like a fucking hog, I eat.'

'Well, bro,' I said, 'you owe it to yourself.' That was one of the old lines. He smiled when he heard it.

'How about you?' he said. 'I heard you got jugged down in Mississippi.'

'Alabama,' I said.

'Killed some guy?'

'He deserved it.'

'I'm glad you survived, partner. So far, I haven't had to do any time. Come close. I'm not sure how I'd hold up.'

I nodded.

'So,' he said, 'now that we've taken care of all the formalities, why don't you tell me what brings you to Washington and why you looked me up? I don't imagine this is purely a social call.'

'No. I'm working on something.'

I told Stackhouse as much – and as little – as I could. He listened, very intent and still, not taking any notes or asking any questions, then he told me to meet him at his office in an hour. He gave me the address, stood up, and left the grubby little restaurant with half a bottle of beer still sitting on the table. I paid. Then I wandered around the little shopping center like some kind of desperate mall rat until it was time to meet Al.

His office was in a nondescript five story building a couple of miles from Langley. The building was probably new when Nixon was president. I wondered, idly, just how many old spooks were renting office space and consulting out of the building which, like them, had seen its glory days.

Stackhouse's office had a computer and a phone, a desk and a chair, a file cabinet and one framed black and white picture on the wall. The picture showed a very thin, very young Stackhouse, wearing tiger fatigues and a rucksack and carrying an M-16. He was looking straight into the camera. His eyes were tired but, when you got past the fatigue, you could tell you were looking at a happy man.

'Welcome to my cave,' he said. 'Have a seat.'

'Thanks.'

'I made a couple of calls. Some of these guys, I could have dialed you up a dossier in a heartbeat. Back when they were trying to put me and some of North's other troops in jail, a couple of us decided to fight back. Amazing, the shit we found out about some of our nation's leading elected representatives.'

'Did you use it?'

Stackhouse gave me a long, level gaze and said, 'I told you I've never done time. So you draw your own conclusions.'

I nodded. Stackhouse would bullshit you. He wasn't one of the worst but he wanted you to be impressed. Most of the time, he didn't need to bullshit. Now and then, he did and he would.

I didn't really care if he was telling the truth, or not, about getting the goods on people in congress. It was a fight and when Stackhouse was in a fight, he didn't hold anything back. He could have easily been telling the truth.

He opened one of the lower drawers on his desk and took out a bottle of Fundador – Spanish brandy – that was about half full. He turned around in his chair and reached for two small snifters that sat on top of the file cabinet. I didn't want to drink brandy in the middle of the day but Stackhouse was one of those – always had been – who wouldn't trust a man who didn't drink with him. He and alcohol were old intimate friends – there was a lot he'd done that he couldn't have done without the help of booze – and Stackhouse stuck by his friends. He would never quit drinking. Brandy in the middle of the day? Why the fuck not?

I raised my glass and we silently toasted ... what? The old days, I suppose. When we were young and indestructible. The brandy tasted hot, with a faintly oily residue. I could remember liking the taste.

'Too bad your man Vincent wasn't around back in those days. We might have had something really good on him.'

'You didn't find anything, then?'

Stackhouse held up his hand, palm out. 'Not so fast,' he said. 'He wasn't one of those who was trying to put me in prison ... That's all I'm saying. He wasn't even around here then.

'But I made some friends back then and some of them know about life on the Hill.'

'The Hill?'

'Capitol Hill,' Stackhouse said, 'you know, where the senate and the House make sausage.'

'Oh.'

'I made a couple of friends up there. But I don't believe it was because of my winning personality.'

He finished his brandy and looked, for a moment, like he was thinking about another. Then he changed his mind and put the glass back on the file cabinet.

'I might be a badass and a renegade and every other thing I've been called but I have never walked on little people just for the sport. You know what I mean?'

I nodded.

'Some of the clowns, up on the Hill, they have a serious problem that way. They like to get up in the morning and, right away, start putting boots to the secretaries and the little guys with glasses who write their speeches. I suppose it makes them feel like they are tough.

'You hear that all the time. "Old Senator Shitforbrains is really *tough*." What it means is – he can make his secretary cry and generally knows how to be rude to anyone he knows can't cause him any trouble. Anyone who can ... well he slobbers on them like an old beat-up dog. I never could figure out what makes people think this town is so fucking *tough*. I mean, the most anyone around here is likely to lose is an election. You and I both know guys who've lost body parts and cried less about it than the average hack around here does when he gets kicked out and has to go get a real job.'

I smiled and nodded.

Stackhouse said, 'Let's have another drink,' got out the bottle and glasses and poured.

'Anyway, I was nice to one of the assistants in this dipshit senator's office. Sent her some flowers after the dipshit jumped all over her for sending me some papers I asked for. They were public documents but the Honorable Dipshit wanted to jerk my chain. He screamed at this young woman – who must have been two years out of college and making eighteen grand for working ninety hours a week – like she'd been leaking coded radio traffic to the fucking Russians.

'After I sent her the flowers, she called me. We even went out to dinner a couple of times.'

I raised my eyebrows.

Stackhouse shook his head. 'She's young enough to be my daughter.' I remembered that he'd been one of those sentimental family men who carried around pictures of a wife and children he very seldom saw and knew hardly at all. Which made it that much easier to idealize them. For

Stackhouse, there were two kinds of women – whores and everyone else. The young senate aide no doubt belonged in the second category, which meant he not only kept his hands off her but probably offered to pay her tuition to graduate school so she could quit her terrible job.

'So you have a source on the Hill?'

He nodded. 'She is a sweet kid. Or was, anyway. Every year she stays there, she gets harder and meaner. Kind of sad to watch.'

'Does she work for Vincent?'

Stackhouse took a sip of brandy and shook his head pensively. I remembered the dark, moody streak.

'Doesn't matter. She is very well wired, up there,' Stackhouse said. 'What she doesn't know directly ... well, she knows someone who does. I called her and told her just the basics. She picked up quick – I mean, right now – when I mentioned Vincent's name. Said she would call me back later. After work.'

I nodded.

'You staying someplace where I can reach you?'

I told him the name and number of the motel.

'One of those airport dumps, huh? I thought you'd be in the Madison, with the Chippendale furniture and the Arab oil thieves.'

'I'm a cheap date,' I said.

'Well listen,' Stackhouse said, suddenly distracted and checking his Rolex, 'I'd love to drink the afternoon away but I've got a couple of people coming in. It's a job – or it might be – and I can't afford to turn those down. But I'll call you, just as soon as she calls me. And maybe this weekend, if you're still around ...'

'Absolutely,' I said, standing and finishing my brandy. 'And I appreciate your help.'

'Yeah,' Stackhouse said, reaching over the desk to shake my hand. 'But it sure does seem like small shit, don't it, compared to the old days?'

I said it did. Just to make him feel better.

Ten

There was a little room on the ground floor of the motel, with a universal machine and a couple of stationary bicycles. I spent an hour or so down there, sweating off the brandy. Afternoon drinking was too tough for me.

Back in the room, I was lying on the bed, with a towel wrapped around my waist, trying to get through the *Washington Post*, which was the thickest daily paper I had ever seen. After the brandy, the workout, and a hot shower, the stories about a rumored shakeup in the State Department were easily enough to put me to sleep.

The phone startled me back to consciousness.

'Mr Hunt?'

'Yes.'

'This is Adrian Lowe. I imagine Al Stackhouse spoke to you about me.'

'Sure,' I said, coming entirely awake. 'Thanks for calling.'

'Well, I'm hoping it is in a good cause.'

'I am, too,' I said.

'I'm busy right now and I don't want to talk on the phone,' she said. 'Can we meet somewhere, in an hour or so?'

I looked at my watch. After four.

'Fine,' I said.

She suggested a coffee house, in Cleveland Park. I told her I could find it – I'd bought a map – and that I would meet her there in an hour.

The route I picked made sense as an exercise in pure map-reading. But the map didn't tell you anything about the terrain the streets went through. All that white space, between the streets, looked the same. Maps are antiseptic that way, and can't tell you much of anything about the kind of neighborhood I found myself driving through.

Cars sat derelict along the curb. All of them stripped and most of them burned for good measure. They gave the street the feel of an urban boneyard. You could imagine these old cars had come here, from all over the city, to die.

A few of the apartment buildings looked like they had been burned out, too. There were black scars around the holes in the brick that had once been windows. No doors. No roofs, either.

Those buildings looked like the last standing structures after some fierce house-to-house combat. The buildings that had not been burned and still had people living in them weren't much better. The biggest difference was the raw plywood where the windows had been. That was the sign that there were still people living inside.

There were debris and garbage on every corner and in every yard. I saw three old sofas and a set of box springs in the space of one block. The empty beer and wine bottles were so thick they could have been dead, fallen leaves. Except there weren't any trees.

On every corner, there seemed to be at least one young man – older than ten but younger than sixteen – standing and shivering and watching. They wore big high-topped athletic shoes, baggy pants, and hooded sweatshirts. It was the style in their world. A look that originated in the jails.

One of these boys turned his head to watch my passing and I caught the reflection from the gold ring he wore in his nose. There was no expression on his face; no life in his eyes. The gold ring could have been adornment for a corpse.

I suspect if I had stopped the car and opened the door, he might have shot me. And it wouldn't have surprised anyone. Or made much news. It would have been just one more street killing and those were routine. There had been two yesterday, and neither made the front section of the *Post*, much less the front page.

Life here was hard and cheap. Up on the Hill, they talked billions for Mexican bailouts. Down here, they would blow you away for a couple of bags of crack.

The coffee house could have been on the other side of the moon. It was just a few blocks from the National Cathedral, in a neighborhood where the homes had windows and doors, the cars were not abandoned, and there were trees along the sidewalks. It was clean and bright inside the coffee house and smelled faintly of warm milk.

There were couples at three of the tables. No single women who could have been Adrian Lowe.

I took a seat at one of the small tables and when the waitress asked for my order, I told her I was meeting someone and would wait.

No problem, she said, and left me to read the menu, which was written on a blackboard behind the counter and above the gleaming, stainless espresso machines. Something about the place struck me as very civilized.

Adrian Lowe was ten minutes late and did not apologize for it. She was thin and it looked like it came from overwork, not exercise. She was also pale, probably for the same reason. But she had blue eyes that were deep and direct and a smile that was genuine and winning and probably would have gotten her called 'vivacious', ten years ago, when she would have been in college and, as they say, 'a lot of fun'.

She didn't look like she had much fun these days.

She was wearing a trenchcoat over one of those suits that goes with a blouse that has a built in scarf that covers up a woman's neck. It was an outfit that could make a fifty-dollar hooker look prim. She was carrying a briefcase.

Once we'd introduced ourselves, she put the briefcase on the floor, took off the trenchcoat and draped it over an empty chair, then sat down. She studied me, like a gambler trying to see through a bluff.

'How do you know Al Stackhouse?' she said.

'We worked together, several years ago.'

'*Work?*' she said, dryly. 'Is that what you call it?'

That didn't leave much room for an answer.

'You know I came here, to this city, because I wanted to put a stop to the kind of "work" you and Al Stackhouse used to do. I wanted to put you out of business first, and then put you in jail, if that was possible.

'Now...' she said, with an ironic variation of what I imagined had been her trademark smile, 'now, I find

100

myself doing favors for Al and his pals. How's that for a story on how Washington corrupts idealists?'

I was glad to see the waitress.

Adrian Lowe ordered cappuccino, with non-fat milk and extra cinnamon. I asked the waitress to recommend a strong, dark coffee.

'Try the Kenyan,' Adrian Lowe said. 'It is *très* funky.'

The waitress agreed, so I ordered a cup.

'When I first came here,' Adrian Lowe said, while we waited for our coffee, 'I expected it would be the easiest thing in the world to tell my allies from my enemies. Look for a senator who was for abortion rights and against dirty little CIA wars – those make-work programs for you and Al Stackhouse – and I would find a friend.

'I found one. And I went to work for him, no problem. I had a good degree and lots of recommendations and summer internships. Turns out I had other qualifications that impressed the senator. He told me I had "nice tits".'

I didn't say anything.

She drummed her fingers on the table for a few seconds, then went on. She was looking hard into my face while she talked. Her eyes glowed.

'Of course,' she said, 'he said that to all the girls. He nailed the weak ones on the office couch. The rest of us just fought him off and smiled. You couldn't slap the piss out of him or knee him in the balls because he would fire you and say it was for incompetence and you would never work on Capitol Hill again. And for all of us idealistic young women – willing to work eighty-hour weeks at slave wages for the cause – that would have been worse than death.'

The waitress arrived and served us. My coffee was as

good as advertised. Adrian Lowe took a sip of hers without seeming to realize she was doing it and then went on with her story.

'When my repulsive boss wasn't pawing you in the office, he was out on the floor or out on the road or on one of those Sunday morning television shows, talking about "women's rights". He was the American woman's greatest friend. He was pro-choice; he was for equal pay; he was for family leave; and day-care. Christ, he was still talking about ERA after it had gone down in flames. He was great in public. It's just that, in private, he was a disgusting sexist pig.'

Hypocrisy in Washington. Imagine that.

'He liked to go out bar-hopping with other senators. They would get drunk and grab waitresses. There was a story in one of the papers about how they tore the clothes off this one waitress at a restaurant where they had a private room. She was in tears. Crying hysterically. And these two fat, drunken senators are laughing like a couple of Bourbon princes, raping a peasant girl after a hard day of fox hunting.'

I made a face and drank a little more coffee.

'Al Stackhouse, on the other hand,' she went on, 'stands for everything I despise. But he has always treated me with respect. At first, I thought he was doing it just to get to me. But, after a while, I realized it was sincere. There was something ... oh, *touching* about it. He honestly believes that I possess some kind of superior refinement that is going to always be out of his reach.'

She smiled, a little wistfully.

'I honestly like Al, as a person, even though I still despise his politics.'

I nodded.

'When I heard that story about my old boss tearing that poor woman's clothes off, you know what my first thought was?'

'What's that?'

'I wished that it had been Al Stackhouse's daughter. It would have been marvelous to see the old bossman when he heard that Al was looking for him. And Al *would* have come looking for him. No question about it.'

'Yes,' I said.

'My politics haven't changed,' she said, sighing softly. 'So I have had to make a lot of pacts with a lot of devils. But I fight a guerrilla war too, against some of those same devils. That's why I told Al I would meet with you.'

'I appreciate it,' I said.

'God, are you going to be courtly *too*?'

'I suppose,' I said. I'm opposed to easy intimacy. Don't believe it is truly possible.

'Just like Al Stackhouse.'

'And unlike your old boss.'

'*Touché.*'

She smiled and drank a little more of her coffee.

'I don't know Senator Vincent, personally. Our paths have never crossed, not even on committee assignments. He's relatively new – second term – and not particularly flamboyant, so there isn't a lot of hot gossip about him. A really good, salacious story about a member or a senator can make it around the Hill at warp speed. But I can't remember a single one about Dan Vincent.

'The buzz is that he works hard and is hard on the people who work for him.'

103

That wasn't what I was looking for and the disappointment must have showed.

'Don't give up too quickly,' she said. 'All that means is that he isn't a party boy, like my old boss, and lots of others around here.'

'All right.'

'You aren't looking for a drunken party boy, anyway, from what Al said.'

'No.'

'More like a brutal animal.'

'That's right.'

'Nothing about Vincent's reputation eliminates him, as far as I'm concerned.'

I wondered just who *was* eliminated, as far as she was concerned. But didn't say anything about it.

'The Hill is a big place. Twenty thousand people work there and a lot more pass through on temporary assignments of one sort or another. People come and go. But, for some reason, a lot of them seem to go from Senator Vincent's office. And most of them are young women.'

'You said he is a tough boss.'

'Show me somebody up here who isn't.'

'Still . . .'

'People work on the Hill for a lot of different reasons,' she said, 'but none of them work there because it is a good job. They believe it is important or – God help us – glamorous, or something. So they don't quit. They put up with crap from their bosses that people wouldn't put up with any other place in the world, except maybe Hollywood.

'They get screamed at in the most degrading ways. They do the most demeaning personal errands. Take dirty laundry to the cleaners. Take the dog to the vet. I know somebody who had to take a senator's dog to the vet to get it artificially inseminated. They'll babysit for the senator's bratty little kids. They will eat all kinds of shit before they will quit their jobs.

'When someone does quit,' she said, 'it is big medicine.'

'And a lot of people who worked for Daniel Vincent have quit?'

'A lot of *women*,' she said. 'A lot of *young* women.'

'Do you know them?'

'No. But I've got some names.' She reached for the briefcase, opened it, and took an envelope from a pocket. She handed it to me and said, 'You might learn something by talking to these women.'

'Thank you.'

'You and Al Stackhouse have your kind of guerrilla warfare,' she said, smiling and finishing her coffee. 'And I have mine.'

Eleven

'He hurt me,' Gwen Lopez said. 'And he scared me.'

'Is that all?'

'You want to know if he raped me,' she said. 'That's what you want to know, isn't it?'

I hesitated before I answered.

'Yes.'

'No,' she said. 'He didn't. But it wasn't because he suddenly developed a conscience.'

She had been sitting on the small sofa in the living room of her small apartment in Chevy Chase. Now she was standing. Pacing.

'He was out of his mind. It was terrifying. One minute he was the boring man we all knew and hated. The ex-prosecutor who didn't know how to relax or smile. Then, the next thing I knew, he was this madman with this wild look in his eyes ...

'I thought he was going to kill me at first and then, when he grabbed for me and I knew what he wanted, I couldn't believe it. It was like he was another person. A monster.

'I hit him and kicked him. I screamed the whole time. He grabbed me by the arms. Here ...'

She pointed at her upper arms.

'I had bruises later. He shook me so hard I thought he was going to break my neck. Then he slammed me against the wall and my head hit so hard I almost passed out.'

She was breathing hard. Almost hyperventilating. She was pacing faster now. I waited for her to go on.

'I fell. Went down to my knees and he was on top of me. I think he expected me to give up then. And for a minute, I did. I was stunned. But I came too and I kicked him. Actually, I drove my knee right into his crotch. As hard as I could. I don't think it was a direct hit or he wouldn't have been walking for a week. But it was close enough.

'He screamed and rolled off me and I got to my feet. He was in too much pain to come after me. But I was still scared. I just told him to get out. I was hysterical. He looked at me on his way out. His eyes were like – oh, I don't know – like you see on a dog – a real mean dog.'

She stopped pacing and stood in the middle of the room with her arms folded tightly around herself.

'Where did this happen?' I said.

'In an apartment. Like this one. We'd been working late. He told me he would take me home. He said he was worried about me. How's that for a fucking joke?'

'What did you do after he left?'

'I locked all the doors and crawled in bed and cried for an hour. Then I got up and took a bath. In the morning, I called in and said I wouldn't be coming back to work. I thought about leaving and going back home. To Sarasota. But instead, I just moved out and got another job.'

'On the Hill?'

'No. I didn't want to go back there. I work for one of the

trade associations – a lobbying group. No matter what you hear, they are a nicer class of people.'

'Did you tell anyone?'

'No,' she said, 'and you know why I'm telling you?'

'Why?'

'Because you wouldn't be asking unless he'd done it to some other woman. Maybe more than one. That means he's in trouble and if I tell what happened, then maybe I can help put the rotten bastard away.'

I nodded.

'That's right, isn't it?'

'I sure hope so,' I said.

It was late evening when I left the apartment. Gwen Lopez had a roommate who had been waiting in the bedroom the whole time I was there. I wondered if she would have let me in her apartment if the roommate had not been there. Probably not. She probably didn't see any men alone in her apartment any more. Not any man, for any reason.

I drove back through the city, past the great marble edifices all bathed in light. I wondered what Senator Daniel Vincent was doing in the imperial city on this night. I had written his schedule in my notebook. I took it out and while I was stopped at a light, I read down it. At the bottom, it said that he would be attending a reception sponsored by something called the Institute for New Communities – or INC. It was a black tie affair with somebody whose name I did not recognize giving a speech about 'Neighborhoods in the Nineties'.

The dinner was being held in a ballroom at the Madison Hotel.

My, my.

My dinner came from a little Chinese place in a shopping
center near the motel – fried rice and hot and sour soup. I
ate in my room while I ran through all the stations on the
television. There were at least one hundred. And nothing I
wanted to watch. I left the news on until I'd finished eating,
then I turned the set off and wrote some notes about the
conversations I'd had with Adrian Lowe and Gwen Lopez.
I filled in four pages of my notebook. By then it was after
ten.

I was just about asleep when the phone rang. I picked it
up expecting that the hotel had put the call through to the
wrong room. Who would be calling me in Washington at
this, or any other, time of night.

'Mr Hunt?'

'Yes.'

'This is Louise Quiller.'

'Yes?'

'You left a message on my machine.'

It took a second or two for all the circuits to close, then I
remembered. Her name had been at the top of Adrian
Lowe's list. I'd called her first, before I reached Gwen
Lopez.

'Right,' I said. 'Sorry. Thanks for calling.'

'What can I do for you?' she said. Her tone was cool and
suspicious.

I told her I was an investigator and that I wanted to talk
to her about Senator Vincent. It seemed like a good idea to
be straight with her.

'How did you get my name?' Extremely wary, now.

'I talked to someone who works on the Hill. I can't tell you her name but she knew of several women who had worked for Senator Vincent and then left.'

'Are you with somebody's campaign?'

'No. I work for a lawyer. This is part of a possible criminal matter.'

After a long silence, she said, 'Have you talked to anyone else ... any other women who worked in his office?'

'Yes,' I said. I didn't say how many.

'Is this about what I think it is about?'

'Probably.'

After another long silence, she said, 'Let me think about it. Will you be there in the morning?' She sounded frightened now.

'Yes.'

'I'll call you,' she said and hung up.

I got out of bed and made a few more notes. Then I stood at the window for a while, looking at the river and the city and thinking, but not very coherently. My thoughts were like hot fragments, angling off in random directions, hot and bright for a minute or two, then growing dim as they burned out and died. I couldn't shut them off, even after I turned out the lights and got back in bed. It was a couple of hours before I finally got to sleep.

I was up early feeling edgy and eager to get started. I ran in the park with the hard chargers. Then I sat in my room, drinking coffee and reading the papers. It was still a little early to call the other women on Adrian Lowe's list.

The truth was that I didn't need to call them. And I didn't

need to hear from Louise Quiller. I knew what I needed to know about Daniel Vincent.

But that didn't mean it would be accepted in court which is where the only conclusions that count come from these days. If you've got a serious question that needs to be resolved, then you either go to court or you do a poll.

I was too agitated to concentrate on my paper which was fat, again, and full of long stories about some scandal at the Pentagon.

Well, I thought, if I couldn't call any of the women on Adrian Lowe's list, there was one call I could make that would ease my mind some.

Nat Semmes would be at the office. He got there around five, every morning, so he could spend the first couple of hours of the day in solitude. He used it for reading. Virgil, lately. Before that, it had been Dante. He kept moving backwards, it looked like. Next year, it would probably be Sophocles.

This morning, though, it would be a phone call from me. And I was sorry about that.

He answered in his usual courtly, patient voice and for a second or two I regretted intruding on his devotionals. But I didn't hang up.

'Nat,' I said, 'this is Morgan. I'm sorry to interrupt this way.'

'Not at all, Morgan,' he said, and I could imagine him carefully marking the page and putting the book aside, 'good to hear your voice. How is it going up there?'

'Good,' I said. 'Or bad, depending on how you feel about Daniel Vincent.'

'I see,' which meant he didn't.

'I talked to one woman who says she went through the same kind of deal with the senator. Except she managed to fight him off. It was a near thing, though.'

'Do you believe her?'

'Yes. I think I do.'

'Anything else?'

'I've got several other leads. I called one of them – another woman who'd worked in Vincent's office, once. I got her machine and left a message. She called me back. Late last night. When I told her I wanted to ask her some questions about Vincent, she said, "Is this about what I think it's about?"

'I've got to tell you, Nat,' I said, 'it might be meaningless – or maybe worse – in court, but it made a believer out of me. Vincent is a creep. Board certified.'

'All right,' Semmes said calmly.

I took a breath and said, less calmly, 'If he's the client, I want out.'

'He's entitled to a defense,' Semmes said.

'Good luck to him, then. My life is too short to spend it walking point for creeps. I'm sorry, Nat.'

And I was. I'd never turned down work from him before. Never thought it would come to that. I expected to hear him tell me, in the cold, curt voice I'd heard him use once on someone who had let him down, that he was sorry to see me go and that he wished me well in the world.

'Write if you get work,' in other words.

Semmes cleared his throat and sighed and then said, 'Morgan, I'm going to ask you to trust me on this one. Can you do that?'

'Well...' I said, a little off balance, 'well, sure. Of

course. Hell yes, Nat, I'll trust you on anything. Just tell me what's going on.'

'I can't. Not just yet.'

I'd done enough things in my life without knowing why – without having the foggiest idea – that it didn't bother me to be doing it once more. And, anyway, Semmes was in charge of this one.

'All right,' I said. 'What do you want me to do?'

'Just what you've been doing. Follow up all your leads. Keep in touch. I'll explain in a day or two.'

'All right,' I said.

'I owe you one, Morgan.'

And at this rate, I thought, we would be even in a couple of thousand years.

So I went back to waiting for Louise Quiller to call. And to reading the paper. By the time I finished the front section, I felt like I had run some kind of mental marathon. Hard to believe that anyone can process that much information about the government, day after day. I started on a section that was called *Style*, hoping for a lighter workout.

Three or four pages in, I was staring at a picture of Senator Daniel Vincent.

He was wearing a tuxedo which made him look even more starched than usual and his smile looked like he'd been practicing it every day, after school, for two hours. He held a champagne glass in one hand. His other arm was around the waist of a woman who was also looking into the camera and flashing one of those same professional smiles. Her shoulders were bare and her dress was moderately low cut. She looked good on the arm of one of the country's youngest senators and most eligible men. And she made him look good. They looked good together. Which, I'm sure, was the point of the picture.

Her name, according to the caption under the picture, was Barbara Hanley. She was a television producer. The picture had been taken at the INC banquet.

I tore it out of the paper and stuck it in my notebook.

I wondered what sort of stories she would tell about Senator Daniel Vincent.

Twelve

By the end of the day, I had talked to three more women. They all told essentially the same story about Senator Daniel Vincent. He was a hitter and a rapist. It was merely an accident that he wasn't a killer as well. His needs had taken other forms.

He was vastly more powerful – and not just physically – than any of those women. He would not lower himself to ask them for anything and he would punish them for making him do what he had done.

None of them had gone to the police. They were afraid and there hadn't been any evidence. And, since this was Washington, they had feared his power. He was a senator and that made him a lord. In spite of all the talk about equality – and Vincent could talk that old talk with the best of them – women were disposable if it suited him.

The woman from Georgia, however, might not be dazzled by his light. In Lisa Hutchinson's world, senators were still people. They couldn't necessarily get away with *anything*.

Driving back across the 14th Street Bridge in the wet, gray afternoon, I wondered if she had filed charges yet. Or, for that matter, if she ever would. I found myself hoping that she would and that she would make them stick. But a conviction was a long shot, even if she did.

The stories of the women I'd talked to should have been a help, but they probably wouldn't be. The case would be tried in Florida where the rules say that if you bring in stories of past acts, they must clearly demonstrate a pattern. It had come up in a Palm Beach rape trial. The prosecutor had found some women who said the accused had done pretty much the same thing to them, but the judge would not allow them to testify. There were enough differences between each episode that no clear pattern could be said to have emerged. If you beat hell out of your first victim, kicked the bejesus out of the next one, then pushed one's head through the wall, those people couldn't testify against you when you used a knife.

One more absurdity in the law. The law is an ass and everybody knows it. No news there.

If the Georgia woman did press charges, Daniel Vincent would get off. Semmes could do it. So could a lot of other lawyers, and I was hoping that it would work out that way.

I had the evidence but it wouldn't be allowed. I'd done my job. But there wasn't much point in it. Which left me with an urge to call Al Stackhouse about going out and drinking Fundador until my head hurt.

There was nothing for me at the motel but a room with a view of a shopping mall so I drove on over to the tomb of the unknowns to watch the changing of the guard. It was cold with a wind blowing off the river and a low, gray sky hanging sullenly over everything and trapping the sounds of the airliners as they took off from National every minute and roared overhead. In the silence that followed, the only thing your numb ears could make out was the steps of the guards as they paced the concrete.

They were polished and starched and their creases could have cut steel. The big marble tomb they guarded held, I suppose, scraps of bone from men who had been blown to bits on pointless ground, like some where I had run the same risks and come out a lot better, no fault of mine.

Luck of the draw.

There were thousands more, whose pieces had been big enough to recognize, buried down the hill. You might say they were luckier, though I don't suppose it made a rat's ass tc them that their names were known and carved in stone above their heads. They'd been snuffed just as cold as the men whose bones rested anonymously up here on the hill.

Down there, they lay in regimental ranks, under small, Spartan stones, perfectly dressed and perfectly still. I'd put one of them here. Long time ago. He'd been my friend and, after he'd bought it on the trail in Laos, they let me fly home with the body on a C-141. I'd hugged his wife while she cried on my shoulder and then I had come out here, somewhere, and carried the casket to the hole in the ground. There was a firing squad, dressed just like the men pacing now, in front of the unknowns. While the chaplain was saying his prayers, I'd heard one of them mutter, 'Ashes to ashes, dust to dust. Let's drop this fucker and get on the bus.'

I looked down at the rows of stone. And then back at the

guards, walking their posts. And then across the river at the imperial city. I suppose, in the end, you belong over here or over there. I belonged over here.

I waited until the guard changed again. By then my fingers and feet were numb and the thin light had bled out of the sky, leaving only gray gloom. Still, I kind of hated to leave.

The message light was blinking when I got back to my motel room.

I punched the phone number with one hand and the television remote with the other. There was the usual clutter on the television. The afternoon junk. I believe if that was all I had to keep me interested, then I would as soon be lying up in Arlington with a stone on my head.

I found CNN and hit the mute just about the time Randolph answered.

'I've got something for you, Morgan. On the thing you were asking about.'

'You work fast.'

'Wasn't as hard as it first looked,' he said. 'Some of these things, you just knock and the door swings open. I figured your boy probably had a cellular phone and that he was signed up in Washington. I started looking at the companies there. Got him on the third company I tried.'

'You make it sound easy,' I said.

'Well, you've got to tease them a little. They've all got security systems. Phone companies, especially, are freaked about hackers. But you can get in.'

'Maybe *you* can,' I said.

'I could show you.'

'Sometime, maybe,' I said.

'Once I had the company,' he said, 'it was a cinch to check the calls he made on Sunday morning, like you wanted.'

'Uh huh,' I said, holding up my end.

'There were five. Four of them to the same number, in Washington, and one to Delta Airlines, reservation department.

'The calls to Washington started at three thirty in the morning. They all went through a cell in Tallahassee. The last one was at about ten till six just before his new flight left.'

'How long did he talk?' I said.

'Yeah, I wondered the same thing,' Atkins said and I could hear him tapping keys.

'The first one was the longest. A little more than five minutes. The next two were about a minute each. The last one was real short. Fifteen seconds.'

'Who was he calling?'

'I tried looking up the number, in one of those reverse directories, but it was unlisted. So I had to get into the local phone company computers.'

'Hard?'

'Yeah,' he said. 'Took me hours ... well, maybe three or four hours.'

'What did you get?'

'The phone belongs to someone named Anita Lepage. That didn't do anything for me so, just for fun, I ran a quick search of the local papers. Same way I did on the investigator down in Miami, remember?'

'Right.'

'Anita Lepage works for the senator. She's called his "chief of staff".'

'You didn't by any chance check...'

'Check her calls,' Atkins interrupted. 'Yeah. I couldn't help myself. I mean, I'm not blind. I can see where this thing is heading. If he wants to claim he rushed back to Washington because of some emergency that had come up while he was gone, then he would have gotten a call from Washington sometime early Sunday morning, right before he called Delta to change his reservation.'

'And?'

'He didn't get any calls from Anita Lepage. Not from her unlisted phone, anyway. She hadn't made any long distance calls since late Saturday afternoon.'

'Good work, Randolph,' I said. 'Real damned good.'

'One more thing,' he said, ignoring the compliment, probably because, coming from me, it didn't count for much.

'What's that?'

'I studied the senator's phone records to see when he first called Lander White, the lawyer down in Miami.'

'Bless you,' I said.

'Called him at home, seven thirty on a Sunday morning. That was while he was in Atlanta, waiting for his Washington connection.'

'I doubt he was calling just to talk.'

'I was impressed,' Atkins said, 'that the senator knew White's home number. But, then, he could have gotten it from Lepage.'

'Why would she have it?'

'I imagine White is a contributor. Lawyers pony up big

when the politicians pass the hat. I mean, somebody has to *write* all those fucking laws. The lawyers figure that the politicians can't write them fast enough.'

Like most computer people, Atkins was an anarchist. To his way of thinking, laws belonged in the agrarian and industrial epochs, which were over.

'How long did they talk?'

'About ten minutes.'

'Okay, Randolph,' I said, 'I appreciate all this. A lot.'

'Proud to do it, Morgan,' Atkins said.

'Send me a bill.'

'How about I E-mail it to you?' he said. 'Over the internet?'

I felt, suddenly, both old and dumb. Randolph Atkins could do that to me. I told him to send the bill regular old mail and he sighed.

'When you get back, I'll come around and check you out on the Internet. It ain't in the future anymore, Morgan; it's right now.'

I told him that sounded fine. Then I hung up and watched the television. Four grown-ups sitting in chairs yelling at each other. They were having a political discussion. It was what people in Washington watched on television, instead of wrestling.

Thirteen

Since I was staying in town to finish what Semmes had sent me to do, I decided that I would start thinking and operating like I was building a case *against* Vincent. I planned to nail it down so tight that once Semmes had seen my work, he would cut the senator loose and let him find himself another lawyer. That was the theory, anyway.

There were two more calls I needed to make and there was still enough time left in the day. I checked my notes, then the phonebook. I wrote the number for Insider Productions in my notebook, then dialed it, hoping the office hadn't closed. It was not quite six. A woman answered crisply on the second ring and when I asked to speak to Barbara Hanley, she said, 'Your name, please?'

I told her.

'Is Ms Hanley expecting your call?'

'Nope.'

'Does Ms Hanley know you?'

'Nope.'

'Can you tell me what you are calling about?'

'Nope.'

'Sorry,' she said. 'Put it in writing.'

Fair enough. I wrote a one-page letter, tore it out of my

notebook, and left the room to find a Fed Ex drop. The envelope would be collected, shipped to Memphis, sorted, and shipped back here for delivery to Barbara Hanley's office which was less than one mile, straight line, from where I was standing.

I was back in my room in fifteen minutes. I looked through my notebook and called another number.

I was about to hang up when a woman answered.

'Yes?' She sounded agitated.

'Ms Lepage?'

'This is Anita Lepage. And I do not take solicitations over the phone.'

'I'm not selling,' I said. 'I'm investigating ...'

Before I could get any further, she interrupted and said, 'Investigating *what*?'

I figured I could try to explain politely, in which case she would hang up and I would have to make another trip to the Fed Ex box. Or I could say something to get her attention.

'A crime,' I said. 'A felony. As serious, just about, as felonies get. Your boss is a suspect. You might be an accessory.'

'Are you with the police?' Still on the attack, but checking her flanks.

'I'm an investigator for a private attorney.'

'Who?'

'Not Lander White,' I said. 'That's who your boss called Sunday morning. From the Atlanta airport after he'd already talked to you ... four times. The first time, it was three thirty in the morning.'

She didn't say anything for a few seconds. Then, when I

had just about decided she was going to hang up on me, meaning I was going to have to make another trip to the Fed Ex box, she said, 'I can't talk now. I'm on my way out.'

'Later would be fine.'

'In the morning,' she said.

'Fine.'

She would be in her office at six, she said. 'Is that too early for you?'

'No.'

'I'll expect you,' she said and hung up.

I was at the door of the Dirkson Building at quarter to six. It was still dark. And cold. There were a few other cars, looking for spaces around the big office buildings, but not many. I wondered what kind of people got to work, in Washington DC, before six in the morning.

Good thing, I thought, that there weren't many of them.

The guard called up and asked if I was all right. He gave me a pass, made me sign a sheet on his clipboard, and waved me on. I walked through the metal detector, rode an elevator, walked down a long hall, and found the number I was looking for. I knocked on the door and a voice said,

'It's open.'

I walked in.

The room was big and felt bigger than its actual dimensions. The ceilings were high. The windows were tall. The doors were vast. The whole effect was like what you experience in an old church. The scale is meant to diminish you, to make you feel small, frail, and insignificant. The building – or in this case, the office – was designed to convey the majesty of the enterprise, the institution.

The paneling was old oak. Very dark and sturdy looking. The furniture was made of the same stuff and looked almost too heavy to move. At the far end of the office, under the windows, there was a huge old wooden desk. A woman wearing half glasses that looked like they came from the drug store sat behind the desk. She was reading a newspaper.

'Have a seat,' she said. While I was crossing the room, she took a sip from a coffee cup but didn't ask me if I'd like some.

I took a chair next to her desk. She was somewhere around forty years old. She wasn't pretty because she didn't try to be. She looked tired and dry and brittle. Her eyes were filmy and sunk deeply into her skull. Either she was frowning or she wore too much lipstick on an unfortunate mouth. But you could see some beauty there and you could imagine that a few days on a beach in the tropics would make her look, if not young again, then at least like someone whose flesh was more than nuisance baggage. There were a lot of women who were considerably older and looked a lot better. Came down to attitude. Life for this one had become the job and nothing more.

She leaned across the desk and looked at me. Skeptically. As though she was trying to decide if I was worth bothering with.

'All right,' she said. 'I'm waiting.'
'For what?'
'For you to tell me what you want.'
I let her wait for a second and then I said, 'It's not a

matter of what I want. If there is a trial, you'll be called to testify about those conversations you had with your boss starting at three thirty last Sunday morning.'

'A trial?'

I didn't say anything.

'Who do you work for?' she said, abruptly, 'the *National Observer*?'

Before I could answer, she said, 'Am I the only one in this whole country who has just had it with the scandals? I mean, Jesus, enough already. Let's all get the fuck back to work. There are a few things that still need to be done before we just stretch out on the couch and watch the scandals on *Inside Edition* and *Court TV* for the rest of time.'

She kept her eyes on me while she gave this speech. When she finished, she shook her head, very slightly, side to side.

'It does get old, doesn't it?' I said.

'It's people like you,' she said. 'Looking for the career maker ... the scandal that will carry you over the top.'

'Not me,' I said. 'I'd rather be home, where it is warm and safe, if your boss could just learn to behave.'

'Keep it in his pants, you mean,' she said.

'People are tolerant,' I said. 'They can live with a little of that. Long as it is discreet.'

'He's a widower,' she said irritably. 'He's still young and ... *robust*.'

I nodded.

'And discreet.'

I waited.

'So what is the problem?'

'How many young women have quit this office in the last, oh, four years?'

'Oh come on,' she said. She waved her hand like she was chasing away a fly.

'You know what he is, don't you?'

'He is a United States senator. A pretty good one, too, even if that isn't saying much. But it is all I can do, in his hectic life, to stay on top of the affairs of state. All other affairs are his business. Not my problem, irrelevant to the real work that goes on around here and a goddamned bore on top of all that.'

'You probably weren't surprised,' I said, 'when he called you at home, three thirty in the morning.'

'All right,' she said, 'that's enough. I've got real work to do. You go on out and see if you can't find some scandal to amuse your public.'

'Like I told you last night,' I said, 'I'm an investigator.'

'I don't care if you are an astronaut,' she said. 'I have work to do. Goodbye.'

I liked her. In fact, I liked her a lot. She would make a lot of difference in the life of a prince. She would do the necessary, ugly, distasteful things. Do them well and enjoy it. You could see why she would be the first, and only, person Daniel Vincent would think to call in the early morning, when he was afraid for his political life ... and worse. Her throaty, no bullshit voice would be pure reassurance, not least because you would know that she wouldn't sugarcoat it. However bad she said it was, one thing was for sure – it wouldn't be any *worse* than that. Princes get used to hearing what they want to hear but even they know when they need it straight.

130

'Loyalty is a fine thing,' I said. 'But I don't think he would risk a felony charge for *you*.'

She waved me on my way. 'Look, friend, I may be a lot of things but one thing I am not is stupid. I made a few *inquiries*. You are not with Lander White and you are not with any State's Attorney's office since none of them have sent anyone to Washington on business in the last two weeks.

'So, I don't know who you are; but I damn sure know who you are *not*. If you are working for some little contingency fee-creep looking for a settlement then you are sucking eggs. There are more sluts looking for a payoff than there is money in the Treasury. No payoffs. Go find yourself a whiplash somewhere. Tell your client the air has gone out of that one.'

'I think you've made your position clear,' I said on my way to the door, 'and I'd like to thank you for your time.'

The sun was rising, anemically, over Washington when I left the Dirkson Building. But the cold drizzling rain felt clean and I didn't mind the walk to my car or the drive back across the river to my motel, against traffic. The cars coming the other way were creeping relentlessly into the District, like ants returning to the hive. I enjoyed the old reliable satisfaction you always feel when you go against the flow.

It was too early for Barbara Hanley to have gotten my Fed Ex package, so I changed clothes in my motel room and drove back down to the park where I ran through the drizzle for an hour or so.

Nothing Anita Lepage had said, I thought as I ran, had

131

changed anything. She'd put up a hell of a show but she hadn't denied anything, which was the same as admitting it. If there had been any doubt in my mind about Daniel Vincent before I went in to see his chief of staff, there was even less when I left her office.

Not enough in that for me to think about. So I counted a soft cadence to myself, dodged the puddles, and made myself think about other things.

Why does Anita Lepage work for him? Where is the real dependency? She wouldn't call *him* before dawn, in a box, desperate, needing help. Not in a million years.

Of course, every time he did it – or did something like it – it made her that much more ... *essential*. She was probably so essential, by now, that he might as well be working for her, except that she didn't want that any more than he did. And she knew it.

Nothing a strong counselor likes better than a weak prince.

I switched gears – or locations – when I got down to the last mile or two. What about Semmes? I thought. What was he doing, back in Panhandle Florida, and why couldn't he tell me?

He wasn't working for Vincent. Not yet, anyway. Lepage had made that plain.

So, maybe he was working for Lisa Hutchinson. Like Lepage said, the whole thing could be a shakedown. I can believe a lot of bad about my fellow man – with experience to back most of it up – but I couldn't believe that Semmes would play that game. Semmes liked a straight-up fight. He didn't pick pockets.

But ... suppose the woman had come to him and said,

'Look, he raped me. But no jury is going to convict him; not after the defense gets through with me. So what about this? You investigate and I'll pay for it. If you believe, after you've finished investigating, that I'm telling the truth, then you go after him for a settlement. I may not be able to put him in jail, but I want to hurt him. I want to make him pay and I want it on the record that he paid. What about it?'

If you were fishing for Semmes, could you catch him with that bait? I didn't think so but smarter people had been wrong about easier things.

But there was one riddle I couldn't solve. Why wouldn't Semmes tell me? I'd been working for him for a long time. It bothered me. And ... well, hell, it hurt.

Which, in the great scheme of things, counted for nothing.

Fourteen

Barbara Hanley said, simply, 'This better be good.'

She had the big hair and the straight white teeth, the good muscle tone, and a lot of appetite in her eyes. She didn't like me but, then, I suspect that she didn't like anyone she considered beneath her on the society/power pole. I wasn't a senator or a columnist or a celebrity lawyer. Not only wouldn't I be invited into the owner's box for Redskins games, I couldn't even get tickets. In her view, when I breathed, I was just using up air.

'Well,' I said, 'how about this? You are going out with a big, dirty story.'

We were standing on the grass, not far from the reflecting pool. There were tourists all around us, taking pictures, in spite of the weather which had cleared just a little but was still dismal. When she called, after she'd gotten my Fed Ex, she had suggested a place where we could get coffee. I was tired of those places. Tired of the air inside. The green had been my idea.

We were standing three feet apart and she was looking at me like she would just as soon squash me. She wasn't big enough to scare me. But if I'd worked for her I would have been faxing out résumés. And if I had been married to her, I would have been ordering flowers.

'What business of yours is it who I go out with?'

'That's the business you're in,' I said. 'You made a splash last year, with the story about the congressman and the lobbyist from Taiwan. I didn't know it was some kind of monopoly. Do I need a license?'

'You've been spying on *me*?'

'Never heard of you,' I said, 'until day before yesterday. But I have taken kind of a shine to that boyfriend of yours. First name Senator.'

'Daniel?' she said, mad enough now that she was losing her hard practiced composure. 'Jesus, you're not just slimy; you are also dumb. Where did you come from? Georgia or someplace?'

'Close enough.'

'Daniel Vincent is straight as a string. He doesn't even *like* money.'

'That comes with growing up around so much of it.'

'It is not a crime to be rich.'

'It isn't an alibi, either.'

'Look,' she said, staring hard and plainly expecting me to blink, 'you talk straight, and give me some details, or you fuck off. Are we clear on that?'

'Ask him what he was doing at three thirty last Sunday morning,' I said. 'And ask his chief of staff. Her name is Anita Lepage...'

'I *know* what her name is,' she snapped.

'And if they won't tell you, then see if you can find out. If you don't, someone else might.'

And I didn't have to tell her how terrible that would be.

Then she would be seen as the newswoman who was sleeping with a story and either did not know it, which would make her look dumb, or didn't report it, which would make her look corrupt. Either way . . .

'Why don't you tell me?'

'Me?' I said. 'I'm just a cracker from Georgia. You're the one who does stories for *60 Minutes*. You've got the sources.'

But other people did, too. Which she knew all too well. She wasn't even thinking about me anymore, even though I was standing a yard away. Her mind was on the story and what it could do for her . . . or to her.

I'd wanted to put a little heat on Senator Daniel Vincent. I had developed a real case about him. I wanted to see him in jail, at least. But I didn't think there was much chance of that.

So I would make him sweat a little under the hot lights of the media. It made it a little better that a woman he escorted to the black tie shakedowns they held every night, somewhere in Washington, would be the one behind the lights, grilling him.

'You know,' she said, 'if you are pulling my chain, then I'll get even. I know how.'

'I'm sure you do.'

'I don't think Daniel has anything to hide.'

'Then it can't hurt to ask him.'

'Where can I reach you? If I need verification?' She opened her large handbag to take out a notebook and pen. I could see inside the handbag. It would have been hard to miss the grip of the pistol. An automatic. One of those modern, highly engineered nine millimeters.

I looked at her and raised an eyebrow. She scowled and closed the handbag.

'You're on your own,' I said. 'Nice talking to you.'

I flew back that night. I might have made an afternoon flight except that Al Stackhouse had left a message at the motel. When I called him, he said, 'Let's do some drinking,' and it sounded like a good idea at the time. So we sat for three hours in a dirty little place in suburban Virginia, drinking Fundador and telling war stories. We were the only people in the place except for the bartender, who treated us with a kind of excessive, attentive politeness that made it plain he thought we were both crazy and dangerous. But he couldn't keep himself from listening in on our stories. Stackhouse had a million of them.

My plane got in to Tallahassee at midnight. I had a headache from the Spanish brandy. A prudent man would have found a motel and slept. So I got in my truck and drove two hundred miles.

I drove with the window down. It was a cool, clear night in the Panhandle, with a sky full of stars and the air smelling of river bottoms and pine trees. My head cleared in thirty or forty miles and I felt good enough to drive all the way to New Orleans; eat beignets and drink café au lait for breakfast.

But I stopped before I got to the Alabama line; first turning off the interstate and on to a two-lane state road, then a little county section road and, eventually, a driveway that was surfaced with crushed oyster shell. That road led to the house where I lived.

It was a big, old place; built by a ship's captain more than ninety years ago. He'd started small and added on rooms every time his wife had another baby and that seemed to happen just about every time he went off to sea. It was a twenty-room house.

It had been derelict for years when I bought it, right after I got out of prison. If it had been in a city, the building would probably have been condemned and it would have been against the law for me to live in it. After I bought it, I started out in the least decrepit room I could find, a tiny bedroom on the back of the first floor. Moved a cot in there and started working on the place one room at a time. It figured to take a long time but I was in no hurry.

I called it my River House because it sat on a little piece of solid ground a few feet over a bend in one of the little backwater rivers that are fed by limestone springs and flow through the low, swampy country of the Panhandle on their way to the Gulf. This particular river was called the 'Perdido'. Spaniards were the first Europeans to settle this part of the country. They didn't have much luck with it. They were lost the whole time.

Starting out, I considered the River House as lodging, therapy, and an investment. I needed a place to live; I needed something to do; and eventually, when I sold it, the money would be nice. It had kept me out of trouble, rebuilding it board by board, and now that I was nearly through, I sometimes wondered if I would be able to let it go if I got a good offer.

The answer, inevitably, was – probably. I'd put a lot of work into the house. But I had put a lot of work into other things that were nothing to me now. You keep moving.

But the house looked good, looming over the river in the

early morning stillness. It was surrounded by old, spreading live oaks that were draped in Spanish moss and there were no lights on inside. For some reason, that made the house seem even more massive and formidable than it was.

I let myself in and turned on enough lights to find my way to the room where I slept. I stripped and lay on the bed listening to the sound the river made a few feet from my window, and went fitfully to sleep.

I was up in three and a half hours.

And, an hour after that, I was drinking coffee with Semmes, in his office.

'A wretched place,' Semmes said. He was talking about Washington. 'Full of people who've dreamed all their lives of getting there and doing big things and are just so proud of themselves for doing it. I believe it is the sign of a malignant spirit for one human to dream of governing others. And Washington is full of just such cancerous shits.

'But ... you don't look so bad. Little tired. Must not have been too hard on you.'

I shook my head. 'I wasn't sorry to leave,' I said.

'I don't doubt it. But you did good work up there and I appreciate it.'

I nodded.

Semmes spun his chair a quarter turn and looked out of the office window at the view of the bay, the barrier island, and the endless green Gulf beyond. The sun was up and you could make out whitecaps.

His office was on the tenth floor of an old bank building. The bank, like just about everything else in the old, downtown section, had left for the perimeter where the malls and office buildings and the brand new suburbs were sprouting relentlessly. Semmes stayed, I suppose, because he liked the view and because he was a contrarian, by nature.

'Pretty day,' he said.

Semmes was usually direct by nature. But he could be evasive when he had to.

'Fine day,' I agreed. 'Mighty fine.'

He looked back at me and grinned. 'You getting weary of the mysterious bullshit?'

'A little.'

'What was that story you told me once, about the insignia you had printed up when you were in the service?'

'It was the order of the mushroom. Picture of a sorry looking toadstool with lettering around it. The letters were ... let's see, KITDFOHS. Stood for Kept in the dark; fed only horseshit.'

'You feeling that way?'

'Some,' I said.

'You ought to,' Semmes said. 'This isn't the way I like to do things, ordinarily. I think you know that.'

I nodded again.

'But in this case, it couldn't be helped. I gave my word.'

Which meant a lot to him. In addition to being a contrarian, he was old school. Maybe they went together.

'I can explain it to you now,' he said, 'but I'm going to have to ask you not to discuss it for the next few hours. You'll know when it is all right to talk about it.'

'Fine.'

Semmes finished his coffee and put the cup to one side, then leaned across his desk and gave me the look that meant he was not merely on a case but that he was on a hunt. His eyes seemed to glitter and the bones in his face seemed closer to the skin. His nostrils flared a little and there was a slight growl in his voice.

'I'm not defending Senator Daniel Lee Vincent,' he said urgently, 'and I never was. We're prosecuting the sonofabitch.'

Fifteen

'*We?*' I said.

Semmes looked at me and there was real concern in his face, 'I was counting on your help,' he said. 'Maybe I shouldn't have been so quick to assume. I apologize.'

I waved that away. My feelings didn't hurt that easy. 'You're too far ahead of me, Nat. All I'm seeing is your tail lights in the dust. When did you become a prosecutor?'

'It's what I started out doing. Million years ago. I liked it. The cases and the courtroom side of it.'

'But?'

'I never learned how to do it by the numbers; the way they like in big offices. I worked for the Justice Department for two years and then I quit.'

I could understand that, I said, in a heartbeat.

'It wasn't the prosecuting.'

I could understand that, too. What I couldn't understand is how he could all of a sudden decide to be a prosecutor again. And on this case.

'The governor asked me,' Semmes said.

'The governor?' I said. Semmes dealt with governors all the time. To me, they were sort of like bobcats and

143

GEOFFREY NORMAN

panthers, out in the swamps. You knew they existed, even
though you seldom actually saw one.

'He knew about that rape the morning it happened,'
Semmes said. 'His people keep a close watch on the cops
and he doesn't miss much. He called me, in the morning.
Called before breakfast.

'What he said was, the state had done a lousy job on
these high profile rape charges – going back to the Kennedy
kid down in Palm Beach – and it was causing problems. He
wanted to see a conviction, if this thing ever came to trial.

'And, he said, there was another problem. One of these
high profile cases can just overwhelm you. Prosecutors
aren't exactly sitting around waiting for work and in one of
these cases, you cannot cut corners. It takes a lot of time
and, sometimes, all the money. You see these little
jurisdictions that suddenly find themselves trying one of
these circus cases, and it will eat up the whole budget for
prosecutions. They can't try a common breaking and
entering, or anything else, for the rest of the year unless
they get help from the state or the feds. You even saw it in
Los Angeles. It cost the city so much to prosecute O. J.
Simpson that it had to go begging the state for money.'

'Did the governor ask you to work for free?' I said.

Semmes smiled. 'That would look like a vendetta, don't
you think?'

'Looks sort of like that anyway,' I said.

'I'll be a special prosecutor,' Semmes said. 'These days,
the world is full of them.'

'For those political deals, maybe,' I said.

Semmes shook his head. 'Not exclusively. When Mike
Tyson was on trial, in Indiana – for rape, as a matter of fact

144

– the governor wanted to make sure the state wasn't overmatched. He appointed the best criminal lawyer in the state as special prosecutor. Man named Garrison. Damned good lawyer. But he looked and talked like a country boy from the cornfields and swine farms. Tyson came in with his high-priced team from Williams and Connally – same firm that got the kid who shot Reagan off on an insanity plea – and everyone figured Tyson would be back fighting again after a two week trial. Garrison waxed them. Sent them back to Washington with no asses in their pants. Sent Iron Mike to jail for a few years, too.'

'I remember.'

'This is the same,' Semmes said, 'more or less.'

'I wonder.'

'Why?'

'Maybe it's out of my league,' I said, 'but I'd say there's more going on here than just straight up law n'order.'

Semmes grinned. 'What could you possibly have in mind, Morgan?'

'Could it be that the governor wants to bring in outside talent – you know, a gunslinger . . .'

'That's exactly what the reporters called Garrison,' Semmes interrupted, '"a gunslinger." It started right after everyone recognized he was winning. The big city reporters didn't think it was fair for the state to have its own hot-shot lawyer.'

'My point,' I said, 'is, once you get past the actual case, what you've got is the governor and a US senator. And they're political rivals, aren't they?'

'Absolutely,' Semmes said, cheerfully. 'They hate each other's guts. Or, actually, it isn't that good. They *fear* each other. They figure there is only so much power to go around and they both want all of it.

'Florida is the third largest state in the country. Growing faster than any state. People come here to retire and there is no block more conscientious about voting than old people. If a politician suggests changing the ink they use to print social security checks, then he'll be looking for work after election day. A young, rising political star from the state of Florida would make a strong vice-presidential candidate. And after a term or two of seasoning, he could run for president.

'But there is only going to be one star from Florida. It is a big state; but it's not that big. So it's either the young governor or the young senator.'

'Seems like,' I said, 'that if there is a trial, the senator is finished, no matter what the verdict is.'

Semmes shook his head slowly. 'No,' he said. 'You're thinking old, there, Morgan. I'd agree with you, if it was twenty years ago. Being charged with rape would have finished anyone. But this is a different age. If Vincent is tried and acquitted, then he could go out and sell himself as a victim. A man unjustly accused. He'd say he was persecuted by a political rival. And I suspect we would see a real sly, oily campaign, the kind that some of these spin doctors know how to run. They'd make Vincent into a clean-living, church-going widower whose good name and reputation had been smeared by one of these immoral, dope-smoking, Jezebels. They'll make it sound like he did a noble thing by going to court to clear his good name and that he has been tested by the fire of malicious, unfair accusations and made hard; that he was ready now to go out and fight the same way, for all the good causes good people believe in.'

I shook my head. 'You believe they could make that work?'

'It wouldn't be the first time,' Semmes said. 'This is for high stakes. Too high to worry about shame or embarrassment. Those are non-factors.'

'Along with the truth.'

'Yes,' Semmes said. 'But there isn't anything new, or surprising, in that, is there?'

'Nat, listen,' I said, 'if Vincent is acquitted, the governor will be toes up ... and so will you.'

'I understand that, Morgan. Believe me.'

'If he's convicted...' I hesitated here and Semmes smiled. It was the kind of wise, vaguely benevolent smile he used on you when he knew what you were thinking.

'You're wondering what the governor will owe me?' he said.

'Sort of.'

'There's no payoff.'

'I didn't mean that ...'

'I know,' Semmes said. 'And I didn't take it like that. But there isn't any understanding between me and the governor. I told him I expected to be paid, like a junior member of the State's Attorney's staff, and that I expected a boilerplate letter of thanks – an official attaboy – when the case was over ... If it was successful.'

'You drive a hard bargain,' I said. 'Shouldn't you have let up on him a little?'

'The governor understands, even though I didn't tell him,' Semmes went on, 'that if one of his backers calls me with an offer to serve on some board or an opportunity to get in early on some "investment opportunity", then I will go straight to the papers and scream "bribe", a lot louder than the woman in this case cried "rape".'

I nodded. And I thought for a moment or two.

'I'm not surprised by that, Nat. I mean, I suppose if I thought there was some money in it; or a job or two tickets to the Sugar Bowl, right on the fifty, and you were the kind to take the payoff, then I wouldn't be so goddamned curious. I wouldn't be wondering why you are, all of a sudden, a prosecutor.'

'You want to know why I'm *really* doing it, right?' He smiled.

'I suppose.'

'Okay, Morgan,' he said, 'I'll tell you why I'm *really* doing it. But you've got to promise that it will never leave this room. If you spread this around and it winds up in the newspapers, I'll be ruined as a criminal lawyer in this country.'

'I understand,' I said.

'Are you sure?' he said. 'Because what I'm going to tell you is the kind of thing that could haunt me to my grave.'

I nodded. I'd never known him to serve it quite this thick.

'All right,' he said, 'the reason I agreed to do this, when the governor asked me is ... well, because it seemed like it was my duty.'

Sixteen

I had to get back to Tallahassee. Semmes had been told that Lisa Hutchinson was going to press charges that afternoon and, when she did, the circus would be on.

'You will be working for me in an unofficial capacity,' he said. 'I'm not sure the State's Attorney can hire convicted felons. Even if they have been pardoned.'

'I wouldn't work for them anyway,' I said.

Semmes wanted me to be his eyes and ears for the next few days. He wasn't sure when he would be coming over to set up shop. Probably not for a while. Shortly before the trial, which was a long way off.

'I'll be dropping in, though,' he said. 'Probably in a few days.'

I said I would call him. Then I went back to the River House to pick up a few things and to check on the place. While I was there, I tried to call Jessie Beaudreux. We hadn't talked in a while.

Her answering machine said that she would be out of town for three weeks and would not be checking her messages.

Well, that was the way things were between us. Without ever saying it, we had agreed not to cling to each other like a couple of desperate lovers since both of us would suffocate if we did. Sometimes it seemed like we carried it a little too far. The River House had that dusty, melancholy look that a house gets when it hasn't been lived in and I was getting tired of small motel rooms and the empty companionship of television. I'd been hoping Jessie would be free for dinner.

But ... she wasn't. So I decided not to hang around and drove back to Tallahassee that afternoon. I got there just in time for the opening act of the circus.

The reporters and photographers looked like a nest of yellow jackets after somebody had stirred them up with a stick. It was a familiar scene, even if you'd never seen it before. These people were here to spread the news. The news is what people do for fun here in the late innings of the twentieth century, now that we don't have public hangings. It wasn't a Hollywood murder but it was a Washington rape and that was better than nothing. Lots better.

Lander White was saying something to the hive. I couldn't catch all of it but it didn't make any difference. If you had been paying any attention at all, you had heard it before.

'Client is not guilty ... welcome his day in court ... reclaim his good name ... etc. etc. and blah, blah, blah.'

But if it was an old song, the people crowding around White, pushing and shoving and sweating from the strain of it all, they were prepared to dance all night long. They couldn't get enough. You would have thought White was some kind of modern-day prophet, just down from the mountain with the secret of more money and thin thighs. The crowd was just eating it up.

I was making a big effort to stay back, away from the press of strange bodies. I could imagine a smell coming from all those excited glands. I didn't want to breathe it and I didn't want it on my clothes.

But somebody crowded me, just the same, and put his mouth close to my ear. His breath was warm, with a strong tobacco scent.

'Looks like your man got screwed,' the voice said.

I turned and was looking into one of those long, angry country faces with prominent bones and pale-green eyes that were set so deep they looked like stagnant pools in the bottom of caves.

'Say again,' I said.

'Looks like the senator found himself another mouthpiece,' the man said. 'Too bad for you.'

I didn't get it and it must have showed in my face.

'I know who you are,' he said, 'and I know who you work for. I expect you must be wondering who I am.'

'Now that you mention it.'

'You talked to my sister, a while back,' he said. He smiled in a kind of cruel, conspiratorial way, 'about what that senator done to her.'

I still didn't know what to say, so I just said, 'Oh.'

'I couldn't believe that you worked for Semmes.'

'Oh,' I said again. Then I gathered my forces and said, 'Why not?'

'Because I know about him. From the papers and the television. It ain't his style.'

'Uh huh,' I said.

'This creep, now,' the man said, nodding in the direction

of Lander White who was still talking, 'he's *perfect*. I mean, just look at the sumbitch.'

I looked at White again. He was wearing a blue suit that looked like linen to me. Cut casual and tropical but also cut perfectly. His shirt was white cotton and so bright that it almost hurt your eyes to look at it. When he raised one arm to make a gesture, you could catch the flash of gold from his wristwatch. His hair had been waved in something and his tan was the kind you don't get without working on it, even if you live in Miami.

'He is a vision,' I said, 'no doubt about it.' Actually, when you got past the costume, you saw White's nervous eyes and weak mouth and you recognized what he was – a man who needed constant validation. For some it comes from voters. For some it is women. For White, it was jury verdicts. When they went his way, he was alive. When they went against him, he was in despair.

Which explained why he would do anything to win.

'I'm trying,' the man said, 'to decide if I'm going to kill him, too.'

I led him away from the scene in front of the courthouse so we could talk without shouting. He told me his name, which was Earl, and that he had made up his mind to kill Dan Vincent and maybe kill his lawyer, Lander White, too, while he was at it.

I didn't have to ask him why. So I said that I believed he might do it but that if he did, he would almost certainly regret it.

'You done the same thing, when you had the chance. You sorry you done it?'

'I went to prison for it,' I said.

'That ain't what I asked you.'

'I did what I did in anger. Heat of the moment,' I said.

'That's still not what I asked you.'

'They'll charge you with first degree murder and send you to Raiford. And, unless you are lucky, they will fry your ass in the electric chair.'

'Could be,' he said. 'But did you stop to think about that?'

'I told you . . .' I started, but I could see in his face that arguing with him would be pointless. He had a stupid, complacent look, like an animal that had been hungry a few minutes earlier but had eaten now and wouldn't have to think about anything until it got hungry again.

'Have you picked a time for these killings?' I said.

'When I get ready,' he said. 'The one I really want ain't even here yet. He's still up in Washington. Passing laws.'

I told Semmes about the press conference and about Earl Hutchinson, when we talked on the phone that evening.

'Was it a specific threat?' Semmes said.

'No. More like something he was thinking about doing,' I said. 'The same way some people think out loud about dyeing their hair or giving up drinking.'

'If he makes a serious, specific threat, Morgan,' Semmes said, 'then you'll have to go to the police.'

'I know,' I said. 'But I'm thinking once he hears you're prosecuting the thing, he'll hold off. At least until there is a verdict.'

'Uh huh,' Semmes said. 'And then, he'll come after me.'

'I don't think so.'

'Just a talker, then?'

'No,' I said. 'I believe he's one of those who would kill if he believed he had a grievance. He'd be one of those who believes that if you want justice – or anything else – then you've got to supply it yourself. And I suspect he'd like to have the excuse, something that would make him feel like he had the right to kill somebody. Then he could really enjoy it.'

After a long silence, Semmes said, 'I might mention something about him to the sheriff, when we talk. Just so he'll know to keep an eye on him. What we especially don't need is some midnight justice. Let me know if you run into him again.'

'Right,' I said.

'Anything else?'

'Well, you can read about the press conference in the papers. It was the usual frog show. Lander White couldn't get enough.'

'He is a man who likes the spotlight,' Semmes agreed.

'Is he any good?'

'He is, indeed. One of the best. But you know,' Semmes said, his tone dropping a note or two and becoming pensive, 'like a lot of people who've become celebrities, he's started enjoying it so much that he sometimes forgets what it is that got him there. He's like a ballplayer who likes the postgame press conferences so much that he dreams about them during the game and loses his concentration. Then, the only thing anybody wants to talk to him about is the play he blew.'

'I see.'

'Lander White is so in love with seeing himself in the papers and on the television that he just might forget that he needs to do his job. He'll be like old Narcissus, admiring his own reflection in the pool, while I slip up behind and cut his throat.'

I told him it sounded like a good plan.

'Well,' he said, 'it's still a little vague. But I like the general design.'

'How do you plan on handling the reporters?' I said.

'I believe I'll follow Admiral King's example,' Semmes said. 'You remember who he was?'

'No.'

'Ernest King. Chief of Naval Operations during World War Two and a very hard man. He wasn't like MacArthur and Patton and Halsey and Montgomery and the rest of the commanders back then who considered it a bad day if their names weren't in the papers. Some of those men just lived for publicity. King hated it and he hated reporters.

'Somebody asked him, early in the war, what his plan was for dealing with the press and you know what he said?'

'No,' I said, 'what?'

'He said, "My plan is to tell them not one goddamned thing until it's all over. Then, I'll tell them who won."'

'That's my plan, too, Morgan,' Semmes said.

I said I hoped it worked.

'So do I,' Semmes said. 'Call me tomorrow evening. Sooner, if you've got something hot.'

I said I would and hung up.

Seventeen

The circus was in town and Lisa Hutchinson could have been one of the prime, center-ring acts. Barbara Walters wanted her; promised her an entire one hour show, in fact, with just the two of them talking.

When I heard about that, I recalled the old line about fame. Something about how, in the future, everybody will get a fifteen minute ration and then return to obscurity. This was a benediction. Four lifetimes. And it came from Barbara herself, who was prime time. Not some daytime hack.

Geraldo, Oprah, Donahue and countless lesser after-noon and morning specimens also called with their offers.

'They can all,' Semmes said, 'go straight to hell. Where their talents will be vastly appreciated.'

And Semmes was calling the shots. He had talked to Lisa while I was up in Washington and she trusted him entirely. Which was a good thing, since it meant she would do what Semmes told her to do.

She would have her day in court, Semmes had explained to her, and after that, she could speak from whatever forum suited her and tell her story on her terms.

'And you won't be doing it to pimp somebody's ratings,'

157

he said. 'Barbara Walters isn't interested in you for any other reason and if Barbra Streisand called and asked for your night, they'd cancel you in a heartbeat. To them, you are just *material*.'

She plainly believed that whatever she was to Semmes, it was more than that.

So, immediately after she filed her formal complaint, so the sheriff could issue an arrest warrant for Senator Daniel Vincent, Lisa Hutchinson went into hiding – in the guest house of a hunting plantation, ironically enough, this one owned by friends of Semmes, named Atwood. Eliot and Ruth. He had done well in lots of ways but especially in mining and shipbuilding. He was a courtly sixty-year-old man who hunted quail every day when they were in season. His wife gave parties and grew prize-winning camellias. They had known Semmes for years and, like most people who had, they would do just about anything for him.

They looked in on Lisa to see if there was anything she needed and they made an effort to be friendly. But the social chasm that separated them was just too wide. She stayed to herself and the Atwoods stayed out of her way.

Dixie Price drove out to visit Lisa and kept her company for an hour or so every day. Her visits were social. Mine were business.

'I've been over that a hundred times,' she said, petulantly, one afternoon, a few minutes into my interview. She was wearing jeans and a faded red Florida State sweatshirt, sitting on a leather sofa with her legs folded under her. She looked tired.

'You should probably plan for two hundred, at least,' I said, 'or maybe three hundred, just to be on the safe side.'

'Why?' she said, in a whiny voice. 'I can understand once or twice, just to make sure you've got everything right, you know. But why do I have to do it over and over. It doesn't make any sense.'

'That's the way the law works,' I said, 'and the law doesn't have to make sense.'

She made a face. It wasn't self-pity but a kind of real pain and I realized at that moment just how trapped she must feel. All the rest of us had something to do. It was action for us but she was just hiding out, telling her story over and over, and waiting to see what would happen next. Waiting to see if people would believe her, even after the inevitable attack on her story and her character and anything else that looked handy to the lawyers whose job it was to destroy her. And there would be people, she knew, who would distrust her or, worse, pity her because she was a victim. It was one of the world's most demeaning roles – victim – and in that moment I felt compassion for her.

'Mostly,' I said, 'it is a mystery. In my experience, the law is just *different*. The rest of the world runs on timetables and deadlines but not the law. The law has all the time in the world. You can't tell your story often enough to satisfy the law.'

'It's crazy,' she sulked.

I nodded and thought, I believe you will find out it is a lot worse than that.

'Stay involved,' I said. 'Don't sit back and let it happen to you. Ask questions and be a player.'

She shrugged.

'You know,' I said, 'I talked to your brother the other day. During that first press conference.'

159

'Earl?'

'He said he was going to kill the senator. And maybe kill Lander White, too, as long as he was at it.'

'He's like that. He'll fight anyone.'

'We're talking about something a little worse than fighting here. Double murder. A US senator *and* a prominent attorney. Be hard to get more serious than that.'

'You think he means it?'

'I thought maybe you'd be able to tell me.'

'He could. Wouldn't surprise me none.'

'Why do you say that?'

'I don't know,' she shrugged. 'On account of how he sounded last time we talked.'

What I like is a precise answer.

'What did he say?'

She wrinkled her forehead. 'He was carrying on – mad, you know – about how the senator was going to get off. About how there wasn't no justice for people like us unless we made our own. So I told him about what you done.

'He said that sounded like the only way and if the jury didn't do the right thing, then maybe he would.'

So I would be remembered for committing the murder of a Coca-Cola heir and for inspiring the murder of a senator and his celebrity lawyer. Well, the good that men do, etc. etc.

'You tell your brother,' I said, carefully, 'not to do it. Not to even think about it.'

'Why not?'

'I went through it with him,' I said. 'But try putting it to him this way. If he is trying to avenge your family's honor, he is not going to feel a lot of satisfaction. And your family is just going to pay in pain, every day he sits down at Raiford, waiting for his turn in the electric chair. It is only worth it if he could get away with it. And he can't.'

I left the Atwood plantation to drive back into town. The pine trees out here were tall, old, and widely spaced with tall yellow grass growing in the gaps between them like some kind of deep carpet. This was the way God and nature had meant for the piney woods to look. Big and open and restful. The paper companies had other ideas. They planted trees like corn, in close rows, so thick you couldn't walk through a stand without breaking branches. It was dark and close, almost claustrophobic, in there among them.

But the yields were good and that's what counted.

I preferred it the old way. In pine trees and everything else.

Back in town, packs of reporters were chasing marginal stories like dogs on scent. I drove past the Gator Pit, scene of the crime, and there were so many television vans and rental sedans in the parking lot that a thirsty construction worker would have had a hard time finding a place to park so he could go inside for a cold beer.

So, while the Gator Pit was all over television and the papers, it also might go broke. Which is a pretty good illustration of the high price of fame.

Inside, the pack would have Pete, the bartender, surrounded by now. It was his fifteen minutes in the barrel.

The herd would be yapping at him. Questions about when the senator and Lisa left. Did they leave together? Did they drink a lot? Did they dance together? How close?

And, they would be asking Pete – and anyone else they could find with something to say – about other nights when Lisa Hutchinson came to the bar alone. Other men she might have left with. They would be asking, without saying the word, if she was a slut.

'Count on Lander White to ride that horse just as hard as he can,' Semmes had said. 'At first, he'll let the media carry his water for him. But I doubt they'll turn up much on their own. They mostly use what someone gives them. So Lander will have ... what's the name of that investigator whose trail you ran across?'

'Longacre,' I said.

'Right, him. Lander will have Longacre out beating the bushes, looking for people who got drunk and slept with Lisa Hutchinson. Or claim to have. Or claim to have a friend who did. I suspect he'll find some.'

'Will he use them?' I said.

'Dog have fleas?'

'How much will it hurt?'

'We'll see,' Semmes said, concealing his cards, for now. But I was dead certain he had a plan.

So did I. My plan was to go work out, then eat supper, then write up some notes and go to bed. Uninspired, but it was the best I could do. It was getting to be Spring, with the woods showing that first sweet tender shade of green and I would have rather been in other places doing other things. But that was just speculative. Fact was, I was here and this is what I was doing. I just hoped that it would quiet down for a while, around the time the dogwoods came into bloom.

I did my weightlifting in the police department weight

room. One of the investigators at the State's Attorney's office got me a pass. None of the young cops who told war stories, stroked their moustaches, and admired their pecs in the mirrors paid any attention to me. Probably thought I was assigned to some kind of undercover drug operation. Or maybe they knew who I was and just didn't care.

Fine with me. I worked out alone, like I had when I was inside the wire. Back then, I'd kept my mind totally on the steel, shutting out all the illiterate conversations around me. I wasn't interested in building up muscle, more in burning off rage. The lifting area was outside, in the yard, and I worked there every day. I worked when it rained and when it froze. There were days when the rain hit the bar and turned to ice. I just wrapped my fingers a little tighter, no gloves, and kept lifting. I had heat to spare.

I didn't have the same deep reserves of rage these days. Why would I? But I'd kept the same kind of focus on the steel and the movement of the weights. Old habits, I suppose. I didn't hear the conversations going on around me and I didn't see myself in the mirrors.

I worked for two hours and felt blood weary when I finished.

I ate speckled trout and coleslaw at a seafood place where they stuck to local ingredients and didn't try anything too fancy. The fish was sautéed but they didn't go overboard on the sauce. It was just fine.

It was actually pretty early for supper but I can't get excited about eating alone and wanted to get it out of the way. I missed Jessie. I'd left a couple of messages but she hadn't called the motel. I tried to put that out of my mind.

I got back to my motel room in time for the news. Local, then national. Then more local. If you juggled the dial skillfully, you could watch two hours of news, uninterrupted except for commercials. I couldn't understand why anyone would want to do that, unless he were being paid, which I was ... after a fashion.

So I took a beer from the cooler I'd stashed in the bathroom, opened it and sat down in front of the television. The beer was good and cold. There was that to be grateful for.

The local news lead off breathlessly with a report from the Gator Pit. It had probably been filmed while I was driving by, earlier that afternoon.

The bartender said all the same things he'd said to me about that night, sounding like he couldn't understand why people didn't get it the first time.

'Did you see them leave together?' the reporter, a blonde with an epoxy face said earnestly.

'No.'

'Did you see either of them leave?'

'Yeah. I saw 'em both leave.'

'Who left first?'

'He did.'

'And she left after that?'

The bartender gave her a look that said, *Now what kind of dumb shit question is that?*

'Approximately how long after he left did she leave?' The epoxy was about to crack.

The bartender shrugged. The tension was definitely not getting to *him.*

'Fifteen, twenty minutes.'

'Thank you,' the reporter said, with relief, and turned away from the bartender to focus all her concern on the camera. Which was plainly the way she liked it.

'The remaining question is,' she said, in that voice they all use, 'what happened *after* the senator and Lisa Hutchinson left the bar that Saturday night.'

She paused to let that one sink in.

'Now back to you, Phil.'

There was more. Praise Jesus. Lots more. Including a long report about Semmes being appointed special prosecutor by the governor. They had the details of Semmes' career more or less right. But I didn't recognize the man. They made him sound like some kind of piney woods Perry Mason, the kind of person who could make lightning flash and thunder roar just by filing a writ of *habeus corpus*. You could see them casting the movie.

The Semmes I knew was a lot more interesting than that. But he came out of another time and he believed things that were considered laughable these days, especially by the kind of people who made movies. If Semmes had been alive during the Civil War, he would have owned no slaves but he would have also raised a regiment to go off and fight in Virginia. And he probably would have been killed leading that regiment up Cemetery Hill. His men would not have left his body in the field.

But he was not a grandstander. He despised that kind of vanity, which made the way the pretty boys and girls on television called him a 'high profile gunslinger' absurd. Semmes had done remarkable things but he hadn't done them to call attention to himself.

But to hear the newsies describe him, you'd have thought

he was F. Lee Bailey or Leslie Abramson or Alan
Dershowitz or one of those other, magazine cover, television consultant lawyers who ride into town by chartered jet
and block-long limo to give interviews and turn a fat fee.

Semmes hated them.

'But what can you expect,' he once said to me, 'when you
live in a world where *speech writers* for the president are
famous people? Trying to make heroes out of lawyers is
bad enough but it's no worse than *that*.'

Fact was, Semmes was prosecuting Daniel Vincent
because a) the governor had asked him to and b) he had
satisfied himself that there was something there to prosecute.
Now, he would do it faithfully. Which meant that Senator
Daniel Lee Vincent had best buckle his chin strap.

Eighteen

Vincent gave his own press conference from Washington and said, not surprisingly, that he was an innocent man.

He said it forcefully, with a lot of indignation; but there was no surprise in that, either. They are all good actors. Among the best, in fact, since no matter what it is they are saying, they believe it entirely.

What *was* mildly surprising about the press conference was Vincent's theory about why this was happening to him. It was, he said, political.

Somebody was trying to set him up and do him in. Presumably because he was a threat.

'Now that,' said one of the men at the bar of the Hilton hotels where all the out-of-town media was staying, 'is a load of horseshit. I can't believe Lander White, who is supposed to be a smart goddamned lawyer, let him say something like that.'

'What should he have said?' a woman standing next to him demanded, slightly loud and slightly belligerent, mostly from beer. She had been drinking with the rest of them, since the end of the press conference. That meant they had been at it for about two hours. They would all go back to their rooms in time to watch the news broadcasts. Then they would come back to the restaurant next door to eat dinner. Some, who were tired of the hotel food, would crowd into a rental car and go looking for a new restaurant. They would all be back here for a nightcap.

'What he should have said,' the man answered loudly – it was noisy in the room, but not that noisy – 'what he should have said is that they were a couple of grown-ups looking for a loveless fuck on a Saturday night. That he didn't have to force her or even talk her into it. She was willing and he was able – straight consentual sex. Heterosexual and everything. Juries can understand that. Even here.'

He was with a newspaper, but I wasn't sure which one. The woman was a stringer with *Time* magazine. I'd learned that sitting around the bar, pretending I'd been hired by someone who wrote true crime books, to do his legwork.

When they asked me who, exactly, I was working for, I told them I couldn't say. Sorry. Part of the deal.

One of them mentioned a name I didn't recognize and one of the others said, 'Yeah, that's it. Got to be. He wrote the shittiest book yet on Teddy Kennedy, so this is a natural for him. Another young senator has a shot and blows it because he can't keep his pants zipped. He can probably catch a seven figure advance on that one. How much is he paying you?'

I just smiled and let them believe what they wanted. That night one of the news programs reported that the famous author of true crime books had hired an investigator to follow the early developments in the Vincent case. The writer denied it immediately, which settled it for the crew at the Hilton bar. It had to be true.

So they accepted me – after a fashion – and allowed me to sit at the bar and listen in on their conversations. I never said much, which made my role even more convincing.

'If they argue consentual sex,' the stringer from *Time* said, 'they are going to have to prove it ... sort of.'

'That's easy,' the man said, still shouting, 'they just convince the jury that's what the Hutchinson woman did for fun on Saturday night. Other nights, too.'

'Can they do it?' a thin, black man in glasses, up from Miami, said. He sounded Cuban.

'You know Lander's investigator?'

'Longacre? Sure.'

'Well, I hear he is putting together a list. Lisa Hutchinson's ten greatest fucks.'

'And I hear,' another man said, 'that it is a crowded field to pick from.'

'And *that* is supposed to be enough to prove that he couldn't have raped her, right?' the woman from *Time* said. 'She can't be raped unless she is a virgin?'

'Oh come on, Sue.'

'No, fuck you. It's always like that, isn't it. Always. She asked for it. Or even if she didn't, she *wanted* it ...'

'Hey, Sue, nobody said it's *right*. Just that it's going down that way.'

'Right.'

'Yeah, chill.'

'Well it pisses me off.'

There was a silence. Thirty seconds or so. A way of showing respect, I suppose, for the solemn fact that Sue

169

was pissed off about the way the criminal justice system treats rape victims. Then, somebody tried to change the subject.

'I heard that there is a guy from *Penthouse* in town. He's got money and he's looking for stories and pictures. Especially pictures.'

'What kind of pictures?'

'Now what kind of pictures do you *think Penthouse* would be interested in?'

'Do we know they exist?' said an older man, thin with lines in his face and very straight, well combed, gray hair. He looked out of place in this group.

'Well,' one of the young reporters said, 'you can't be sure. But these days, it seems like whenever a young woman gets her name in the papers, no matter what it is for, some boyfriend shows up with pictures he took of her. She's lucky if she is just standing there with no clothes on. Sometimes they are action shots.'

'Sometimes,' another man said, 'it's even a video.'

'I'll tell you what's hard to believe,' the stringer from *Time* said. 'What's hard to believe is that somebody who had said the things it would take to talk a woman into letting him take those pictures would turn around and sell them. That's what's hard to believe.'

'Well,' somebody said, 'love isn't always for ever. It isn't always kind, either. And sometimes you need the down payment on a new truck.'

'Men are pigs.'

'Agreed. And the women who'll let them take pictures are fools.'

It was still going like that when I left.

* * *

It would be months, I thought, driving back to the motel, and maybe more than a year, before the trial got started. Interest would die down from the high heat of today to a bed of coals which the tabloids and the heavy breathing television shows would keep glowing until the major players got back to town and the big show got started. Inquiring minds wanted to know. Not just inquiring minds. Also minds that read *Time* magazine. And the people who bought the books written by the man that everyone believed I was working for.

I could not understand it. I was already sick of it.

There were two messages at the motel. One from someone named 'Frank' at a local number. The other was from Jessie. She was in North Carolina somewhere. I called that number first and got an answering machine. It wasn't her voice so I hung up and tried the number again. Same machine, same voice. I hung up again. I would try later. I wanted to talk to her. Seeing her name on the pink message slip had made me momentarily light headed, like taking a double shot of bourbon after a long time dry.

I tried the other number.

'Yeah.' The voice at the other end was rough as a flat file.

'This is Morgan Hunt,' I said. 'Someone left a message for me.'

'Huh,' the voice said. I could hear a television in the background.

'Maybe I've got the wrong number,' I said. I looked down at the pink sheet.

'No, wait a minute.' The television noise faded. Sometimes

it seems like before anything can get started, you have to turn off the television.

'Hunt,' the voice said, 'this is Frank Swearingen. Remember? Public defender's office. Friend of Tom Pine.'

'Right,' I said. 'Sure. How are you doing?'

'The same,' he said. 'Taking it one day at a time and all that other happy shit. You?'

'Hanging in there,' I said.

'Good,' he said. 'That's good. Looks like you and Semmes have got your hands full.'

'That's a fact.'

'You remember how you told me to keep an eye on the Hutchinson woman, and her apartment?'

Actually, I had forgotten. I'd asked back before I left for Washington. When I thought Vincent would be our client and I'd assumed we'd want anything we could get on Hutchinson that would make her look bad in court. Now, if Swearingen had something, I didn't want to know about it.

'Sure,' I said. 'Absolutely. Listen, figure up your time and fix up I bill. I'll get you a check.'

'I appreciate that,' Swearingen said. 'But I'm sure you're good for it. I thought we ought to talk, actually. I turned up something, back when I was watching Hutchinson's apartment. You probably need to know about it.'

'All right,' I said.

'Can you meet me somewhere?'

'Pick a place,' I said.

'Well, I don't much like the bars these days. And it's a nice afternoon. Let's meet outside.'

There was a small green area. A park, of sorts, across from the capitol building, and we met there. It was a cool,

Spring evening and the air was warm and fragrant.
Daffodils and narcissus were blooming in the beds next to
the walks and the dogwood buds were swollen and ready to
burst.

'Strange place for guys like us to be meeting,' Swearingen
said. He was wearing wash khakis, a white shirt, a green
blazer. He looked like a retired city cop, dressed for golf,
which he had never played.

'You sure you don't want to find a bar somewhere,' he
said. 'It won't bother me.'

'Nah. I just left a bar,' I said. 'This is better.'

'I still can't get used to that about Florida. In the city,
every bar looks better than anything you can find outside. I
probably got heavy into the sauce because bars were such
nice places to go into, coming off the streets, you know.
Warm, friendly, orderly. The way the bottles were lined up
on the back bar, sparkling, and the glasses were clean and
racked. Nice soft light, that didn't hurt your eyes, and
maybe some nice soft music – Sinatra or something –
coming from the juke box. Bars were prettier than the
streets every single fucking time.

'Here in Florida, though, outside is better. My problem
is, I haven't figured out anything to *do* outside. In a bar,
that's a no-brainer. You drink and that leads to all sorts of
interesting things. But here, it's harder. You can walk
around and smell the flowers, but that gets old pretty
quick.'

'Try fishing,' I said.

'Yeah. That's what everybody says.'

We had walked the length of the park. There was a bench
under a tall hickory tree. He sat and shook out a cigarette.

Put it in his mouth and lit it with a kind of ceremonial care. Exhaled in a way that made it clear that, with smoking, he was down to pretty much his last pleasure in life. He pinched the tip of his tongue thoughtfully, then took another deep drag from his cigarette.

'I watched Hutchinson's apartment while you were gone. Like you asked me.'

He exhaled the smoke.

'I wasn't the only one.'

'There was Longacre, right?' I said. 'From Miami. He works for Lander White.'

'Yeah ... him. No surprise there. He came and went. But there were a couple of others, came by when Longacre wasn't watching.'

'Did they go inside?'

'Both of them. First one stayed an hour. Second one, a little longer.' He took a last drag and flipped the cigarette on the grass.

'I got descriptions. And the plate numbers. And, since I didn't have anything better to do, I ran them down.'

'You give good service,' I said.

'Fucking time on my hands. Anything to keep busy. Tell Semmes, if he ever needs somebody to back you up...'

'I will.'

'Anyway, I wrote it all up.' He reached inside his jacket pocket and took out an ordinary envelope. 'Bill is in there, too,' he said as he handed it to me. 'Fifty an hour, plus some expenses. Mostly mileage.'

'Sounds fair.

'I did a little research,' he said hesitantly. 'Couldn't help myself.'

'Are you worried about poaching?' I said.

'Yeah. A little.'

'Don't be,' I said. 'If there's enough work, you'll get the call. From either me or Semmes.'

'Well, it just seemed like nobody can be two places, one time, you know. When you're not here, I can cover. I wouldn't crowd you. But I wouldn't mind the extra work. I'm not ready to start fucking around with wood carving, you know, or leather tools. That's the kind of stuff they tell you to do ... keep busy, you know. I'm just not ready for that program.'

He shook another cigarette out of the half-empty pack and lit it. His gestures were less methodical. This was not a devotional smoke; it was about nerves.

'This thing will probably last for a year. Just keep me in mind, would you?'

'Sure,' I said. 'Absolutely. Glad to know you're available.'

'Anyway,' he said, leaning against the back of the bench, 'the two dudes who went in to see Hutchinson ... one was from around here and the other came from down around Gainesville, between there and the coast. The one from here is Tim Fulton. He works for Patrick Ewell, who owns a big hunting plantation up on the Georgia line. That's the place where Vincent was staying – in the guest house – when ...'

'Right,' I said, 'I know. How long was he in with Hutchinson?'

'He was the first one. Stayed inside almost exactly an hour. Parked at three in the afternoon and pulled out at four.'

'The other one?'

'More interesting, actually. Man's name is Tom Lewellen. Ever heard of him?'

'No.'

'I hadn't either. So I asked around. Some of the old timers around here remembered him. He was up here for a couple of sessions of the legislature. One of the hot young representatives, you know what I mean. Fucking first class political horseflesh. People had him pegged for a long run and a big finish. So who do you think he went up against when he decided to move up in class, run for congress and go to Washington?'

'Wouldn't be Vincent, would it?' I said. 'Just to take a wild stab at it.'

'You could be on *Jeopardy*, my friend. Or bet horses. You ever go to the track?'

I shook my head.

'That's something I miss. Much as anything. I tried the dogs, over Green County, you know. Just not the same. Look like a bunch of goddamned mutts chasing a fucking bus.

'Anyway ... Lewellen came to see Hutchinson the day after Tim Fulton made the trip. He comes a little later in the day and he stays a little longer. Drives a little better vehicle, too. Fulton was in a Ford pickup. An F-150 that needed a bath. Lewellen was driving a BMW. Red. Like wine.'

'Anything else?' I said.

'No. Not really. The only other people came to see her, while I was watching, were Dixie Price and her nasty ass brother. You know about him?'

'Met him the other day,' I said. 'We discussed the paradox of vengeance.'

'Yeah? Did he drool while he talked?'

I smiled and shook my head.

'He's a badass,' Swearingen said. 'Some guy cut him one night, outside one of these fighting and dancing clubs. He must have bled a gallon but he wouldn't let go of the guy who cut him. Had him around the neck. Held on until the guy passed out. That wasn't enough for Earl, though. He kept holding on, strangling the guy, until he damn near died. He was in a fucking coma for a couple of weeks. They had him on tubes and ventilators. Badass Earl came by the hospital one night, after he'd been sewed up, and snuck in the guy's room while the nurses weren't looking, and pissed all over him. It shorted out the fucking monitors. That's how they caught Earl.'

'That is an inspired gesture,' I said. 'Do you suppose he thought it up all by himself?'

'If he did,' Swearingen said, 'it is sure to have left him with a bad case of brain strain.'

'I'll take care of this,' I said, indicating the envelope Swearingen had handed me. 'You'll have your check in a week.'

He shrugged. 'I appreciate that.'

'And I'll let you know if there is more work.'

'Bless you,' he said.

He stood up and we walked out of the park together, then went our own ways.

Nineteen

Tim Fulton lived in a small, new-brick house on a red clay road that marked the property line of Laverly Spring's Plantation. The grass was carefully mowed and the trim was carefully painted. There was a Dobermann chained to a pecan tree in the front yard.

I kept my eye on the dog on my way to the front door.

Fulton opened it almost before I knocked. He managed to make it into an aggressive gesture. He was wearing old, working jeans and a faded cowboy shirt with pearl buttons. His face was tired, lined, and perpetually angry.

'What,' he said very slowly, 'do you want?'

'Do you want to talk,' I said, 'or would you just like to bite your dog there?'

'Talk about *what*?' He stepped out on to the little front porch. He was always closing the distance between us. Maybe because I had a few inches of reach on him. Like a lot of small, tough men, he stayed on the attack and he fought best from the clinches.

Your instinct is to take a step back or at least to lean away. I resisted it.

'Talk about what you were doing at Lisa Hutchinson's apartment the other afternoon.'

'Who wants to know?' Staying on the attack.

I didn't say anything.

'Some reason I *shouldn't* be talking to her? You've got some kind of problem with that? Maybe she's your sweetie? You and half the other men in the county.'

'I'd bet money,' I said, 'that you weren't visiting her on your own business. You were running an errand, right? That's what you do. Run errands for gentlemen?'

His jaws went tight. Like he was biting a nail.

'Just doing what you were told, I suppose. And that is understandable. You like your job.'

He bit down a little harder, chewing on the nail of resentment.

'The problem is . . . this is not about chasing poachers off the property or killing off a couple of old feral dogs that have been running deer. Those are housekeeping chores. This is different.'

'Is that so?' He had to force the words past his rigid mouth.

'Yes. It is.'

I paused.

'Look,' I said, trying to sound like sweet reason. 'It doesn't have to be a pissing match and there is no reason at all for you to be involved. Unless that's the way you want it.'

'That a fact?'

'But if that *is* the way you want it,' I said, keeping my voice level, 'then you'll get steamrolled. Flatter than a smashed cat.'

He kept his eyes on me and said nothing.

'This is strictly a social call. Casual dress and all that. But you could be subpoenaed. They could *compel* you to testify or they could charge you with contempt of court. If you lied, it would be perjury. And there is always obstruction of justice. That's a good, general purpose club they can use to beat the living hell out of you.'

'Are you a cop?'

'No. Not exactly.'

'You drink beer?'

'Absolutely.'

'Come on around back.'

Fulton had built a little patio and a bar-b-q pit in the back yard, under the shade of an aging magnolia tree. There was lounge furniture made of raw cypress. I suspect he'd built that too. It was a restful spot.

There was beer in an Igloo cooler. He handed me a bottle. Opened one for himself.

'Have a seat.'

When we were both sitting, he said, 'I guess you must work for that lawyer they made special prosecutor.'

'Semmes,' I nodded.

'Good man to work for?'

'Yes.'

'Ever ask you to do something you shouldn't do? Break the law or just go against your own self some way?'

'No.'

'My boss hadn't neither. Up till now. He could be a high-handed sonofabitch. But I could live with that. It was too good a job to quit just because your feelings got hurt. I should have told him to shove it when he asked me to talk to Lisa Hutchinson. It would have been the same as quitting. But now, I'm out anyway.'

He sighed and sipped an inch off the top of his beer.

'Ain't that a bitch? The boy senator goes screwing off the reservation and I lose my job. That's the way it happens, isn't it? Rich man sneezes, the poor man gets pneumonia and dies.'

'You'll get fired,' I said. 'For sure?'

'Oh yeah. And I've got a wife. She'll probably divorce me.'

He looked at me over the top of his beer bottle and gave me a smile that was full of old, familiar bitterness. He'd been through it before.

'I've had this job for five years, now. Best job, probably, I've ever had. You can't hardly get a good job anymore, working outside, in the woods. So I was willing to eat a little shit. This time, I expect I took too many helpings.'

He sighed again. Sipped indifferently at his beer.

'I'll have to get my ass out of this house. I pretty much built it, but the land still belongs to the man. Not much different from the sawmill days when my grandfather lived in a house that the mill owned. He made it pretty. Kept it painted and planted zinnias in the front yard. But they held the deed.

'I'll see if maybe I can line up something selling cars or insurance. Buy me a couple of suits at Penny's. Find a house to rent because I don't have enough in the bank to buy one. Starting over will be too much for my wife, I guarantee. She'll pack.

'And it all started with that senator losing it and raping a woman, early Sunday morning, with me in bed for hours since I have to get up at dawn thirty and saddle horses for the day's hunting. For something that happens while I'm sound asleep ... I lose my job!

'And the senator? Well, according to the story I saw this morning on the television, he's in better shape than I am. If Lander White can get him off – and if he can't, then nobody can – well the senator has a good chance, a real *good* chance, of getting himself re-elected. At least that's what the latest poll says.

'What Lander White will do, according the story I saw, is make Lisa Hutchinson look like bad medicine. You know, like she had a real hard time keeping her pants on.'

He paused to take a sip of beer and sigh, with more resignation than satisfaction.

'He'll probably do it, too,' he went on, looking past me to a gum swamp a couple of hundred yards away, where a few wood ducks were coming in to feed.

'Lisa was always pretty wild. Still is, I suppose. I'm not in that crowd, no more.

'But the thing is, her being wild makes me believe it probably happened the way she said it did. She didn't mind men and she liked doing what men and women do together and she didn't much care who knew it. She wasn't like some of them, who like it but are ashamed to admit it – to themselves or anyone else. So they'll say, "He got me drunk," or "He raped me."

'Lisa liked it, no question about it, but she had to like you and she didn't like being forced into it. And I know without asking that she didn't like being beaten up. She has some pride and she wouldn't let anyone treat her like she was trash.

'So ... I believe her. But that doesn't help the price of

cotton much. Lander White will have the jury, and most of the rest of the country, believing that Lisa *is* trash. So she'll get it twice. Once from the senator and once more from his lawyer.

'Me and Lisa, a couple of little people, we'll pay for what the big dog done.'

He'd sounded resigned up to this point – weary and ready to give in – but that changed abruptly.

'I'd like,' he said, in the old clipped, snarling voice, 'to kill that sonofabitch. Like to do it slow. With my own hands, looking right into his eyes while he shit his pants and died.'

What I've always liked about people like Fulton – call them rednecks and maybe I am one – is that they can be ignorant, intolerant, violent, and a few other things we all know about but you'll generally know right where you stand. They do not go in much for ambivalence.

'Well,' I said, 'you might not have to do that.'

He showed me the bitter smile again.

'Because you and Semmes are going to see that justice is done? Put Vincent on trial and convince a jury to convict him?'

I nodded.

'You and Mr Semmes have got to be the only people anywhere who believe that ... If you really do.

'And, anyway, even if you do get a conviction – six months or a year from now – that won't help me none. Once Ewell finds out I've been talking to you, I'm finished.'

'Maybe not.'

He shook his head.

'He may not have to know you've been talking to me. He won't learn it from me. But you've got to tell me what he wanted you to say to Lisa Hutchinson ... and if there was any money that went with it.'

He hesitated. But just for a second. Then he said. 'Okay, let's do it quick. It's sundown and I've got to feed the dogs.'

The circus was still in town when I got back and found myself standing at the Hilton bar, waiting for the bartender to bring me the beer I had ordered.

'Hello mate,' a man said. He was loud and standing three inches from my ear.

'Good day,' I said, mimicking what I thought was a fake Australian accent.

'No, no mate. You don't say it like that. It's *g'day* and you have to make sure to swallow most of the soft sounds. But you're from these parts, a southerner, and you blokes won't ever learn to do it properly. You dawdle over too many sounds. Some you squeeze up together and others you spread wide apart. But no offense. I'd buy you that pint but I think I might have a better offer. My name is Patterson. Ian Patterson, that would be. I know yours.'

'Pleased to meet you,' I said, raising my bottle. 'Sorry about the weak beer.'

'Oh don't bother,' he said, smiling. 'Some of the microbrewery stuff is drinkable and, anyway, I've been living here for fifteen years now. Gotten to where I can even swallow a little Budweiser when there's nothing else available.'

'I thought you were probably with one of the Australian

papers,' I said, to no real point. Seemed like I had to say something.

'Well, yes, I was. That's where I learned my craft. Finest tabloid training in the world. If you want a man who can smell when a story has got low sex and high society in it, then you look for someone who has cut his teeth on one of the sheets in Sydney.'

'Who do you work for now?'

'I'm coming to that,' he said, happily. His face was so fair it looked like it had been bleached. He had a sandy moustache, ineptly trimmed, and watery blue eyes that seemed to go in and out of focus, which was probably due to the beer. He was tall and he had a little fat around the middle. He seemed like the kind of man you could drive to Memphis with and he'd never run out of stories or the steam for telling them.

'All right,' I said.

'But first,' he said, 'let's discuss my offer.'

'What offer?'

'The one for a hundred thousand dollars.'

'What could I do for you that would be worth that kind of money?'

'Tell your story.'

'*My* story? Why would anyone be interested in my story?'

'Because you are part of the big story. You are Nathaniel Semmes' trusted investigator.'

'Bee Eff Dee,' I said.

'Beg pardon?'

'BFD. Big fucking deal.'

'Oh I see. Well, actually there is a bit more to it. The

color, we call it. That's the part about your going to prison for killing a man and how Semmes helped you get out on a pardon.'

'You're going to print that?'

'Certainly. Human interest, don't you know. Readers lap it up.'

I felt the heat creeping up my neck.

'So,' he said, 'what about it. You game? Take maybe five or six hours. You sit with me and tell the whole story into a tape recorder. I ask a few questions – what do you feel about this case and your own case and the big picture … life, you know. We take a couple of pictures and you walk away with a check for a hundred thousand. Sound all right to you?'

I shook my head and said, smiling because it was hard to be mad at him, 'Listen, I appreciate your offer. But … Well, can I speak frankly?'

'Absolutely,' he said, 'oh, entirely so. If it is not enough money … well, I don't control the purse, personally, but things can be worked out. Especially if you can tempt the check signers with something. An inside deal or two, if you know what I mean.'

It was a bribe, of course. And it was hard not to appreciate Patterson's style in soliciting it.

'Well, listen,' I said. 'It's a generous offer. Too generous. But the truth is, I wouldn't sell you, or your magazine, the steam off last year's shit. Not for any amount of money. Nothing personal.'

'Oh no,' he smiled and his mouth was crowded with the usual bad teeth, 'not a bit of it. But I do think you are making a mistake. You see, we'll do the story – some kind

187

of story – anyway. Do it from clips and anything we can find in the trash can, if we have to. Doesn't matter. One week job and then it's for wrapping fish. But we'll do it and if there's money in it, then it seems you ought to have it. D'ya see what I mean?'

'Sure,' I said. 'I don't suppose there's anybody I could speak to. Explain how, you know, I don't really want to be written up in your newspaper. Or any other, for that matter.'

He shook his head sadly. 'No,' he said, mournfully, 'no, there's no chance in the world of that. They get it in mind to do the story, then they'll do the story. You can make a book on that. That's why I say, you ought to go ahead and take the money.'

This was the threat. Either take the bribe or see my name – and the most unflattering picture of me they could find – on the cover of a tabloid, for sale in the checkout counters of supermarkets everywhere, for all the fat, gum-chewing shoppers to read. If I did take the money and give them the interview, the story probably would never appear. The relationship would have been established. Ian and I would be talking a lot, especially as the case got closer to trial. If the relationship were exposed ... Well, that was just fine. They lived off scandal like buzzards on road kill.

'What made them decide to do the story?' I said. 'Who brought it to them?'

'Why d'ya say somebody brought it to them?'

'Because I haven't talked to anybody about it and I don't believe you people were doing a lot of deep document research and just stumbled over it. You haven't been out of the bar since you got to town.'

'You found me out,' he said happily.

'So who gave you the lead?'

'You're asking me to reveal a source,' he said, turning arch. 'I can't do that.'

'That,' I said, 'sounds like bullshit when it comes from the *New York Times*. Coming from you, it is a joke. Who has been slandering my name around?'

'You don't really expect . . . ?'

I was looking hard into his eyes.

'I don't scare that easy.'

'And I don't care about consequences,' I said. 'Just remember *why* I went to prison. You go ahead and write your story. The dumbshits who read your magazine don't matter to me. But I'll have that name.'

'I might make a deal . . .'

'Okay. You keep your hundred thousand and I don't crush your skull. Your side is . . . you give me the name.'

'Sounds fair enough,' he said, smiling a weak, feverish smile. 'How about another pint?'

'Sure,' I said. 'But I'll have the name first.'

'Well, all right, then. It was Mr White.'

'Lander White?'

'Himself.'

'Well I'll be damned,' I said.

Twenty

I was still boiling when I got back to my sterile little cell with the view of the interstate. I didn't mind Ian Patterson so much. He was a rogue and didn't care who knew it. Lander White, though, was another thing. I'd seen him do the television interviews and talk shows about his solemn duty to his client and the sacred claims of the Constitution and how, in all modesty, he was pretty much doing God's work here on earth.

Just then, my goal – my dream and my sacred ambition – was to strip the skin off his back and pour salt on to the raw flesh. I'd tell him the whole time that it might not be pretty but it was in a good cause.

But for now, back here in my little room, what I would do is ... cool down, drink a beer, and call Jessie.

This time, she answered. On the second ring.

'Well hello, Morgan,' she said. 'Nice to hear your voice.'

Like that.

'How are you?' I said. Cautious. Like one of those diplomats, opening a negotiation by discussing the shape of the table.

'Just fine,' she said, and she did sound good. Happy, in

fact. Which made me even more apprehensive. 'How are *you*?'

'Good,' I said, wishing that I had never made the call. 'Real good.'

Jesus.

'That's nice, Morgan.'

'Well, I just wanted to call because it has been a long time and I ... uh, missed you.'

'You did?'

'Yes,' I said, feeling both miserable and stupid, 'yes, I did.'

'*Really?*'

'Yes.'

A long silence. I listened to my heart beat. Called myself names.

Then she sighed. And said, in the throaty voice I like, 'Well I missed you, too.'

I started to say something but she cut me off.

'When you miss me, Morgan, you ought to call me. You've got a phone. Couple of them.'

'I know.'

'So call me up on one of them. I like talking to you. Even if you don't have anything to say to me, I like talking to you. I like it when you say you miss me.'

'I'm sorry.'

'You don't have to be sorry. You didn't want to call me. I wish you had. I got this job, here in North Carolina. They wanted me to come up here.'

'For good?' I said, already thinking I would sell the River House and move up there too.

She laughed.

'You sound worried.'

'I am.'

'Good,' she said, happily. 'That's good. I like that. I want to see more of it. No, I ain't moving up here. It's nice, though. I expect I could live here and like it, if I had to.'

'North Carolina is all right,' I sulked. Stupidly jealous of the place.

She laughed. 'That's right. You used to live here, didn't you?'

'Long time ago,' I said.

'Well, I just came up here because these people who are making a movie wanted me to do some technical consulting. They make a lot of movies in Wilmington, of all places. Did you know that, Morgan?'

'No.'

'Well they do. They call the studio area "Wilmiwood". A friend of mine is working on one and since I knew something about the story, he got me a job. You ever watched someone make a movie, Morgan?'

'No.'

'Well it's some wild times, let me tell you.'

And she did – tell me. For the next ten or fifteen minutes. She told me about all the sitting around. The doing one scene over and over until they decided they had it right even though she couldn't tell the difference between the first time and the last time. The feeling everybody had of working together, like a team, on something important. And, of course, the vanity of some of the actors. She liked to talk this way and I liked to listen. She was a grown woman in her thirties who had done a lot of things in her life, including getting rich in oil when she was just out of college. But she was the farthest thing from being jaded or cynical. She still got excited about things. It was one of the reasons she was such good company. She was plenty tough but she was not cynical. Or bitter.

'I'm probably going to miss it when it's all over,' she said, when she finished telling me about life on the set.

'When will that be?'

'Around two weeks,' she said. 'Maybe sooner.'

'Can I come see you?'

'Hey, Morgan, I understand you got your own hands full down there. You got to put that sorry senator away; get his worthless ass off the streets. You don't have time to be coming to North Carolina, hanging with the movie people. Besides, you wouldn't like them. They ain't your type, *cher*.' Every now and then, she said something to remind me that she grew up in one of those bayou parishes, west of New Orleans. Her daddy worked on the rigs until she bought leases so he could retire and fish.

'I'd like to see you,'

'I know,' she said. 'And I'd like to see you. Why don't we wait until I'm finished up here? Then I'll come see you in Tallahassee. Or maybe you can get away for a couple of days. We'll go to New Orleans. It ought to be pretty with all the flowers blooming. We'll take some walks, listen to some music, eat some food, and make some love. All the good things.'

'Yes,' I said. 'All of the good things.'

'Two more weeks,' she said. 'Maybe three. You call me in the meantime, okay?'

'Okay.'

'Is it going all right? You and Semmes going to put that man in a cage?'

'We're working on it.'

'Good for you. Call me when you want to talk about it.'

'I will.' I wasn't very good at talking about it but sometimes, when I did, she helped me out. But she didn't push me. And I preferred to listen.

'Thanks for calling, Morgan. You take care of yourself, now.'

'You too.'

'Bye.'

I stood there, in the middle of the room, for a few minutes after I'd hung up. I wasn't thinking about much of anything and I sure wasn't enjoying the view. It was, I suppose, some kind of afterglow. It made me feel good just to talk to her. One of the ten warning signs of love, I imagine. I probably ought to see somebody about it. Get some help.

But you can't make a phone call last for ever. Ten minutes was my personal best and I almost matched it. Then, other thoughts began infiltrating my brain. I started wondering what I ought to do next. Besides eat some supper and go to bed.

First, I decided, I ought to ask Lisa Hutchinson to tell me what Tim Fulton had said to her and check it against his account of their conversation.

Then I thought maybe I ought to talk to Tom Lewellen first. Find out what he claimed to have been talking to Lisa Hutchinson about and ask her about both conversations. It was still early enough to call Lewellen. I flipped through my notebook until I found the page where I'd written his number. Sat on the bed and dialed it. The phone was cool in my hand. It had been warm when Jessie and I hung up.

'Hello.' The voice was big. And hearty.

'Mr Lewellen?'

'If you're selling,' he said, 'put it in the mail. I don't do business over the phone.'

'I'm not selling. I'm an investigator, in Tallahassee...'

He interrupted before I could go on.

'Tell me,' he said, 'just *please* tell me, that this is about our esteemed Senator Daniel P. Vincent.'

'Yes,' I said. 'It is.'

'Praise God and halleluiah,' he said. 'Mine enemy has been delivered into my hands.'

I waited.

'What can I do for you, my friend?' he said. 'Anything at all. Just name it.'

'I'd like to ask you a few questions,' I said.

Just as few as possible, I thought.

'That,' he said, 'is no problem at all. I'll talk as long as you want and answer any question you ask.'

I didn't have any trouble believing that.

'You want to do this interrogation over the phone or in person?'

'In person would be better.'

'Your place or mine?'

'I can be down there in the morning,' I said. 'If you've got some time.'

'Friend,' he said, 'I shall make some time. Just as much as you need. How soon can you be here?'

'Seven o'clock?' I said. 'I'll drive down tonight.'

'Fine. I like to get an early start myself. Let me give you directions...'

At three in the morning, I was on my way to see Lewellen. I got off the Interstate after a few miles and took Highway 19, east and south. It was the old highway that you took, once upon a time, to make it from the Panhandle to Tampa and the other west coast cities of Florida. It had been a main artery back then but now it was mainly local traffic. This time of night, it was just me and the occasional possum or deer.

I drank coffee, listened to the radio for a while, then turned it off and let the road carry me along. I did some thinking, I suppose; the kind that seems achingly profound, out there on the blacktop late at night, and adolescently silly once the sun has come up and you're parked somewhere.

Still, if I could go back, it would have to be to a time when I was indestructible and twenty years old, driving across Wyoming at night, drinking beer for nourishment and stopping now and then, to drain my bladder and to listen to the antelope that I couldn't see whistling out on the desert.

Highway 19 to Cedar Key wasn't Wyoming but it wasn't bad. I was sorry to see the sun come up.

I stopped outside of Homassassa for breakfast and gas and to put some cold water on my face. And I pulled into Tom Lewellen's driveway at precisely seven o'clock.

Lewellen lived in a low brick place shaded by pecan trees and surrounded by a couple of hundred acres of soft, green pasture where a dozen finely muscled horses grazed, hides glistening in the early morning light.

'Good morning,' he said, stepping out of a side door and letting it slam behind him. 'Right on time. No trouble finding it?'

'No,' I said. 'None at all.'

We shook hands. He was a big man, settling into middle age. His stomach was beginning to droop over his belt. He had a big, bushy moustache that also drooped. And eyes like a basset hound's. He had fair skin and freckles and in a year or two he would be seeing the doctor about getting the cancers burned off.

'Come on in,' he said. 'You had breakfast?'

'About an hour ago,' I said.

'Coffee?'

'Sure,' I said and followed him inside.

He filled a mug for me, in the kitchen, and said, 'I'd introduce you to my wife but she seems to have left me.'

'Sorry.'

'I'm not,' he said and I wondered how many other people he'd set up for that line. I didn't care about his domestic arrangements so I let it drop, told him I'd take my coffee black, and thanked him when he handed me the mug.

'What do you say we talk in my office?'

'Fine.'

It was what you would expect from a lawyer with horses for a hobby. Dark paneling that looked like red gum to me, leather-covered furniture, built-in bookshelves, cut-glass decanters, a gun case with leaded glass doors, and the mounted head of a ten point buck that almost surely had not been killed in these parts.

Lewellen took the big swivel chair behind the big mahogany desk and indicated that I could have the couch. He put his feet on the desk so I could see his snakeskin cowboy boots.

'All right, Mr Hunt,' he said. 'how can I help you? I think you'll find that, when it is a matter of causing problems for Senator Daniel P. Vincent, I'm willing to cooperate in any way I can.' The line was delivered like a political speech. He made Vincent's name sound vile, like it left a bad taste in his mouth.

'What were you doing in Tallahassee?' I said and read the date off the page in my notebook. 'At Lisa Hutchinson's address?'

'I went there to talk to her,' he said.

I waited. He was a bullshitter. He liked to talk. I'd learn more by letting him open up and ramble than by trying to pull it out of him, question by question.

'I wanted to offer my services to Miz Hutchinson, as her attorney. *Pro bono*, of course. She listened most attentively – Miz Hutchinson seems like a very smart, capable woman, even if she was raised country – and she said she appreciated my offer and would let me know.'

'What's your interest?' I said.

'Well,' he smiled in a sinister way. 'Well, I suppose that I could say I just want to be a good citizen and look out for the rights of the little people. Would you believe that?'

I shook my head. His smile grew wider.

'No,' he said. 'I didn't think so. You look like a man who would know bullshit when he's standing in it. And I know Semmes. He has a romantic, noble streak – would have made a good Confederate colonel – but he wouldn't hire any sentimental idiots.

'So I'll tell you the truth. More or less. The reason I want to help Miz Hutchinson is so I can maybe hurt Senator Daniel P. Vincent. I would go considerably out of my way to do anything that might have a small chance of hurting him. You know much history?'

I shrugged.

'You know what Churchill said, when people criticized him for making an alliance with Stalin in World War Two? He said he would form a pact with the Devil himself in order to defeat Hitler. That's a mild version of the way I feel about that sonofabitch Vincent. You know why?'

I shook my head and resisted the temptation to say that I didn't much care, either.

'Well, partly it is because he beat me in a political contest. It was going to be one or the other of us from this part of the state and either one of us could have gone on to much bigger things. Turned out it was him.

'But that was only the superficial reason. I'm not automatically a sore loser. Life is just too fucking short. I hate Vincent because of what he is and what he stands for and what he's doing to this state and this country.'

I didn't say anything. Let him indulge himself. I'd come a long way and I was enjoying the coffee. He was no more extravagant than the average talkshow guest.

'I came from here. Born and raised. Fourth generation. I have orange grove people, fishermen, and ranchers in my family. One or two real estate barons, but we don't mention them.

'Vincent? Well, his father came down here ahead of the

bankruptcy lawyers. He couldn't get out of New York fast enough. The only thing he loved Florida for was its homestead protection laws. He bought the biggest house he could find, with the money he'd looted from his business and his creditors. They couldn't touch him. Then he started over down here and got rich during a time when, if you started with money, you just about couldn't help it.

'The old man was into everything except gator poaching and the only reason he didn't touch that is he didn't want to get his hands dirty. He let other people do that. But he was into insurance, banking, and most especially real estate. He could make a swamp breed money better'n it would breed mosquitoes. He was just a deal-making sumbitch and you couldn't stop him with a stopping machine.

'But he raised his boy Daniel to be different. He wasn't going to have to make money to prosper. Daddy would own the state and sonny boy would rule it. He was going into politics. And that's exactly how the old sumbitch raised Vincent. Groomed him, he did, like some of those tennis mommies and daddies groom their little boys and girls to make it to Forest Hills, only they never do. But Vincent, well, he never even foot faulted. Never had an honest emotion or an original thought in his entire young life, but he had iron control.

'His Daddy sent him to the right schools – Vandy and Yale Law – but he made sure he was back here, during the Summers, not off in Europe with his college buddies. And when he graduated, Daniel had to sign up for military. And not the JAG, either. He was infantry and airborne, the whole bit, even though the draft was over and Vietnam was done, and people were supposed to be down on the military. But Daniel's old man knew this was Florida where people are old and conservative and a lot of them are veterans. When we ran against each other for congress, Daniel made a lot out of that uniform and reminded people I hadn't ever served. Well hell, the war was over and there wasn't no draft and my family needed help with the orange grove business. I suppose I would have joined up if there'd been an enemy somewhere, but the only invaders coming across the coast was Japanese cars. So I took a pass. Vincent made me sound like a coward, without ever exactly saying so. That was the way he did things. And he was real good at it.'

He shifted in his seat, took a swallow from his coffee mug, looked out the window as though the view of his fine spread might help him get over the memory of what Daniel Vincent had done to him. Then he frowned, as if to say there was no chance of that.

'He was always *running*. He was running for class president way back in high school. And he was always lying. About himself and about whoever he was running against. By the time he ran against me, he'd had a lot of practice and he was real damned good at it.

'My family had some bad years, like anyone in agriculture. Shit, in agriculture all it takes to be a good year is not to be a real bad year. Anyway, there were a couple of years when we didn't pay any taxes; even though we owned a lot of land. Well shithouse mouse ... you would have thought we were just simple, straight-up tax cheats and thieves the way Vincent and his people put the story out.

'I could have taken that, maybe, from some little guy who owned a hardware store and never made any money or missed a tax payment in his life. But Vincent, shit. That sumbitch sprang from the loins of one of the biggest crooks and cheats ever to shit between shoes. I mean, Vincent himself didn't cheat. He paid every nickel of taxes he owed and he never took any funny deductions and he was always charitied up to the very maximum limit. But his daddy had done enough cheating to last the family for about six biblical generations. Junior was just cruising down smooth blacktop that the old man had already poured.

'And that, my friend, is what really dumped acid into my soul. It was like being called a bigot by the top Kleagle in local Klan. The goddamned *effrontery* of it. And you got the feeling that's what Vincent liked. An ordinary garden variety slander didn't get his juices flowing; there had to be a big dose of hypocrisy in it before it gave him any pleasure.

'That's why it got to me so bad when he started the rumors about me and women.'

Another long pause. Long enough, this time, that it seemed like I had to say something, even if it was just to remind him I was here.

'What were the rumors?' I said, gently as I could.

'Oh, you know,' Lewellen sighed heavily, 'he and his boys spread it around that I was a little too fond of the ladies and spent too many evenings away from my wife. And, you know, the thing about those rumors is ... They were true. I like ladies. Like 'em too much and for the wrong reasons and I'm not good enough to the ones I marry.

'I give 'em presents and flowers but that's because I can't give them what they really want. It's the way I am. Some days, I spend ten or fifteen minutes regretting it.

'Vincent, now, he married a good middle class girl – her daddy was a doctor, I believe, but he'd done fairly well in some land deals – right after he came home from the Army. She did all the right things. Went to the ribbon cuttings and smiled like an ingenue selling toothpaste. When he made a speech, she'd sit there with her hands folded, looking up at him with such adoring eyes that, even if it was a speech to the Future Farmers of America, about composting manure, you would have thought she was listening to Pericles addressing the Athenians.

'She had two kids and they managed to get in about half the pictures that were ever taken of Vincent. Sumbitch might as well have been campaigning for the job of running a nursery school.

'But all that time, there were rumors. Not like the rumors about me. Those things that were pretty much common knowledge. I never was very good at keeping a secret. But the talk about old Vincent was ... Well, it was kind of dark and ugly. People said he went after girls, the way his father had. But it wasn't like he *enjoyed* it. More like he couldn't help himself and then hated the girls for making him feel weak. And the girls were always from way below him on the social pole, you know what I mean. He didn't screw his friend's wife. He screwed his mechanic's daughter. And then, he made her pay.'

I slipped a question into the silence, before it grew too long.

'He hit them?'

Lewellen shook his big head. Mournfully.

'There were some people said so. But I don't believe that he was doing that back then. I think he would get pretty rough, during the dance, and then leave 'em cold when the music stopped. He couldn't figure out who he hated more – them or himself.

'I expect he might have gotten rougher when he got more powerful. Tends to work that way. He's a bully. Nothing more despicable. But I wasn't surprised when I heard about that little bit of trouble up in Tallahassee.'

When he seemed about to drift off on a wave of memory, I said something, the first thing that came to mind, to bring him back.

'What about his wife?'

'A nice girl,' he said, wistfully. 'She even called me, after the race, to say good luck. Damned awkward conversation but I appreciated it. People said he was colder than Winter in Finland to her. Treated her like she was an actress who was being paid to play a part and get it right, every time she performed. She was unhappy and lonely and then she died in a car wreck. Right in the middle of his first run at the senate.'

'What happened?'

He shrugged, ponderously, and looked down at the floor. 'She missed a turn on a piece of slick road, ran through the ditch and into a power pole. She was going faster than a scalded dog. People like her don't drive that way, unless they are in an emotional state or trying to get away from somebody or driving to the hospital in an emergency ... There have got to be some unusual circumstances involved.'

'You saying he killed her?'

'I tried for six months, maybe a year, to make that case. But that was mainly a matter of me wanting the thing to be true; bad enough that I made myself believe it. After a while, I had to admit that he wasn't out on that road when it happened. He was somewhere giving a speech. But I still blame him. I believe she either did it on purpose – with no proof and a sheriff's investigation that says otherwise – or that he had her so worked up that she didn't even know how fast she was driving when she hit that curve.

'But the worst thing was after the accident. All the pictures of Vincent at the funeral, holding the older kid's hand. Kid wasn't much more than four. He didn't have to go to the funeral. It was a campaign appearance for Vincent, who was in a tight race.

'Then, when I thought it couldn't get any worse, the sumbitch gives a speech saying that while his grief tells him to quit the race and mourn his sainted wife, her memory tells him to carry on the fight. And he just can't let her down. So he is going to see this campaign through to the end. For her.

'I tell you, it was the worst, smarmiest speech I've ever heard. It made the hogs puke.'

'But he won?'

'Yessir. And rode on to glory. But he may have tripped on his tool here. And if he did, then I want to do everything I can to ruin him. Hell, it may be my only chance. And I'd never forgive myself if I passed it up.'

Twenty-one

Nothing that Lewellen had told me would be useful at a trial. He could make you believe, by the force of his own conviction, that Daniel Vincent was not just an ordinary weak man, that there was something rank and dark at his core, but in my case, he was preaching to the choir.

We had been talking about an hour – or, he had talked and I had listened – when he seemed to wind down. The tension went out of his face and he looked tired. His voice lost its snap and he began speaking in a monotone.

Time for me to leave. Turn my ass around and make the same drive I'd made last night; this time in the other direction. Back to Tallahassee.

Lewellen rinsed our mugs in the sink – that was probably near the high end of his domestic skills – then followed me out the screen door, into the driveway and the bright sun which had climbed to a high, hot angle while we were inside, talking.

'About to be warm,' he said. 'I like it when it gets hot. I believe I liked Florida a hell of a lot better before they came up with air conditioning.'

'Amen,' I said. I felt tired. Especially of talking. And I hadn't said that much.

'You know, it's funny,' Lewellen said, 'I've spent a bunch of good years trying to incinerate Vincent and now, when he's standing naked, out in the open, I can't come up with anything. I'm shooting blanks. I can't even give you a real good lead because I've checked them all myself.

'But, now,' he grinned, 'if you wanted something on Vincent's *lawyer*, that would be different.'

It was like I had been slapped.

'Lander White?'

'Yessir,' Lewellen said.

'You know something about him? Something he, ah, doesn't want known.'

'Absolutely.'

We were standing next to my truck, now. He was looking away, admiring his horses.

'What is it?'

He turned back.

'Well, now, from the sound of your voice, I'd say you want Lander White as bad as I want that lizard Vincent.'

'At least that bad,' I said.

'What's your aim? You going to teach him some manners?'

I nodded.

'Well, I'm all for that. Lander White is one of those lawyers makes people want to put a bounty on them. I, personally, would like to horsewhip him. But I'll let you decide on the punishment.

'Me,' he said, smiling grandly now, 'I'll just provide the evidence of the crime.'

And he was off, again, talking almost as long outside,

standing in the sun, next to my truck, as he had talked inside, in his study. His shirt turned damp with sweat and his face glistened as he talked. I listened.

It was late morning when I left. He wanted me to stay for lunch but I wanted to get back and go to work – breaking Lander White.

About an hour down the road, I stopped and called Randolph Atkins. I got the recording. He picked up after I identified myself and said I needed to talk to him.

'How's your time?' I said. 'I believe I've got a live one here.'

'I'm not doing anything important,' he said. 'Just trying to figure out a lumber straddle. Whatever you've got, it's certain to be more exciting than that.'

It took about ten minutes to outline it for Atkins. When I finished he was eager. Ready to drop the lumber contracts and get started.

'I can't wait,' he said. 'It'll be a pleasure to help crucify that man.'

I gave him my number and told him to call me.

'No cellular,' I said.

'Certainly *not*,' Atkins said. 'Of course, if you'd learn how to use E-mail and encryption, we could have totally secure communications.'

'Okay,' I said. 'After this is over, you give me the short course.'

'It'll be a pleasure,' he said. 'Bye.'

The evening session of drinking and posturing was underway when I arrived at the Hilton bar. It was close and smoky; with a smell of something a little glandular and urgent, a scent that made some people feel alive but that just reminded me of jail.

Ian Patterson thrived on it. He was standing at the bar looking serene and he saw me right away. His eyes were glittering.

'Hello, mate,' he said. 'Stand you a pint?'

'No,' I said. 'I'll buy. There's something I want to talk to you about.'

His expression changed. 'Not going to threaten me with bodily harm again, I hope. I've just gotten over the last time.'

'No,' I said. 'And I apologize for that. I've got a hot head.'

'Well,' he said, 'I always thought a temper showed character in a man.'

'Maybe. But I apologize. I went off half-cocked.' I signaled the bartender with two fingers. He nodded.

'And,' I said, 'I've been thinking about your offer.'

'Oh?'

'Is it still open?'

'Absolutely.'

The two mugs arrived and I paid for them. Patterson and I raised them and drank.

'As long as I'm going to be written about,' I said, 'seems like I might as well have something to say about what's written...'

'Absoluto.'

'You want me to sit down with you and do an interview, right?'

'That's right. Absolutely correct.'

'We talk about my life and my brush with the law?'

'Righto.'

'You write the story? Not somebody else?'

'Correct.'

'When will you publish?'

'Oh ... I don't suppose it would be for a while. Not for a matter of weeks, actually. Maybe months. And ... of course, we wouldn't want to just stop with your incarceration and release.'

I looked at him over the rim of my mug and waited.

'Our readers would want to be ... Ah, *current*.'

So there it was.

'Of course,' I said soothingly. No big deal.

'So you and I would be meeting and chatting right up until the time we decide to go public. Whenever that is.'

'Naturally.'

He grinned. 'Wonderful.'

'But I'll want to be paid up front.'

We were surrounded by the din of a dozen conversations. But between us, at that moment, there was a chilly silence.

'Up front?'

'Sure. I'm not going to stiff you. If I tried it, there is no way of telling what you might publish about me. What you might say about our arrangement. And courts take a dim view of people involved in a case talking to the tabloids. You write about me, and I'm in contempt of court and most likely out of a job.

'You risk money. A lot to me; petty cash to you. So, up front. That's how it has to be.'

'Unorthodox.'

'You have a rule book?'

He waved his hand, as though to dismiss it all as a technicality.

'I'll check it out. But it might help if I had some kind of down payment from you. Token of good faith and all that, don't you know.'

I didn't say anything. Studied the last of the beer in my mug, as though giving it heavy thought. The truth was, I'd already made up my mind.

I sighed, reluctantly, like a man taking the first step along the path of sin and ruin. I worried that I was playing it too thick, but he seemed to buy it. He eased closer, to increase the intimacy.

'A lawyer named Tom Lewellen,' I said, 'has offered to represent Lisa Hutchinson, *pro bono*.'

It was strictly chickenfeed. Lewellen knew. Semmes and I knew. Lander White probably knew because his investigator, Longacre, would have told him. Now, the readers of Patterson's newspaper would know, too. And he would have a scoop on the rest of the media. No harm.

'Lewellen?'

'Old political enemy of Vincent's.'

'Oh, good,' Patterson said. '*Very* good. We love vendettas.'

'I thought you'd like it.'

'I'll look into it,' he said, draining his mug and putting it on the bar. 'We'll talk about the ... ah, *package* tomorrow.'

'That would be fine.'

I was on my way out of the bar when a hand reached out

from one of the booths, grabbing my arm and stopping me. I looked down. Barbara Hanley was looking up at me through narrow eyes full of malice.

'Digging through garbage?' she said. 'It's probably *much* easier here. Your home turf and all.'

'Could be,' I said. 'But there is a lot of garbage in Washington. What brings you to town?'

'It seemed like somebody ought to come down here and do a little real reporting and journalism,' she said. 'Up until now, you sleaze merchants have had a monopoly.'

'Sleaze merchants?'

'People with a stake in a lurid story; whether it is true or not,' she said, her tone of voice somewhere between a growl and a purr. Every time I looked at her, I thought *cat*. 'People like tabloid journalists, gunslinging lawyers, and their sneaky investigators.'

'What about afternoon television stars?'

'They,' she said, almost snarling, 'are a cut above the sleaze merchants.'

'How so?'

'They are just out to entertain an audience. The sleaze merchants are out to ruin people.'

'I wonder,' I said. 'Does being raped ruin you?'

She looked at me hard and then looked around the room. Nobody was paying any attention to us, except the three people she had been sitting with in the booth. They were intensely interested.

She looked back at me. Her eyes were hard and hot. The big hair looked like it was full of stray electricity. Her face was tight so the bones showed as clean ridges, catching what light there was in the bar and leaving a lot of shadow

213

around her eyes and mouth so she looked mysterious and sinister.

'Let's talk outside,' she said to me. Then, without waiting for an answer, she turned to the people in the booth and said, 'Excuse me just a minute. Business.'

I followed her out of the bar, through the hotel lobby, and into the parking lot. It was dark now and getting cool. Felt good to be out of the bar.

We stood on the cooling asphalt, facing each other. Her face had not softened any in the night air.

'I want you to understand something,' she said. 'Maybe if you understand it, you'll pass it on to your boss, the great Semmes, dean of the redneck lawyers.'

She paused to relish the sarcasm. Name-calling gave her a lot of satisfaction. I suspect it made her feel tough as hell to say 'motherfucker'.

'Talk real slow,' I said. 'I'll see can I make myself understand.'

'Very funny.'

I shrugged. What the hell.

'This is a ridiculous prosecution,' she said. 'And you know it.'

'If you say so.'

'What's your motive here? Are you doing this to get your picture in the paper. Do you think maybe *you* will get invited on to afternoon television?'

'Gee, I sure hope so.'

'This,' she said through her teeth, 'is not some carnival show. It's the real world.'

'So is rape.'

'Rape? What do you know about rape?'

'Well, I know that there is a real world woman who claims your friend the senator raped her.'

She looked ready to spit. 'That is the newest hustle. All these little trailer park Lolitas are hip to it. How much do you know about this woman?'

I shrugged. 'Not a lot. I know what her story is.'

'Well, I *do* know a lot about Daniel Vincent.'

She left herself wide open there. But I did not say anything. Catfights leave me feeling like I have fleas.

'And,' she went on quickly, 'I'll tell you what this is. It is a shakedown.'

'Say again.'

'Listen, there are people trying to destroy Daniel Vincent.'

'Why?'

'Because of what he represents,' she said and I tried hard not to roll my eyes.

'Look around you. All these churches. These fundamentalists.'

'Do they have a beef with Vincent?' I said.

'Oh, come on.'

'What's their problem?'

'Everything,' she said. 'It's what he represents. He's no radical. But, on the social issues, he is a moderate and that is enough.'

I looked at her.

'I mean, I can't believe you don't see that.'

'I don't pay much attention to those things,' I said.

'Because you are superior, right. Too good to pay any attention to the messy things.'

'No. Nothing that pure. I just don't give a rat's ass about

Vincent or any of the rest of them or what they do in Washington. I'm just interested in his hobbies and the way he spends his free time.'

'Listen to the radio some time. It's scary out there.'

I knew that already, even without listening to the radio, I thought. But didn't bother saying it.

'You need to know what kind of people you are dealing with.'

'Okay,' I said. 'But what do they have to do with the price of fish?'

'Who do you think is behind this woman? Urging her along. Probably paying her, too. More money than she has ever seen.'

'The whole congregation of the First Church of the Resurrection,' I said. 'But that is just a guess.'

'That's very funny,' she said. 'And it is also very nearly the truth. We've got proof she has been meeting with those kooks.'

She leaned in close, like a conspirator, and said, 'We also know a lot about her. She's not exactly a chaste maiden. There've been men. Quite a lot of them.'

'I thought that was okay. She's a modern woman.'

'A couple of abortions.'

I looked at her.

'That is her personal decision. But it is going to make a jury wonder.'

'What about you?'

'I don't care about her abortions. But down here, in this climate, she probably feels guilty about them and that just makes her vulnerable to these people. I don't blame her. I just want to know why she is lying. I want to know who is behind her, doing the pushing.'

'How do you know she is ... lying?'

'Because I *know* Daniel Vincent.'

The old thing, I thought. You're always reading about it – the kid next door who goes berserk and kills his whole family including the dog, burns the house down, and then drives downtown in the family car for a pizza. Interviewed later, the neighbors say, 'I can't hardly believe it. He was such a nice kid. Real polite you know.'

I remember this doctor, killed his whole family but said he was innocent and managed to sell it for a couple of years. But then, the evidence that he'd done it turned up. Enough for a jury to convict him. But right to the last, and beyond, the new woman in his life said, 'He's innocent. I know he is. The man *I* knew couldn't have done that. *I* would have known.' She came to visit him, every weekend, and she worked faithfully to clear his name. She was an easy mark for lowlife investigators who claimed they could find new evidence that would point to the 'real killers' and free her man, who couldn't have been guilty because *she* knew what kind of man he was.

The people who think they are close, who consider themselves intimate, have a hard time, for some reason, admitting they have been deceived. The more intimate, the harder it is. Especially if you believe in the infallibility of your own intuition.

'Why are you telling me this?' I said.

'Because Semmes needs to drop this ridiculous prosecution.'

'Show me something,' I said, 'and I'll pass it along. Or I'll tell him to talk to you and you can tell him yourself.'

'This isn't going to be some backwoods, good-old-boy trial,' she said. 'This is for big stakes.'

'Yes, I know.'

'I'm not sure you do. How much exposure can your witness take? How much can *you* take?'

'Oh come on,' I said. 'You're threatening me.'

'You're absolutely right,' she said, turning to go back inside. 'And you can tell Semmes I'm threatening him too.'

She started inside and looked back at me. 'You keep going with this prosecution and one day, you'll look back on this conversation and wish you had paid attention when you were warned. But, by then ... You'll be fucked.'

She opened the door and, when she was back inside, let it slam behind her.

Strange, I knew she didn't have anything to threaten me with. And I wasn't exactly afraid of her. But ... I felt like I ought to be.

Twenty-two

I was tired. It was not a case of being short on sleep as much as it was the sense of having been confined. I don't handle that very well. One of many areas, I suppose, for some self improvement; but I don't expect I'll find the time. I never liked feeling confined, right from the start, and I liked it even less after I'd been in prison.

So, after all those hours in the truck, driving to Lewellen's and back, and then another couple of hours on top of that in a close little bar, everything felt too tight, including my skin. It was all closing in on me.

So I drove to the motel and did not call for my messages when I got to the room. I stripped, changed into some trunks and went out to the little pool where I swam laps for an hour. The water was warm and the pool was short. I made a lot of turns.

But I also made a lot of strokes and the movement felt good. Motion does for me what chanting does for the kind of people who wear robes and burn incense. I got into the rhythm and lost track of things.

When I got out I felt better. Still tired; but in a different way. The good way. The kind of tired where you can sleep.

I sat on the bed with a towel wrapped around my waist and called the desk for my messages. There was only one. From Jessie.

I called the number, got the machine, and was about to hang up, when the message kicked in and I heard her voice.

'Morgan,' the tape said, 'I tried to call you. I'm going to be working real late. But I just wanted you to know I'm thinking about you. Try to take care of yourself, you hear me. Call me tomorrow. In the afternoon. I'm gonna sleep the whole morning. Love you.'

Then the machine clicked. There was a pause. Then the long beep that indicated to the caller that it was time to leave your message.

'Love you too,' I said. And hung up.

Then I did what most lonely people in motel rooms do; I turned on the television. When the picture came up, I lay down, on top of the covers, and pointed the remote at the screen. I wasn't looking for anything in particular and I didn't expect to find anything worth watching. It was just a holding action. Like all the rest of the lonely people I was looking for some thin diversion; something to keep my mind off the melancholy image of myself, stretched out on a bed alone, in an institutional little room bathed in lurid blue light.

I was just looking for non-narcotic transition into sleep.

What I got was – the usual clutter. Commercials, mostly. Reruns of shows that seemed like brainworms when they first ran – *Gomer Pyle*, *The Fugitive*, *Starsky and Hutch*. Shows about animals migrating across the Serengeti plain – if they filmed many more of those migrations, they were going to have to start paying the wildebeest by scale. Sports shows. Weather shows. Call in and buy something with your credit card shows. People arguing about politics shows and people arguing about incest shows. Standup comic shows where nobody seemed to say anything funny, even though people you couldn't see laughed just about nonstop. Music video shows where nobody actually sang the words to the songs and where crowds in the thousands and thousands of people worked themselves into a state of orgiastic hysteria, usually at night, in the dark, just like the throngs at Nuremberg had.

I saw all this just by pushing a button on a little plastic box. I know the line about how television has shrunk the world and brought people closer together, but I never feel more alone, and the outside world never seems more alien, than when I am watching television.

Maybe it is because there is so much television in prison. When I remember my days in the steel city, I recall first the smell and, then, the noise. The noise that never stops and that is a mix of metal striking metal, angry inarticulate voices echoing down concrete corridors, and the background din of televisions that are never turned off.

The image on the screen changed in front of me. One picture replaced by another, as though some invisible hand were flipping through the pages of an incomprehensible book. Shopping followed some rock group which followed the weather in Eastern Europe which had been preceded by a rerun of *M*A*S*H*. I changed channels so rapidly that I could not actually watch anything.

It was, in its way, like one of those old terrifying childhood dreams of whirling, image following image until it was all a blur of ionized blue and I killed the power and went to sleep, still lying on top of the covers, my mind an empty white blank.

I ran ten miles before sunrise. I was dressed and drinking coffee when the telephone rang.

'I worked all night, Morgan,' Randolph Atkins said, 'but I believe we got him...'

Three or four hours later, I was on the road again, heading west this time. I crossed the Apalachicola River where the time changed to Central Standard and by mid-afternoon, I was at the main gate to Eglin Air Force Base.

The federal prison at Eglin is called 'Club Fed' because the inmates can play golf and tennis there. But it is still jail and when I walked through the gate I got the cold feeling you get when you come close to stepping on a snake.

The metal detector screamed when I walked through it. I'd handed over the slim little lockback knife I carry – mostly for slicing apples and cleaning my nails – and the belt with the heavy buckle. Also my mechanical pencil. The only thing left was the silver in my teeth.

'Nah,' the guard (I couldn't help thinking of him as a *screw*) said, after looking in my mouth. 'You don't have enough for that. You got any old plates or rods or screws left inside from surgery?'

No, I said.

'Shrapnel?'

Well, yeah. A little. Not enough...

'Doesn't take much. This thing will tell us when some-body walks in with a goddamned razor blade in the seam of his pants. Where'd you get it? Vietnam?'

Yes, I said, feeling a little stupid. I'd known guys who could set off the airport systems. Every time.

'You can go on in, sir,' the guard said.

Respect from a screw, I thought. What next?

The visiting area was standard and sterile. You sat on one side of a partitioned table and the inmate you were visiting sat on the other. If you were a lawyer, or working for one, they gave you a table to yourself, for privacy. There were also soundproofed rooms and I'd asked for one.

Carl Wynn was waiting for me. He didn't bother to stand up, so I took a chair on my side of the table. We looked each other over. He was pale, like everyone in jail, but there was something even worse than that about his pallor. He made you think of the way a flower looks after it has been cut off at the stem. The color is still there, but the essential vitality is gone.

He was almost translucent.

Also thin. And edgy. With a pointed but weak face that made you think of some kind of rodent. A ferret maybe. With sly, nervous eyes.

'All right,' he said, finally, 'what do you want? I've told everybody who has asked, from every jurisdiction, that I'm not turning evidence. I don't want witness protection and I like living.'

'How much more time do you have?'

'Three years,' he said, sounding infinitely sorry for himself. 'That's with good time.'

There were hard cons who would tell you that they could do three standing on their heads. Do it with their hair on fire. But Wynn wasn't cut out for this kind of life.

'You'll be needing some money,' I said.

His expression changed.

'I was disbarred. You know that?'

I nodded.

'Plus the fines and the back taxes.'

I nodded again.

'I won't have any money and I won't be able to work,' he said in a voice drenched with self-pity. 'I guess they expect me to just curl up in a corner and die.'

'I know of a way,' I said slowly, 'that you might be able to get well.'

He studied me, trying to keep the eagerness out of his face. But he couldn't help himself.

'Okay,' he said, 'I'll bite.'

I reached in my shirt pocket for a small, folded sheet of paper. Put it on the table and unfolded it. The paper was a check. From Ian Patterson's paper. The check was made out in Wynn's name. It was for $10,000.

'That,' I said, 'is the up-front money. This money and the rest of it can be deposited in an account for you. Offshore, if necessary. If you don't have an account, somebody can help you open one.'

He studied the check and he studied my face. One eyelid twitched, like he had strained it reading.

'Up front?'

'Ten per cent,' I said.

He thought for a minute. 'I can't,' he said, 'do anything to earn that money that could possibly mean – even by the remotest fucking chance – that I'd have to spend any more time in here.'

'It will be a legal, but confidential, relationship,' I said.

'Confidential because you probably don't need for the Feds to know you've made a little money. What with the fines and the back taxes.'

'No.'

'So?'

'All right,' he said, bending a little closer, like a conspirator, even though we were in a soundproof room. I could feel his breath and smell his aftershave. I don't know anything about perfume but if his was *not* cheap, then he was being robbed. 'All right, tell me what I have to do.'

I leaned back and took out my notebook. 'Tell me,' I said, 'about the trouble you got into with Lander White, back when you two were in law school.'

I left the prison two hours later. I had what I had come for but I still needed a little more, and something cold to drink besides. So I took a two lane that ran north through pine trees and pasture land and stopped when I came to a little country store. They had a case of beer iced down in a galvanized wash tub. I bought a can and drank it, standing out in the parking lot while I talked on the pay phone to Randolph Atkins. The beer seemed to cut the bad taste in my mouth.

'Well, I'd say you struck paydirt, Morgan,' he said after I told him about my conversation with Wynn.

'Thanks to you.'

'Basic stuff, actually,' he said. 'But kind of you to say so.'

'Wynn told me the woman's name,' I said. 'She was a townie and she may have gotten married, changed her name, and moved to California...'

'But you'd like me to find out?' Atkins said.

'Yes.'

'No problem. Can I reach you?'

'No,' I said. 'I'll have to call you.'

'Morgan, you need a cellular phone. Pay phones just don't get it anymore.'

I had a cellular phone, as a matter of fact. I just didn't like carrying it around unless I had to. The trial of Senator Dan Vincent, if it ever came to that, was at least six months away. My calls could wait a couple of hours.

'Thanks again, Randolph,' I said. 'You'll hear from me.'

'Bye bye.'

I got back to Tallahassee in time for the news. The Vincent case was all over the television and I made myself watch it.

The anchorpeople were stirred up over what they kept calling 'new developments'. But, then, I don't suppose newsies would care a lot about 'old developments'. In their lexicon, *new* is synonymous with *good*.

The 'new development' that seemed to have people most exercised was the report, in a tabloid newspaper, that Lisa Hutchinson was getting free legal advice from a man named Tom Lewellen who was an old political enemy of Dan Vincent.

'This,' one of the anchor women said gravely, 'raises very troubling questions, according to some, about the possible political motives behind the charges against US Senator Daniel Vincent.'

And cut to:

Lander White standing in front of a bunch of reporters who were pointing microphones at his face and taking his picture in the sort of frenzy you see when you kick the top off a fire ant mound.

'We have maintained, all along,' White said, sounding like an undertaker quoting prices, 'that this is not a criminal prosecution but a political persecution.'

I changed channels.

Just in time to hear about another 'new development'. There were, it seemed, 'unconfirmed reports' that Lisa Hutchinson had once had an abortion. She was, the anchorman intoned, 'not married at the time'.

I changed channels again. This time I learned that Senator Daniel Vincent, through his attorneys, had agreed to leave Washington in three days to fly down and appear before a judge. Vincent would plead to the charges against him and the judge would then set bail.

Those were the developments. You had to wonder why anyone who didn't have an actual stake in the case would care at all about any of them. It was a circus act, nothing more or less, and I suppose the citizens needed to be amused. They had grown tired of sitcoms and cop shows. These days, they liked real trials. Soon it would probably be public executions and then, maybe, we would start sacrificing virgins.

I turned off the set and went out for dinner.

I decided, on my way, to look in on Lisa Hutchinson. Dixie Price had found another house, closer to town, where she could stay – or hide out, actually. The house was in an older sub-division that was fairly close to town and had probably once been the newest and most exclusive address

227

around. Back then, the neighborhood would have been all white and nobody could have imagined it any other way. These days, it was probably less than half white. Times do change.

The house was small. White clapboard with green trim. The yard was lush, almost overgrown, and the shrubs seemed almost to conceal the house from the road. I imagine Dixie and Lisa liked that. I went around the block twice. No strange cars. I called on my cellular – this seemed like one of those times when it made sense – and when Lisa answered, I said, 'This is Hunt. May I drop by?'

'Okay,' she said listlessly.

I broke the connection and parked five or six blocks from the house then walked the rest of the way, checking over my shoulder to make sure I wasn't being followed. All this security was to duck reporters. You could not simply say 'No. Go stick it in your hat.' You had to hide out. They had their rights, after all.

The rest of us, I guess, could suck eggs.

I knocked on the door. It opened halfway and I stepped inside. It was dark in the living room. Just one light burning and it was a dim little table lamp.

'Sorry about the short notice,' I said.

'That's all right,' Lisa said. 'I wasn't doing anything. Just sitting here ... crying.'

'I'm sorry,' I said.

'What for? You didn't do nothing.'

'I'm still sorry. You shouldn't have to put up with that.'

'Why not?' she said. 'I mean, shit fire, it's a *fight*, ain't it? You use everything you've got.'

'You sound like you're working for Lander White.'

'Maybe I should be. He's the only one in this fight, so far, who is doing any fighting.'

In the dim light, her face looked twisted and almost grotesque with pain and anger. She had been violated again and it wasn't any better the second time.

'We'll get our turn.'

'Well, is that a fact?'

'Yes.'

'Cause of the great Mr Semmes.'

It was easy to see where this was going. She needed someone to cloud up and rain on, and I was handy.

'Well I haven't seen your Mr Semmes do shit. I'm locked inside a house that ain't mine, hiding out. Everything I've ever done, that I might be sorry about and want to keep to myself . . . Well, it's on the news for everybody to see. I've got parents, been going to the Baptist church every Sunday for thirty years, and I don't want them to see that stuff. But Lander White wants to get it out and so it gets out. The great Mr Semmes doesn't seem to be able to do anything about it.'

'That's right,' I said. 'He can't. But he didn't make the rules.'

'Well fuck the rules,' she shouted and slapped the wall with the flat of her hand. 'Just fuck the rules.'

It sounded like a good idea to me but I didn't say so. I just waited. She was entitled to a tantrum. She'd earned it.

'What do you think Lander White is doing tonight?' she said.

I shrugged.

'I'll bet he's out somewhere, enjoying himself. Having a nice dinner. And I'll bet the Honorable Dan Vincent is

229

GEOFFREY NORMAN

doing the same thing. Acting like nothing happened and
he's got nothing to worry about because ... probably he
doesn't.

'And me? I'm hiding out, in a house that isn't mine,
afraid to go out and embarrassed, even, to call my parents.
And I didn't do anything that I deserve to be punished.

'So you know what I think?'

'No,' I said.

'I think I should have never talked to the law, like
everybody was telling me I should. What I ought to have
done instead is gone straight to Earl and told him about that
maggot senator and let him go ahead and kill him for me.
He would have, too. I'd have gotten even, just as sure as
anything that Mr Semmes might have done. Quicker, too.
And without my name and everything I've ever done being
shown all over the television.'

I couldn't argue with her and I didn't try.

'It's rough,' I said. 'I wish I could do something.'

She was about to say something ugly but I interrupted
her.

'Why don't you let me take you out for something to eat?
Maybe a couple of beers. It's not much but it gets you out of
this particular jail.'

Twenty-three

She had a face people would recognize but it wasn't so
distinctive that she couldn't ride in my truck, through
traffic, after dark. She picked out a radio station that
played country, turned the volume up loud, and leaned
back in the seat to let the sound of Randy Travis and the
sensation of moving down the highway wash over her. It
seemed to change her mood instantly.

'Sure feels good,' she said, over the music, 'to be out of
that house. I was going crazy. Nothing but four walls and
the television and every time I turned it on, there was
something I didn't want to see.'

I told her I could see how that would get old.

'Where are we going? You know someplace safe?'

'No,' I said. 'This isn't my territory.'

'Me neither,' she said, sounding like a disappointed
child. 'But we can just drive around for a while. Then I'll
eat back at the house.'

'Maybe I can come up with something,' I said. 'Hand me
the phone out of that little canvas bag.'

Twice in one day with the cellular. A new record.

I called Tom Pine, back in Pensacola, and got him on the
second ring.

231

'You still on that thing with the senator?' he said.

'Yes.'

'Well pity your poor ass, then. Looks like a real Chinese fire and boat drill from here.'

'It is,' I said, 'every bit of that.'

'What can I do for you?' he said. 'I'll do most anything as long as I don't have to get involved in that case.'

'I'm looking for a place to eat,' I said.

'Beg pardon?'

'A restaurant.'

'You lose your phone book? Why don't you call the Chamber of Commerce?'

'I need a place where I can take somebody who doesn't want to be recognized. I'm looking for some privacy.'

It didn't take Pine long.

'Oh,' he said, 'what you want is some funky chicken and rib place where the white folks don't go.'

'Right.'

'No problem,' he said and gave me directions to a place called Eddy's. 'Give it about five minutes. I'll call Eddy and tell him to treat you right.'

'Thanks, Tom.'

'If you're traveling with who I think you're traveling with,' he said, 'then you tell her to hang in there. Tell her Semmes hadn't had his innings yet. But I suspect you told her that already.'

'She can't hear it enough,' I said.

I gave her the phone and she put it back in the duffel.

'Who was that?'

'A sheriff's lieutenant I know. From over in Pensacola.'

'And you were asking him about a place to eat over here?'

'Well,' I said, 'he knows the area. And he's black.'

'Black?'

'Right. I figured he would know someplace where you might stand out but nobody was going to call the newspapers or the television and tell them you were there. That give you a problem?'

She thought for a moment, then said, 'It used to. I was already getting over it. From school, you know. Right now, I think I kind of feel like what those people must feel like their whole lives. You know what I mean?'

'Sure.'

'I mean, I guess I'd just be grateful if they didn't treat me – and look at me – like I was some kind of freak. I suspect that's all they want, too. Right?'

'Yes,' I said. 'And you know what else?'

'What?'

'The truth is, they always make the best ribs. White people can't even come close.'

Eddy himself, all three hundred pounds of him, met us at the door to a sagging clapboard building on the side of a two lane that ran south, out of town, down into the Apalachicola swamps. You could smell the ribs as soon as you parked. It was a smell that was made up of unequal parts of hardwood smoke, probably hickory, vinegar and pepper sauce, and fat meat slowly cooking and steadily dripping grease on the coals.

'You got to be Pine's man,' Eddy said, gripping my hand and rubbing my shoulder. 'Be pleased to meet you.'

I said the pleasure was mine.

He turned to Lisa Hutchinson and said, 'And I know who you are, too. Everybody does. And I suspect I know how you must be feeling. It's a shame, is what it is, the way them lawyers act. And the TV people, too. And can't nobody do nothing about it. Ought to take them people out in the swamp and feed 'em to the gators. But that ain't allowed.

'But maybe you'll feel a little better, you get something good to eat. You like ribs?'

'I love them,' Lisa said.

'Good. Come on in. We'll get you a booth. In the back. Give you a little privacy. And we'll feed you some ribs.'

'Thank you,' she said.

'Sure. But it ain't nothing.'

He led us through a large dark room. There were picnic tables in the center, booths along the wall. All the tables and about half the booths were filled. We got looks, but no comments, on our way to a booth at the far end of the room, in a corner, near the kitchen.

'This is about as private as we got,' Eddy said. 'A waitress will be along. You enjoy your dinner.'

'Thank you,' Lisa said, biting her lip. When Eddy had gone, she started crying.

'He's so *nice*,' she said. 'He doesn't have to do this.'

'Nope.'

'He doesn't even know me.'

I could have pointed out that he was doing it as a favor to Tom Pine and that he did know Tom. But I didn't. It seemed like a good thing for her to realize that there were a few people in the world capable of a kindness toward her along with the millions who were happy either to exploit her or to be entertained by her ordeal. They didn't know her, either, the tens of millions of people who followed the case on afternoon television and called her by her first name.

'I'm sorry,' she said, wiping her eyes, 'I guess the strain was just getting to me.'

'Sure,' I said. 'Now let's get some beer and forget about it for a while.'

We drank two pitchers of beer and ate two large orders of ribs which came with cornbread and coleslaw and we ate that too. Neither of us had dessert.

The ribs were moist and tender, so that you really could clean the meat from the bone. The smoke and the slow cooking seemed to break down everything tough and chewy in the meat so you peeled it away from the bone with your front teeth and then chewed with your back teeth. The meat was dark and rank and with a taste that made you think of black ground and sweet roots. The pepper and the salt made you thirsty so you drank beer to cool your mouth. While you were working on the ribs, you didn't talk much. And when you finished, you just talked about how good they had been. We were there for an hour and a half and I suspect it was the longest she'd gone without thinking about the case since the Saturday night when it all got started.

She was happy, in a temporary fashion, and it was good to see it.

The waitress asked if we wanted another pitcher. I said no and gave her a bill. When she brought the change, she looked at Lisa and said, 'None of my business, honey, but you be strong, understand. Stand up to the bastards. It's what they most fear.'

'Okay,' Lisa said. 'Thank you.'

We got some more looks on our way to the door, where Eddy met us.

'How were the ribs?' he said.

'Sublime,' I said.

'First time in twenty years,' he said, 'I've heard 'em called that. Can I quote you?'

'Absolutely.'

'You see Tom much?'

'Time to time.'

'Well you tell him don't be a stranger. He used to come over every Spring. He said he told everybody he came for the fishing but he was really here to eat ribs.'

'I suspect that's right.'

'Then tell him the ribs are good as always. It's been three or four years.'

'He's busy,' I said. 'Like people get.'

'When you don't have time to go fishing and eat ribs, then you done got yourself *too* goddamned busy. You tell Tom I said that.'

'I will.'

'Good luck to you,' he said.

'Thanks.'

Lisa gave him a kiss and we got in the truck and went back the way we came.

When we got to the little house, in the aging sub-division, I drove around the block a couple of times just to make sure that no reporters were lying in ambush. The coast seemed clear, so I parked in front of the house and killed the engine.

She looked at me and said, 'You got a girlfriend, I expect.'

'Yes,' I said, wondering what Jessie would say if she heard me call her my 'girlfriend'.

'Well,' Lisa sighed, 'it doesn't make any difference. Night like this, when I've had some fun, I'll sometimes ask a man to come inside. Have a drink.'

She laughed. It was an abrupt, bitter sound.

'Funny. Everybody says that. "Have a drink." And everybody has something else in mind. I know I usually did. Maybe it wasn't right but, you know, it's just how I am.'

She slapped the dash. Then balled her fists and hit the windshield.

'How I used to be, anyway. I wouldn't invite no man in for a drink now. Not even you, after you've been nice to me and we had some fun. I think about that door closing behind us and I just go cold. If you came in with me "for a drink", I don't think I could stand it. I'd be screaming soon as we were inside.'

She wrapped herself in her arms.

'That's horrible, isn't it?'

'Pretty bad,' I said.

'That's what that bastard did to me. What he did wasn't just for one night. It made a lot of nights terrible. Maybe every night, from now on, will be terrible. You think so?'

I shook my head.

'Why?'

'I don't know,' I said. 'I'm just guessing. Seems like even

when you don't get over something entirely, you get over it enough.'

'I hate that. It's like being crippled.'

I didn't say anything. The way I saw it, beating on my windshield was healthy.

'I keep thinking that there is one thing that would make me feel better.'

'What's that?'

'Seeing him dead,' she said in a voice full of venom. 'Arrested and tried, that doesn't get it. He still gets to wear his suit and talk to his lawyer and make his speeches. He hasn't lost the way I've lost. Maybe not even when he is in prison and he won't ever go there. We all know that. But dead ... then, he's paid fair.'

I sighed. 'You want some advice?'

'Sure,' she said. 'But I know what you are going to say.'

'Well, then, just consider the source.'

'Okay,' she said sullenly. 'What is your advice?'

'Put it out of your mind.'

'That's it?'

'Yes.'

'Put killing him out of my mind?'

'Either you are thinking about it because you really intend to do it or you are just playing with yourself. Either way ... it's prison thinking.'

'Prison thinking?'

'That's when you make your misery the center of the whole universe, so it just dominates everything. Nothing else counts. You get to where you carry your misery around like a baby and you'd die before you'd give it up. Everybody goes through it. The thing is to get over it.'

'Did you?'

'After a while.'

'I hate him,' she said, 'and it is always on my mind.'

'Yes,' I said. 'And he probably never thinks about you. If he does, it is an irritation.'

She hit the dash, again.

'I want to see him dead.'

I would have said the same thing, in her place. And, maybe, done something about it.

'I would, too,' I said.

That seemed to satisfy her. An ally was enough, for the moment. She tried to smile and managed a sort of bleak grin.

'You're a nice man,' she said. 'I'd invite you in for a drink, in a heartbeat, if things were a little different.'

She let herself out and I watched while she walked to the door. Then I drove back to the motel and watched the late news, most of which was devoted to one theme: that Lisa Hutchinson was a hot pants slut. She didn't seem like the same woman I remembered from Eddy's, eating ribs and drinking beer. But you can get fooled in this deceitful world, I told myself. Good thing I had the news to keep me straight.

Twenty-four

At dawn, I got up and went running at FSU. It was one of those mornings that leaves you feeling a little giddy, a Spring morning with the dogwoods finally blooming and the leaves a tender, sweet shade of green that they lose as soon as the days get hotter. But, for now, everything was fragrant and new and, somehow, innocent. I kept thinking two things: first, that I wished Jessie would come home soon and second, that I needed to get out into the woods.

There were three calls when I got back. All from people who knew my habits. I called Jessie first.

'What does it look like down there, Morgan?' she said. 'Is it pretty yet?'

I told her about the dogwoods.

'That settles it, then,' she said. 'I'm coming home this weekend, no matter what.'

'What time?' I said. 'I'll meet your plane.'

'Nah, hell, Morgan. You don't need to do that. I got my own car and, anyway, the airport scene is just too grim. I swear I've been in Greyhound bus terminals that were nicer than most airports. I'll get myself home. You meet me there.'

'When?'

'Morgan, you sound like you missed me.'

'Must be Spring.'

'How about lunchtime, on Saturday.'

I told her I would be there. Then I hung up and called Randolph Atkins.

'You need to give me a hard one, Morgan; all this stuff lately has been too easy,' he said.

'Sorry,' I said. 'I'll try to do better.'

'Please,' he said, 'everyone loves a challenge. Anyway ... Louise Pender married Jimmy Dale Swilling, in Gainesville, a couple of years after the episode with Lander White and Carl Wynn. They had three kids but the marriage didn't take for one reason or another. I found her under her maiden name, by checking the welfare records. She lives in Perry.'

I wrote the address and phone number in my notebook.

'I already called her,' Atkins said, 'to make sure the number was good. Told her I was with the state, verifying records. I could have been her priest, the way she trusted me.'

'Thanks again, Randolph.'

'No need,' he said. 'Actually, it's fun. But it's more like a warm-up than the real thing. Let me know how it turns out.'

'Will do,' I said, hung up, and called Semmes.

It was still early and he knew the call was from me.

'This is the season for renewal, Morgan,' he said without preamble. 'The time of resurrection. The earth is reborn. Persephone emerges from the land of the dead; the flowers bloom and the birds sing; a gentle sun shines and soft rains fall. The young look for love and the old remember what it was like and envy them. So what in the Sam Hill are we doing busting our asses on a trial for rape?'

'I don't know,' I said. 'Just lucky, I guess.'

'Morgan, this is *not* the season for trials. There has only been one trial of any note done this time of year and most people think Pontius Pilate handed down a lousy verdict.'

'This is just the preliminary stuff, remember,' I said. 'Real trial won't start for a while. Maybe you can schedule it for January, when the weather is nasty.'

'I suppose,' Semmes sighed. 'Still seems like blasphemy, almost, to be thinking of such shit on a day like today. How you doing? You got anything interesting?'

'I thought I'd fax you something later in the day,' I said. 'Nuts and bolts. Nothing dramatic.' I had decided to keep him in the dark on what I'd learned about Lander White and my discussions with Ian Patterson. He would disapprove on the grounds that it was dishonorable and maybe illegal and I couldn't disagree. But I believed you needed to play offense and that you didn't always get to pick your ground.

'If it isn't red hot,' he said, 'then save it. I'm driving over there tomorrow morning.'

'Why?'

'Well, I thought maybe I would show the flag at the pleading and the bail hearing,' he said in the languid voice he falls into when he has something planned. I wondered what it was but knew better than to ask.

'What time do you expect to get here?' I said.

'Mid-afternoon,' he said, 'early evening. Why don't you get me a room where you are staying, at the Redneck Ritz there? We'll have dinner. I know a good place for catfish.'

'See you tomorrow.'

I was back on the road in less than an hour. On my way to Perry, in cattle country. Louise Pender, however, did not live in a big white house surrounded by hundreds of acres of green pasture where the Charlois and the cattle egrets fed. She lived close to town, in a double wide, crowded on all sides by other double wides. Some people have bathrooms and closets bigger than her front yard.

Even so, it was a mess. She hadn't bothered to plant grass, so what covered the ground was a crop of volunteer weeds, along with a lot of cigarette filters and little piles of dog crap. The trailer needed paint and the screen in the front door was ripped. When I knocked, it set off some kind of little dog that yapped for a full minute, at least, before the door opened.

'What is it?' the woman said. She was fat. The kind of fat that comes from eating potato chips and drinking Coca-Cola for the same reasons a child sucks his thumb. She was wearing shorts and the flesh of her thighs made me think of milk curd – shapeless and a kind of off-white color, tinged with blue.

'Louise Pender?' I said.

'That's me. What do you want? You with the state or something?'

'No,' I said. 'I'm not.'

'You looking for money?'

'No,' I said. 'I work for a lawyer. We think you might be able to assist us in an investigation. And, actually, it might be worth some money to you.'

She stared out at me from the gloom of her trailer. Her little eyes looked like finger holes punched into dirty snow.

'This is some kind of con, ain't it?' she said.

'No,' I said. 'We believe you have information that could help us.'

'You want me to be a witness?'

'Not exactly.'

She studied me a little longer, then sighed and said, 'All right. Come on in.'

We sat in a small living room where the most imposing piece of furniture was, inevitably, the television. It dominated the room. She hit the mute button on her remote but did not turn the television off. It was tuned to one of those shows where the host wanders through his audience sticking a microphone into the faces of people who then direct questions to people sitting on stage. There was no way to know what the subject of the interrogation was. But the people in the audience were plainly angry. And one of the people on the stage was weeping. It was, I thought, like watching some high-tech version of a medieval troupe performing a mime.

Louise Pender sat on the couch with her little Pomeranian dog in her lap. She was drinking Coca-Cola from a large bottle. She did not offer me anything. I sat in an upholstered chair that smelled of old cigarette smoke.

'Miz Pender,' I said, 'does the name Lander White mean anything to you?'

The lifeless little eyes went wide for a moment and the surly lower lip began to tremble. Almost before I realized it, she was crying. Just like the woman on television.

'Don't tell me you work for him,' she said. ''Cause if you do, you can just get on out of here. That man ruined my life. *Ruined* it. And it never cost him nothing.'

245

'I don't work for him, Miz Pender,' I said and, to myself, I sounded like a hired mourner doing a day's work at the funeral home.

'What do you want then?'

'I want to make him pay.'

She cried for a little while. Loudly. Then she went away and washed her face. The little dog followed her and left me alone in the forlorn little room where there was nothing at all to distract you from the monolithic television. No books, no magazines, no newspapers. Not even a few family photographs to make you wonder how the people in their high-school graduation clothes had turned out since.

'So you must know something,' she said when she was back sitting on the couch with the little dog, 'or you wouldn't be here. You wouldn't even know about me. So I figure it must have been you who called yesterday, saying you was with the state.'

'Somebody who works for me,' I said.

'I probably wouldn't have talked to him if I'd known this was going to happen. Or maybe I would have. Most of the time, I just try to forget about what happened. But, every now and then, I'll have a kind of day when I think what I ought to do is go on one of those shows, like Oprah or Geraldo or Jenny Jones and just tell my story about how the man who ruined my life, when he was in law school, is now a big-deal lawyer. It's my dream of revenge; that's what it is. But I just keep putting it out of my mind. I've never had the nerve.'

'It would be hard,' I said, trying to sound soothing, like someone trained to reassure.

'I *ought* to want to do it. That's what they all say, on them shows. I ought not to feel ashamed and guilty. *He* is the one ought to feel like that. I can get to that feeling, now and again, but I can't seem to hold on to it. You know what I mean?'

'Sure.'

'I wasn't always fat and afraid ... on welfare.'

'No.'

'I was pretty cute, once. And I liked to have fun. I had a lot of friends. They all thought I'd do things. But you know what I was?'

I shook my head.

'I was a "townie". You know what that is?'

'You weren't a student,' I said. 'You lived in town.'

'That's right. And you know what else it meant? It meant that they thought I was trash and that they could treat me that way because nobody would do nothing.'

She bit her lip and shook her head.

'They were right about that,' she said. 'They took me out one night, to a party, filled me up with vodka and gangbanged me and left me on somebody's front lawn. If my girlfriend hadn't been there, I might have died. She found me and got me to a hospital. They pumped my stomach and, later on, I got an abortion. You know what happened to Lander White and the rest of them?'

'No.'

'Well, it was May. They were about to take their last exams and then graduate. So the school said that, for punishment, they would have to wait until August to take their exams and they couldn't graduate with the rest of the class. That was all. They raped me – more than one of them

247

– and left me for dead. And that was their punishment. They couldn't graduate with the rest of them boys.'

I nodded. That had been what Atkins spotted; the tip that led him, ultimately, to Carl Wynn, doing time in Eglin.

'Lander White was the one who put the others up to it. And now, he's doing fine. And me? There hasn't been one day, since then, that I've been free of it. There's lots of days when I wish I'd laid on that lawn just a little bit longer so I could of gone ahead and died.'

I took out my notebook and an envelope that held another check from Ian Patterson's paper. This check was made out to Louise Pender.

'If you'll tell me that story, slowly, from beginning to end, then I can pay you something for the rights to it. There is a small chance that it might be published in a paper, but I doubt it will come to that. But I can use the story to even things up with Lander White.'

She took some convincing but, a couple of hours later, I had her story, in my notebook. I'd written so feverishly that my hand was cramped. It felt good to stop writing and better, by miles and miles, to get out of that trailer and back on the road.

Twenty-five

It was late afternoon when I got back to my room. There were no calls. After a swim in the tepid little motel pool, I spent four hours typing up reports on my computer. It is an Apple Powerbook. Randolph Atkins recommended it as an entry level machine. Said it was idiot-proof and, so far, it has been. I like it fine. But not as much as my truck.

I typed slowly and made lots of corrections. When I finished, I plugged the machine into the phone in my room and faxed everything to myself at the front desk. I don't carry a printer around with me.

It was dark when I left my room to walk over to the office for the faxes. There is something about letting the night slip up on you that leaves me feeling disoriented and a little down. I feel like I haven't been paying close attention. If you don't notice the world getting dark around you, what else have you missed?

The woman behind the desk handed me my fax. It was one long roll of slick paper. When I got back to my room, I used my pocket knife to divide the roll into three sections. One for Semmes and two for me. I needed one more, for Semmes, to even things up, I thought; and I could do that one in the morning.

Semmes' 911 Porsche pulled in front of the motel office at three in the afternoon. I was waiting for him.

'You like the four-star places, don't you, Morgan?' he said, looking around the motel. It was said with more amusement than distaste.

'I'm a cheap date,' I said.

'And you don't use a motel room for anything except sleeping, right?'

'That's right.'

'Well, let me check in and park. Then I'll come over to your room. You have anything cold? The highway always makes me thirsty.'

'Cooler full of beer?'

'Perfect.'

Five minutes later, he knocked. I opened the door and handed him a cold can of beer and two faxes. One had been typed the night before. The other that morning, after I'd talked to Lisa Hutchinson again. This time about Tim Fulton and what he'd said when he came to see her. She said he had made her an offer. A lot of money to 'just go away'. Tim Fulton had told me the same thing, sitting on the patio behind his little house on Patrick Ewell's plantation. The money for Lisa Hutchinson would have come from Patrick Ewell.

'What's he buying?' Semmes said. He was sitting next to the window in one of the flimsy motel chairs, scanning the faxes and drinking his beer.

'He's paying her to keep quiet.'

'Of course. But what does that buy *him*? She's not saying

he raped her. What does he think she might say that would hurt him?'

'I don't know.'

'Ummm,' Semmes said, his eyes and his attention returning to the fax.

'You're sure about all these times?' he said. 'On the phone calls and the airplane flights?'

'Reasonably,' I said.

'I might want to use them tomorrow,' he said. 'Can you do better than *reasonably*?' It was a command, delicately delivered.

'Stand by,' I said. I picked up the phone, dialed Randolph Atkins, and went through the usual drill with the answering machine. When I got the real Randolph, I told him I wanted to doublecheck the times of the calls that Vincent had made on the morning after the rape. Also the times of his flights.

'No problem,' he said, sounding bored. 'I downloaded all that stuff into a special file. Give me a nanosec and I'll open it. What's the matter, something doesn't fit?'

'No,' I said. 'But there is a hearing scheduled for tomorrow. We're just checking our knots.'

'Okay,' he said, 'here it is.' He read off the times and I checked them against the report which Semmes had handed me. Everything was correct.

'Thanks, Randolph.'

'Call any time,' he said. 'You can find me in cyberspace.'

Semmes nodded when I told him the dates and times were fine. Went back to scanning the report and said nothing until he was finished, had put the fax on the cheap veneer table next to his chair, and had taken another drink of beer.

'It sounds like Miss Hutchinson is feeling the strain,' he said mildly.

'She'd like to hit back,' I said. 'She feels like the other side is getting in all the shots.'

'I can sympathize.'

'So when do we get in our shots?'

He looked at me and smiled. 'You too?'

'Seems like they are in the papers every day,' I said. 'On the television every time you turn it on. They've floated rumors about abortions and what her blood alcohol was that night and the media has gone for it like wolves on a truckload of lamb chops. Last night, on the television, I saw one of those network legal consultants say that Lander White had already won the battle for public opinion. He also said that whichever side won that battle usually won the case.'

I was feeling the same way Lisa Hutchinson was feeling. Like they say, I was tired of being patient and fair. I wanted to kick some ass.

'I saw the same show,' Semmes said. 'That man is a fool. Most of them are fools. They are like the people you see at the racetrack, peddling tip sheets. If they could really pick winners, then they would never sell the information. They could make more betting on one race than they'll ever see selling tout sheets. And they wouldn't have to mess around with layouts and printers. Just buy a ticket and collect the money. The only bigger fools than the people who sell those tout sheets are the people who buy them.

'If that consultant knew as much about the law and courts and criminal cases as he claims to know,' Semmes said, 'he would be trying cases instead of making sixty-second comments on the evening news. Nobody is exonerated or convicted on anything he says. It carries all the weight of a horoscope.'

'Okay,' I said. 'If you say so.'

'But you would still like to play a little offense.' He smiled. Tolerantly.

'Sure. But that doesn't mean anything. I'd a lot more like to win at the trial.'

'Maybe we can do both,' he said. 'I think we may play a little offense tomorrow.'

He did not seem inclined to elaborate and I knew better than to push. Semmes would think about a problem for a long time and then he would suddenly arrive at a solution, almost by a kind of inspiration. There was nothing random or fragmented in his thought process. He didn't try out ideas or bounce them around. And when he arrived at a plan, he did not talk it out. He kept his own counsel.

When I first noticed this about him, I thought he was obsessed with security; one of those people who believe that there is no such thing as a secret once you have told anyone. But I learned, as I got to know him better, that there was more to it than paranoia, though you wouldn't call Semmes' way of thinking conventional, or even entirely rational.

He kept things to himself, I decided, because he believed that once they were out in the open they lost something, some part of their force, and he needed for his ideas and plans to have that power if he was going to make them work. The plan, whatever it was, had to be revealed to him in action. It was the way Stonewall Jackson had planned and fought his battles.

'What do you need from me?' I said.

He looked up. His eyes were not entirely focused on me.

'Right now, nothing.'

'That shouldn't be a problem.'

He smiled. 'Give me an hour with these reports. They look very good, by the way. Up to your usual quality. I want to think and I want to get my game face on.'

For a bail hearing? I wondered but did not ask.

'But how about a little fishing, later on, toward evening?'

'Sounds fine. Where?'

'Eliot Atwood's place. He's got some ponds, full of bass. He wanted to have us for dinner but he and his wife have some kind of charity function tonight, in Atlanta.'

'Call me when you're ready to go fishing,' I said and left him to his work.

The pond on Atwood's plantation was thick with cypress but there was one fairly clear bank and a juniper skiff pulled up on dry land. We paddled out into the pond in the skiff and drifted silently. I was in the stern and made a paddle stroke whenever it seemed like we'd been in one place two long.

I made a few casts but mostly I watched Semmes work a fly rod. The line rolled over and lay on the water straight enough to satisfy Euclid, landing so softly it hardly made a ripple. Semmes had learned as a boy, from his father. On his father's seventieth birthday, Semmes had taken him to Norway where they fished for two weeks on the finest

salmon river in the world. It had been satisfying, Semmes
told me, to finally do something for his old man.

In the early evening, birds seemed to rise in every
direction and begin moving off somewhere for the night. A
few ducks came in to our pond to roost. And vast flocks of
egrets, flying in wavering formation, flew high overhead.
Solitary blue herons left one pond and went to stalk the
shallows of another. The insects and the frogs began to sing
the way they do in that last active hour of daylight. Semmes
caught three or four small bass and released them.

We probably hadn't spoken fifty words, when he said,
'Has it been bad?'

'Bad?'

'Yes, *bad*. You know, as in a disgusting spectacle. A
circus complete with clowns and freak shows.'

'Yes,' I said. 'I suppose it *has* been that bad.'

Semmes shook his head and then made a cast, laying out
fifty feet of line in a sinuous loop and dropping a deer hair
bug tight against a cypress knee.

'I get so tired of it,' he said. 'So goddamned weary of this
need people have to be *entertained*. There are days when I
think Thomas Jefferson did us all a major injury with that
stuff about "the pursuit of happiness". It wasn't much of a
stretch to go from the "pursuit of happiness" to the pursuit
of pleasure and from that to this infantile longing to be
entertained. You see these people who know everything
there is to know about one of these celebrity trials. They
know the life history of every witness, every lawyer, and
everyone who is on the jury; they can run down the whole
roster, the way kids used to be able to recite the batting
average of every player on the Yankees or the Dodgers.'

He twitched the bug and the water bulged around it. Semmes set the hook on a small bass and played it quickly to the boat. He picked the hook from the fish's jaw with his finger and thumb, the way you would pull a sticker from a crying child's foot.

'This need to be entertained,' Semmes said, resuming his argument, as though nothing had happened, while he made a few false casts to dry his fly, 'is just another addiction. You've been entertained by one murder trial for five or six months and when it is over, what do you want? Do you want to go out and plant a tree, train a dog, build a house, make a baby? Do you want to live?'

Rhetorical question. I waited for him to answer it.

'No sir,' he said, sounding now like he was addressing not just me but also some larger jury, out there in the swamp, hiding in the gloom that was settling among the limbless columns of the cypress trees. 'No sir. What you want is a fix. Another murder trial. This time, though, you want multiple victims or, if you can't get that, you want the defendant to be a bigger star than the last defendant at a celebrity murder trial. He should have a hit TV series, perhaps. Or have won an Academy Award sometime in the last five years. There should be more lawyers than last time and the trial should take longer, with more people getting thrown off the jury and more surprise witnesses and more expert commentary. It has to be a bigger high.'

He made another cast. We watched the rings spreading out around the little bug after it landed. When they died, the surface of the pond was black and still, gleaming like spilled oil.

He stopped talking and watched the water for a minute.

Then went on, in a different tone. 'I'd like to go to trial tomorrow. In a case like this, you shouldn't need more than two weeks to get ready. Another week to file motions. A day or two to pick a jury. That's it. Then you start the trial.

'And the trial takes one week. Both sides stipulate what everyone already knows. There is no dispute about anything up to the time those two met in that bar. Nothing else matters. You've got two stories. A dozen witnesses, at the most. You could do it in a week. With that kind of deadline pressure, both sides know they've got to use their best stuff and they've got to make it sing. They can't clutter it up with a lot of meaningless stuff, hoping to put the jury to sleep and, later on, find some reversible error in all the debris.

'But it will take a month – maybe two – just to select a jury. They'll ask about how people feel about politicians and who they voted for and whether they worked in a campaign and if they've ever known anyone who was raped and what kind of movies do you like. It will be a search for the absolutely untainted juror – twelve of them – and it will make Diogenes look like a weenie. The ostensible goal will be epistemological certitude but, actually, it is all just the warm-up act for the main event. Because if they wanted purity, they would hold the trial in a bare room somewhere, with only enough spectators to keep things honest. There wouldn't be any television cameras and the reporters would have to work off transcripts. Because the whole point would be to have a reasonably fair trial in a reasonable amount of time. But we all know that is *not* the point.'

He paused again. Made another cast. We both looked out at the sun, which was hanging just over the horizon, glowing gold, and cool enough that you could look straight into now, for a few minutes before it dropped below the land line.

I liked listening to Semmes when he was like this. And I was willing to do my part, which was ask the occasional simple question to keep him going.

'What is the point?' I said, mildly.

'Entertainment. The show. It is all show business now.'

'Everything,' I said, 'or just the law?'

'The law, certainly,' he said. 'Maybe not everything else. Not yet, anyway.'

He reeled up and I paddled to the bank. The sun was gone and the air had turned a soft, gauzy gray with a slight chill that you felt on the tips of your ears and the back of your neck. Except for a few whistling wood ducks, the birds had stopped flying. A single bared owl called from a tree close by. I called back and he answered.

'Excuse the tirade, Morgan,' Semmes said from the bow of the boat. 'I get carried away.'

'I enjoyed it,' I said.

'I'm sure.'

'Truth,' I said. 'I just wonder what you – anyone – can do about it.'

'Nothing. If that's the game, then you play or go home. I'm playing and I plan to win. Lander White and Daniel Vincent have had their innings. Tomorrow, by God, we get ours. It'll be time to hide the children and spread some sawdust on the floor.'

Twenty-six

Senator Daniel Vincent looked good, considering. Poised. Confident. Carefully and conservatively dressed. I wondered, idly, as I watched him step out of the car and make his way to the courthouse steps, if there were consultants you went to for advice on how to act once you'd been indicted. Did you just ask your lawyer? Or did they bring in a specialist?

Whoever was advising Vincent could make a career of it. He was cleanly barbered, in a way that did not draw a lot of attention to his hair. Seems like a lot of these television trials – especially in California – get carried away by hair, but Vincent was not overdoing it.

His color was good; but not too good. It wouldn't have been helpful if his skin had been pale and waxy. He did not want to look diseased or like he was afraid of the light. But, then, he didn't want to look like he'd been spending a lot of time at the beach or the tanning salon, either. He needed to look like a healthy, normal, robust adult is supposed to look – but doesn't necessarily – because that way the jury would think he had a healthy, normal, robust sex life.

That wasn't my theory. I'd picked it up from one of those television analysts – the kind Semmes had warned me against – and from what I saw, Vincent could have been watching the same program.

Good color.

And good clothes, too. Good cut, good fit; but not flashy and not the sort of suit that would mark him as a man who cared excessively about his wardrobe. He did not look like a fashion model but he did look like a man who had a normal, healthy measure of vanity in his makeup.

He was cleanly shaved and he looked like he'd had a good night's sleep. He also looked confident. Not cocky, like one of those punks who come to court laughing, so the world will know that no matter which way it goes, they just don't give a cold crap. Vincent's face was composed, sober, and eager. Almost as though he relished this day and his chance to stand up and say, in court, that he was innocent. That, also, was how he was supposed to look. According to my source on television.

I knew that I wasn't supposed to pay any attention to that – Semmes had told me so – but I couldn't help myself. I was listening to the expert analysts and a part of me believed what they were saying. I was worried and I was sick of the whole goddamned carnival. I had started this thing, back on a rainy Sunday afternoon, feeling the safety that comes with detachment. Miles and miles of detachment. I wanted to do a good job for Semmes so he would give me more jobs and I could continue to satisfy my old appetite for action. But I didn't have anything at all at stake. My attitude was ... call it, *professional*.

But that had changed. I now hated Vincent with a kind of righteous, personal, vindictive hatred. But that was the easy part. Hating politicians and actors and such doesn't take much in the way of brains or imagination. You can find it in any cheap bar and all over the radio dial, twenty-four hours a day.

Standing on the sidewalk in front of the courthouse, watching Daniel Vincent get out of his car, button his jacket and make his way through the crowd of reporters, I was filled with a loathing for the whole rancid pageant. It corrupted everyone who had any kind of role in the production, and the spectators as well. You could almost prefer the ancient way, with blades, out on some lonesome field. Blood on the earth. It would have been so much cleaner.

'You look like you know you've been beaten,' Barbara Hanley said. I hadn't noticed her standing next to me. Didn't know how long she had been there. Her expression was smug and contemptuous. Gloating. She reminded me of an imperious cat.

'Wouldn't be the first time,' I said. 'And he wouldn't be the first big man to rape a woman and get away with it. That is an old story.'

'But in this case it isn't true,' she said. Purring.

'You really believe that?'

'Yes I do.'

'Why? Because the woman had an abortion? I suppose you made sure that one got into the papers.'

'I didn't have to,' she said, with a narrow smile that revealed only her upper teeth.

'But you would have ... If you'd had to.'

The smile did not change. 'I'm willing to do whatever it takes,' she said. 'Men think that's righteous, don't they?'

'She could have been your sister,' I said.

'Or yours,' she said, still smiling.

'Then Vincent would be dead,' I said and wished, immediately, that I'd had the good sense to keep my goddamned mouth shut.

'Yes,' she said. 'We know that, don't we? All too well.'

She moved away, leaving me standing there with my face burning. I watched Vincent step up to a pod of microphones. They looked like a nest of snakes. He was alone. If he'd had a wife, then she would have been with him. That is proper form in these things. But he was a widower.

He did have children and if they had been older, then I'm sure they would have been with him. But bringing young children into something like this ... That would have been too much even for this circus. Sensibilities are not that coarse. Yet.

So he was alone and I could imagine that his lawyers had thought about that and finally decided that they could make it work for them. Lander White was nowhere in sight. Vincent was a solitary man taking on unfair charges. And, after the stories about how his political enemies had volunteered to help his accuser, it played.

'Good morning,' he said in a firm voice. There was a faint hum of feedback from one of the speakers. Not enough to keep him from going on.

'I would say that I'm glad to be here this morning, in Tallahassee, where my late wife and I spent some memorable years. But I'm not. It would be good to say that even though I am not happy to be here, I can understand why it is necessary. But I can't. I would even like to say that I realize people in public service have to pay a heavy price in terms of their privacy and that I can accept that. But I can't.

'I am an innocent man, accused of a repugnant crime. One of which I will be quickly and thoroughly acquitted inside this building.'

He paused and pointed, solemnly, to the courthouse behind him.

'But,' he went on, his voice quivering slightly with indignation, 'in the larger world of rumor and innuendo and gossip, and in the media where strict rules of evidence do not apply, I will never be entirely absolved. To some, because I was once accused, I will always be guilty.'

He paused again and stuck his jaw out like a coach about to tell the team some gut-check truth.

'But I am going to fight that, too. For the sake of my children. For the sake of my reputation. And for the sake of civility in our public life. I am not going to allow my political enemies to use the lowest, most vile kind of slanders to advance their agenda.'

He paused again. Took a breath. Then lowered his voice. 'This is a sad day. Sad for me. Sad for my children who have lived through enough sadness. But saddest for our country.

'I want to thank all my supporters who came out today and promise them that I will not quit on this fight and ask them, in turn, not to quit on me.

'Thank you.'

He turned away and walked up the stairs and into the courthouse with the crowd following and the reporters circling him, like remoras around a solitary, pelagic fish, waiting for scraps.

'He gave a pretty strong speech out there,' I said to Semmes when I saw him inside, in the courtroom.

'I heard it.'

'You weren't impressed?'

'This isn't a debate about civility in the public sphere,' he said. 'Whenever I hear someone ranting about how his enemies have set him up, instead of talking about the evidence, then I know I'm listening to a guilty man. He doesn't have the kind of political enemies who care that much. He's not John Brown. Vincent made a speech once, saying he thought it was a terrible thing when someone shot a doctor for doing abortions. He's against crime and for prosperity. Not exactly the kind of thing that brings out the long knives.'

'I see.'

'Right now,' Semmes said, 'he's still making speeches to the press. And that's a different game. Different goals; different rules. He's trying to take folks' minds off specifics and get them on to generalities. That's what a campaign is. There's no cross-examination during a campaign speech.

'He can spread bullshit all he wants, today and every day, right up to the trial. But, then, he's going to have to decide what his story is and we get to see how well it holds up. I'm going to make him defend his story and he's going to find that a lot harder than giving airy speeches about standing up to his enemies.'

Semmes' blue eyes glowed eerily with the kind of light you sometimes saw in the eyes of men who'd just been pulled suddenly out of a firefight so their bodies were still flushed with adrenaline and their minds were utterly focused on destruction. They would look at you and, even if you were a friend, would not recognize you. Would look right through you.

Before a battle, Stonewall Jackson's eyes were supposed to have burned with anticipation. His troops had called him 'Old Blue Light'. Semmes was a student of the Civil War and I'm sure he knew that little datum. I wondered if he knew his eyes glowed the same way.

'Still a long time until trial,' I said, 'a long time until you can get at him.'

'It may be a long time until the trial,' Semmes said, 'but that doesn't mean I can't get at him.'

The glow was still there.

Semmes sat alone at the prosecution table. There was one thin file folder in front of him. He wore a dark cotton suit, a white cotton shirt, and a subdued rep tie. He looked comfortable in the clothes and comfortable with himself. Serene. No hurry, no urgency, no pressure. He could have been a real-estate lawyer sitting in on a routine closing. Except for the eyes.

The courtroom was full. Spectators and reporters. Unusual for a proceeding where someone merely entered a plea and the judge accepted it and set bail. But you don't get many US senators up on rape charges and, like I'd been learning, people are bored and crave entertainment.

Me, I would rather have been just about anywhere. It was a pretty day and the woods were ripening. In another few days they would be at peak, with the dogwoods in full bloom, chaste and white against the new green of the hardwoods and the darker, richer green of the pines. It felt like the crime was being inside. But I was working and didn't see where I had any choice. Semmes didn't need me, certainly, but I still needed to be there.

I suppose you could say the same for the reporters. As for the spectators, they reminded me of the old women who carried their knitting to the square so they could keep busy while they waited for the guillotine to begin its work.

Daniel Vincent sat at the defendant's table. Along with Lander White, who looked very dapper in a well-pressed, cream-colored linen suit with what I assumed was an Italian cut. Very slim. His shirt was a pale, tropical blue. His tie was the color of wine and looked like silk to me. He was every inch the prosperous South Florida lawyer, dressing with dignity but still hip.

There were two other men at the table. Both on the young side. Dressed more conventionally. I assumed they were junior lawyers. Spear carriers for Lander White who was turned around in his chair, talking to Barbara Hanley. They could have been discussing a time for tennis and probably were. For a minute, I didn't recognize the woman sitting next to Hanley. Then it came to me. Anita Lepage, Senator Vincent's chief aide. Come all the way from Washington, taking time away from her big desk and busy schedule, to watch her man say, 'Not guilty.'

I wondered why.

I was staring at her and she must have felt my eyes on her. She turned and recognized me right away. The change in her expression, which had been solemn, was barely perceptible but it said about as plainly as possible just how much she loathed me.

Which was no skin off my ass. I wasn't looking for a good word with the EPA or any other favors from her boss. I just wanted to put him in jail.

The judge entered to the usual chanting and everybody

stood. When the chanting stopped they sat back down. A
respectful hush had come over the room.

'Call the first case.'

'Your honor, State of Florida charges Daniel P. Vincent
with ...'

The statute Vincent had violated was identified first by
number and then by what the number stood for and all the
mumbo-jumbo carried me back to the time of my own trial
and that feeling that settles over you, a feeling that you are
part of some vastly impersonal process and that, at bottom,
nobody involved cares much about you one way or the
other. The process runs on indifference. The only person
involved who truly cares is the accused.

And, in this case, Semmes.

Bad news for Vincent.

'How do you plead?' the judge asked and I stopped
daydreaming.

'Not guilty,' Vincent said firmly, like a soldier swearing
his allegiance.

'Motion for bail?' the judge asked in the tone he no
doubt used when he said, 'Bring me the check, please.'

'Your honor,' Lander White said, standing and smooth-
ing his tie, 'defendant is, as you know, a United States
senator. He is well known, not just in this state, but across
the entire country. He has never before been accused of
any crime. He has cooperated freely and fully in the
investigation of these charges, which he denies categoric-
ally. Defendant represents no flight risk whatsoever and
we request that he be released without bail. We believe that
to impose bail in this case, with the widespread interest it
has attracted' – here, White turned slightly and waved a

hand in the direction of the spectators – 'we believe that would tend to unfairly prejudice potential jurors.'

The judge looked at Semmes and raised his eyebrows.

'Mr Semmes?' the judge said. Lofty and indifferent.

'Your honor, the state is going to ask for bail in the amount of two million dollars.'

Lander White jumped up like something had bitten him. It wasn't all theater; he was genuinely surprised.

'Your honor, that is an outrage. Mr Semmes is grandstanding and playing to the press ...'

Before he could go any further, the judge said, 'Sit down, Mr White.'

Then he turned back to Semmes.

'That is a rather startling amount, Mr Semmes. Do you have grounds?'

'Of course, your honor,' Semmes said, sounding like he wanted, more than anything, to be helpful.

'Would you mind sharing them with the court?'

'Not at all, your honor. Counsel for the defendant says that his client is not a flight risk. The state believes that he is.'

'Evidence?'

'He ran once, your honor. We think he might do it again. He has the means and the contacts to get out of the country ...'

'Your honor,' White said, on his feet again, and sputtering, 'I object ...'

The judge held his hand up.

'Just a minute. We'll talk about your objection after I've asked a few questions.'

Again he turned to Semmes and he was scowling.

'What, exactly, do you mean when you say the defendant "ran once"? I think you need to explain yourself.'

'Your honor, on the morning when the events in question took place, Mr Vincent was a guest at a local hunting plantation. He had reservations on a plane leaving that evening. Scheduled departure was, I believe, seven ten. That's p.m. He was going hunting that morning. Then there was a lunch at the plantation. And a small reception, for some of the people who contributed to his campaign, later that afternoon, before he departed for Washington.

'Without canceling any of those plans, Senator Vincent caught the first flight out of town that morning. He had no reservation. Instead, he arrived at the airport, in a hurry, dropped his keys and contract at the rental car counter, went to the airline desk and asked for a ticket. When he was told that there was only first-class seating available, he said that would be fine and he paid with a credit card.'

Semmes paused to give the judge time to consider the image of the senator, who probably hadn't made his own travel arrangements or paid for his own tickets in ten years, suddenly in a hurry to get out on the next flight, at dawn on a Sunday morning.

'We've checked and there was no pressing senate business the next morning,' Semmes went on. 'No roll-call votes. No important committee hearings. The senator's own calendar was clear that morning to make time for a meeting with a real-estate agent who is helping him find a new condominium in Washington. He had a lunch with representatives of the Citrus Counsel. Afternoon meetings with constituents. Two hours with his administrative staff

269

to handle paperwork. An embassy party that night. Nothing that would require that he drop everything and get back to Washington. The logical assumption is that Senator Vincent was less interested in being in Washington than with being out of Tallahassee. I'd say he was in a hurry to get out of town.'

Lander White was on his feet but before he could say anything, the judge raised a hand to silence him.

'Just a minute,' he said impatiently.

Then, to Semmes, 'Is there more?'

'Yes, your honor,' Semmes said, 'but I'm prepared to discuss it in chambers, with the defense present. As a courtesy.'

'Why?'

'While it has clear relevance to fitness for bail, it might not be relevant at trial. I see no need to make it public in that case.'

'All right. Ten-minute recess.'

Semmes, White, and the judge retired to chambers and, in the courtroom, people looked at each other and said, in so many words, 'What the Christ is going on?'

I guessed that Semmes was going to tell the judge about the early morning phone call that Vincent had made to Lander White from the Atlanta airport. Semmes would say it suggested that Vincent already knew he had a problem and was running from it. And that he was keeping the call private because he didn't think that hiring a lawyer should be held against anyone, even if he hired one before being charged with a crime. Lander White could say that he didn't think that when and how his client sought counsel should be in issue or even made public. The judge might agree, in principle, but now he knew. And he was the one setting bail.

Standard legal bullshit. These things were choreographed like Japanese opera and made just about as much sense.

But Semmes knew all the steps.

You couldn't read much in his expression when he came back into the courtroom but Lander White's face said it all.

The judge split the difference on bail.

One million dollars.

The reporters went nuts.

Twenty-seven

When it was over, Semmes and I drove back to the motel in his Porsche. He drove fast, as usual. He keeps a radar detector on his dash but it isn't enough. He is always about one speeding ticket away from losing his license.

He was calm, almost indifferent, as he worked through the gears and told me about the meeting in the judge's chambers, after the hearing.

'Everyone was calm and professional except Vincent,' he said, 'and he was like a petulant kid; agitated and loud one second and, then, sullen and sulky the next. But he was upset over the inconvenience this was causing *him*. He was especially irritated – outraged, actually – over the fact that he couldn't catch a plane back to Washington this evening, the way he'd planned, since he's got to wait around until the bail is taken care of and he can't just put that on his gold card. He's invited to some Washington function and he just cannot abide that he's going to have to miss it for the mere formality of a felony rape charge.

'I remember some kids – high schoolers, you know, years ago, who had gang-raped this girl. When we charged them, they weren't eaten up with remorse. It didn't occur to them to regret what they'd done. But they *were* upset because it

273

meant they were going to be kicked off the football team. Before homecoming. In a year when they might go undefeated.

'Bad enough in high school jocks. In a senator . . .'

Semmes shook his head as though he were genuinely disillusioned. Which I couldn't quite bring myself to believe. He might be old school but he was not naive.

'Senator Vincent?' Semmes said, making a question out of the name – something Southerners do.

'Yes.'

'He's a bad one, Morgan. There's not a doubt in my mind about that.'

'Can you get him?'

'I think so,' Semmes said, downshifting to pass a truck and then cutting back into the turning lane so he could take the exit to our motel. 'I believe we got him this afternoon.' He turned his head just enough that I could see his smile. It was like him to say 'we got him'. I'd been sitting in the audience while *he* got Vincent. But I was part of the team, in Semmes' mind, so *we* got him.

'The problem in a case like this,' he went on, 'is that people are making up their minds on the basis of just about everything except the evidence and the facts. If you like the way Vincent votes on social security, then you'll say he is innocent. If you oppose him on abortion, then he is as guilty as sin itself. I suppose it is a good thing he isn't black.'

'Or an Indian,' I said.

'Lander White plays that game better than anyone,' Semmes went on. 'He's the master. I heard him talking to Vincent when we were finishing up in chambers. White was leaning on him to give a press conference, Monday morning. Vincent will stay in Tallahassee and they'll work on it all weekend so Vincent will be ready. He'll make himself out to be a martyr in some good cause. It will be the people who favor open immigration for Haitians or who oppose Medicare trying to do him in. They'll be behind this case.'

'Nobody is going to buy that,' I said, confidently. And then, after I'd thought for a second or two, I added, less confidently, 'Are they?'

Semmes smiled in a sort of abstracted way.

'A few people will buy anything. Anyway, I was exaggerating. But I suspect that Lander White will be trying something audacious.'

'Why?'

'In the first place, that is his style. It gets him into the newspapers and he likes being there. In the second place, he wants to seize the initiative. That's also his style. He lost the initiative today and it is eating at him like worms. So he'll work all weekend, coaching the senator for the press conference. He'll want him to deliver.'

Semmes paused long enough to turn into the motel driveway and park in a far corner of the lot where he wouldn't be crowded and the paint job wouldn't be nicked by other cars' doors.

He killed the engine and took the keys from the ignition. Then paused before he opened the door to get out.

'White will want Vincent to be Mark Antony, come to bury Caesar not to praise him. Or Clarence Darrow pleading for the lives of Leopold and Loeb. Even Richard

275

Nixon defending his wife's cloth coat and the family dog. Something dramatic, to turn things around.'

'Wanting and getting aren't necessarily the same,' I said. 'He can coach his client all he wants but Vincent has to have something to say. Otherwise, he's just talking. And he doesn't have anything to say.'

Semmes was looking away, as though at something in the distance. But he couldn't have told you anything about the view.

'Or does he?' I said.

'Let's go inside and talk about that,' Semmes said.

We used my room to talk. I took two bottles of beer from my cooler and opened them. We sat in the cheap chairs, across from each other, at the cheap table.

'Morgan,' Semmes said, 'you know as much as anyone about the case. If you were brought in to advise Vincent and Lander White – and thank God you won't be – what would you tell them? What's your strategy?'

Semmes was slipping into his Socratic personality, the one where formal dialogue replaced conversation and he asked the questions and tried to make you think. He did it with clients, a lot. With me, occasionally.

'I don't know,' I said.

'Come on,' he said, mildly. 'I need your help here.'

I thought for a moment. 'Does my side have to tell the truth?'

'Of course not,' Semmes said. 'This is a criminal case. We aren't interested in truth. Strictly a favorable outcome.'

'Okay. Then I would try to make my client – Vincent – into a sympathetic figure.'

'How?'

'Well, I suppose I'd try to make it look like he wasn't just innocent. I'd try to make it look like someone was out to get him. Make *him* the victim; instead of the Hutchinson woman. That's what you do these days, right? You set fire to a hospital for kids and then blame the company that made the matches. They pandered to the latent pyromaniac in you ... for profit. They are the guilty swine.'

Semmes nodded. 'You make the woman the bad guy, so to speak?'

'Nah,' I said. 'Can't do that. She is the common people. Salt of the earth. You don't make villains out of secretaries and nurses.'

'All right,' he said. 'I'll buy that. But if Vincent is the victim, who is responsible for the injustice?'

'I don't know, Nat. I'm not good at hypotheticals.'

'Indulge me.'

I'd had enough of all of it. But since Semmes was asking ...

'All right. I'd make it look like a vendetta. And I'd go high. Big targets can't defend themselves in the media. When they try, it just makes them look guilty.'

'How high?'

I shrugged. 'All the way, I suppose. Say it was the governor, doing it for political reasons. And ... I might make you the governor's errand boy. Or say you had your own reasons. Make the whole thing into a common political pissing match. You and the governor and some shadowy old bulls in the background out to get the herd charging an up and coming young senator. Claim that the Hutchinson woman is being used; that she is as much a victim as Vincent.'

Semmes drank some beer and rocked back in his chair. He was calm. We could have been discussing the price of feeder cattle.

'You could do well in this line of work, Morgan,' he said. 'I'd bet tall money that you have just outlined Lander White's strategy. Exactly. All weekend long, and at that Monday press conference, he is going to be doing everything he can to get the topic of the conversation changed. Instead of "Did Vincent do it?" he wants people to be asking, "Why are *they* saying that Vincent did it?"

'The answer will be – "*It's a vendetta.*" Exactly like you say. But to make that plausible, there has to be a motive. What's behind the vendetta? Who has a grievance? The governor and Vincent aren't overly fond of each other. In their universe, power is a finite resource. If you have more, then I have less. Your misfortune is my good fortune. Nothing personal; just the nature of the business.

'So, the governor has his reasons. Which is why he appoints a special prosecutor. A gunslinger.'

I nodded.

'They will want to smear me. They smeared Lisa Hutchinson with the abortion story and the party girl stuff. They'll want to do the same thing to me.'

'How bad can they make it?'

'Well,' Semmes sighed. 'The last time somebody lived a blameless life, they nailed him to a tree.'

I nodded.

'I don't imagine most people would like to have everything they've ever done made public. Most rock stars would love it, I suppose. And politicians learn to live with it. But they are exhibitionists by nature. I'm a relic. I don't believe the great omnivorous television audience out there has any God-given right to chew on my life. Your non-criminal sins are your own business ... Or ought to be, anyway. God is all the witness we need. More.'

I looked at Semmes and waited. I must have looked stricken because he laughed.

'There's nothing I can't live with. And nothing that would shock you. At least I don't think so.'

I nodded.

'But that isn't the point.'

No, I thought, of course not. It was about the principle. About his pride.

'I was reluctant to take this job. But I don't have to tell you that. I sent you out, running around, looking for the evidence before I'd made up my mind to do what the governor was asking. I was stalling.'

'Why did you say yes?'

'It just didn't seem like I could say no.'

Duty, in other words.

'Do you want out?' I said. I could not imagine Semmes quitting.

He shook his head. Emphatically. 'I'm not quitting, Morgan. And I'm not sorry I took the job. But we are coming up on an ugly time. It will be hard on you, too.'

I nodded again. I wasn't exactly rattled by the prospect of seeing my name in the papers and my picture on television. I'd lived through that before. But I didn't have a wife and children like Semmes. And I knew how he'd feel about putting them through it.

'So what do we do next?' I said.

'Well,' Semmes sighed and put down his beer bottle, 'I'm

going to drive home and tell Bobbie and the kids to buckle their chin straps. I don't see any need to hang around here. What about you?'

'I'll be along. Tomorrow.'

Semmes looked at me with raised eyebrows. 'Are you still working?'

'Chicken feed,' I lied. 'But I've made appointments.' I was not about to tell him about the affidavits and what I had in mind for Lander White.

Most people would have asked for the details. But not Semmes.

'Well, let me know if you turn up anything useful. And I hope that Lander White doesn't cause you too much grief in the next few days.'

Not bloody likely, I thought.

'I'll talk to you next week,' I said.

'Good. And Morgan, listen ... we routed them this afternoon. You get the credit for that.'

'Thanks, Nat.'

'No. Thank you.'

Twenty-eight

After Semmes left for home, I drove to the Hilton bar. There was an urgent, almost erotic edge to the mood there. The case was getting interesting now that Semmes was on the attack and the reporters could smell blood.

I found my Australian sugar daddy, Ian Patterson, in his usual spot, right near the service bar.

'Bloody sensational,' he said. 'Nobody in hell's whole front yard would have guessed he'd ask for bail on a US senator. One million. Just bloody amazing.'

'He asked for two million,' I said.

'And had to settle for half a loaf, poor darling. Utter failure, I'd call that.'

Patterson signaled the bartender to bring us two bottles of beer. We clinked the bottles ceremoniously when they arrived.

'I don't expect we ought to spend too long together here,' Patterson said. 'People will talk.'

'Right,' I said, even though nobody was paying any attention at all to us.

'Give me a call later?'

'Maybe.'

'You and your Mr Semmes … You keep it up, hear. Makes for a great bloody show.'

We moved away from the bar, in opposite directions. I noticed a couple of the reporters looking at me and leaning across their table to say something. It gave me a clammy, vulnerable feeling to think they might be talking about me. I've always wondered how genuine celebrities could stand it.

I overheard someone at a nearby table say, 'I wonder if he'd do a standup for us.'

'Hey,' his companion said, 'you've heard the stories on that guy. You want it, then *you* ask him to do a fucking standup.'

So, the word on me was that I was some kind of badass. That was another aspect of genuine celebrity that I had pondered. How did they reconcile the impossible, lurid reputation with what they knew was the truth? Maybe that is what drives so many of them crazy.

I was still working on the beer and thinking about these things when someone tapped me on the shoulder.

'That was inspired – in a low, sleazy sort of way,' Barbara Hanley said. Her face was moist and her eyes glittered like shattered glass.

'Kind of you to say so.'

'The idea that Daniel Vincent would try to flee … You couldn't possibly sell that to a judge anywhere in the civilized world. That would only fly down here in Kuzuland.'

I nodded and said, 'I'm sure the judges are much wiser in Washington, the Athens of the modern world.'

'They are better anywhere than what you have here,' she said. 'Even in Washington. But *touché*.'

I nodded. She seemed to enjoy having me for an enemy. Which meant, I suppose, that she thought I was dumb and that she wouldn't have any trouble beating me at just about anything.

'I mean, you have to admit that judge is an idiot. I can't believe he graduated from law school ... Not even one of the local diploma mills around here.'

'He didn't.'

'I'm not surprised.'

'He graduated from the University of Virginia Law School,' I said. 'Not too long after Teddy Kennedy. So he's probably qualified to work in Washington.'

She glared at me, then said, 'You pulled off a nice ambush in there today. But you can't do that every day. And if you want to play hardball ... fine. Other people know how to play, too.'

'You're telling me I should bring my lunch?'

'You can put it whatever quaint little country way you like, Bubba. But just remember ... You had a good day. But that's all it was. One day.'

'We'll play 'em one at a time,' I said. It was one of those old sports clichés that I had heard a thousand times and every time I heard it, I thought that it would be a lot more interesting to watch them play 'em two at a time. Or, maybe, three or four at a time. But they all seemed to stick to principle and play 'em one at a time. No imagination.

'Lander White doesn't like being humiliated,' she said and I wondered who did.

'Today,' she went on, 'he got mad. Tomorrow, he will start getting even. And it won't just be the grubby little

283

bimbo. He'll be getting even with everybody who humiliated him today.'

She gave me a look that was full of menace.

'Is that a message directly from Lander White?' I said. 'Can I expect to find a horse's head between the sheets when I wake up?'

'You take it like you want to,' she said. 'The dumb thing would be to ignore it. But I wouldn't put it past you.'

'Well, if you see Mr White,' I said, 'tell him that I got the message and he should be aware that two can play that game. I am way ahead of him. If he looks real hard, he might be able to see my dust.'

'What's *that* supposed to mean?'

'It means I can fight dirty, too.'

She looked at me again, differently this time. Less contempt and more curiosity. She was appraising me and I was getting smarter, in her eyes.

'You came up with all that "evidence" didn't you? The stuff that was supposed to prove Daniel was a flight risk.'

I shrugged. 'Seems like anyone would know enough to retrace the suspect's movements.'

'And check his calls? The ones on his cellular?'

I shrugged again.

'Lander White said that is what really turned Judge Hambone. The call to Miami.'

'Routine.'

'What is your incentive?'

I liked the word choice. *Incentive*. A very Washington word.

'What's yours?'

'I asked you first.'

'I work for Semmes,' I said. 'And I like action.'

She must have called Lander White from the Hilton a minute or two after we finished talking, because there was a message from him when I got back to the motel, thinking about a swim in the tepid little pool.

I called the number and I got someone who wasn't White. But he came on quickly once he knew I was calling.

'You and I,' he said, 'need to talk.'

'Do we?' I said.

'Yes,' he said. 'I think we do.' He had a way of giving every word extra weight. There was something theatrical about it; but he made it work.

'All right,' I said.

'I'm staying up near the Georgia line,' he said. 'At the Ewell place.'

He started to give me directions but I interrupted and said, 'I know how to find it.'

'Oh?'

'It's the scene of the crime,' I said.

'The *alleged* crime,' he said.

'One hour?'

'That would be fine.'

I drove up north, on 19, in the rich yellow light of late afternoon. The pasture land was a dark, lush green and the woods were shot through with bursting white dogwood blossoms. White egrets flew overhead in watery formation. I wanted badly to be out in the woods. On a little river somewhere, in a canoe, drifting through a wood dappled with dogwood and alive with the songs of mating birds.

I was, however, behind the wheel of my truck on my way to talk to a lawyer. It was a lick on me.

I drove into the Ewell place and parked in front of the replicated plantation house, right behind a Range Rover, which is the show-off sport utility among people with money and not much more. It is powered by one of the worst engines ever built, an aluminum block Oldsmobile reject. And the transmission is about as tight as the federal budget. But the car looks good at a dog show or a horse jump.

A black man in livery answered the door when I knocked. Ewell went all out. I wondered if he had a string of slaves out back, chopping cotton.

'My name is Hunt,' I said. 'Mr White is expecting me.'

'Yes sir. Can you wait here just a minute, please.'

The man came back and lead me down a dark wainscotted hallway to a little room that was probably called the 'study'. I expect it was mainly used for drinking. There was a mahogany writing table at one end of the room with floor to ceiling bookshelves on the flanking walls. Brass lamps and a fireplace. Leather sofas and reading chairs. Very traditional, right down to the little butler's table with the cut glass decanters and drinking glasses.

'Come in,' Lander White said. 'Something to drink?'

'No,' I said. 'I don't think so.'

He nodded and waved a hand in the direction of one of the leather chairs. He was wearing khaki pants and a pale green shirt with epaulettes and lots of pockets. The sleeves were rolled up past the elbow, showing his tanned and well muscled arms. He was dressed to relax but he looked even more alert than he did in court. His eyes were deeply, intensely focused; like the eyes of a stalking cat.

'You had a good day,' he said, using a tone that said he could afford to be tolerant.

'Wasn't me,' I said.

'You came up with all that bullshit Semmes used as evidence of "flight risk".'

'It was just lying around, waiting to be picked up,' I said. 'Could have been anyone.'

'A modest man,' he said.

'Yeah, well I come by that honestly too.'

He smiled.

We looked at each other across the room. He pressed his lips together, brushed an unseen speck of dust from his shirt and said, 'I spoke to Barbara Hanley.'

I nodded.

'And she described your conversation.'

I waited.

'If you are going to make my client into a "flight risk", then you have to expect I'll fight back. I owe it to my client.'

'Sure. You owed it to him to tell the papers that the woman he raped had an abortion. It was the only honorable thing.'

He gave me a reptilian smile.

'Lawyers defend clients. The best defense is usually a good offense.'

I knew that.

'You knew my client wasn't a flight risk. You were just picking up a few yards on offense. A couple of first downs, really, but no points. Not even a field goal.'

'So why does it bother you?'

'Who said it does?'

'You wanted to talk.'

'Barbara said you were making some threats. I thought maybe we should talk before you did anything unwise.'

'I try to do at least one unwise thing every day.'

'What is your interest in this?'

'I work for Semmes.'

'And what is his interest?'

'You wouldn't understand it,' I said. 'Not in a million years.'

'I think it is a legitimate question for public discussion,' he said sounding sonorous enough to be arguing in front of some fool judge. 'What motivates a prominent private attorney and his investigator – a convicted murderer and former convict – to persecute a respected United States senator at the request of his political rival? I think the public has a compelling interest in the answer to that question. We can't just turn over the engines of justice to private, unknown parties, can we?'

'You threatening to *expose* me, slick?'

He frowned. 'I'm saying there are obvious questions.'

'Me and Semmes?'

'Where there are questions,' he said, 'I intend to ask them.'

'That's mighty fine,' I said. 'Going the extra mile, like that, to do your duty for your client. You set a fine example.'

He laughed.

'I guess I'll just have to do the same thing ... Look into your background, I mean.'

His face went tight.

'Which I already have, by the way. And talk about interesting questions, try this one. What makes a man who gang-raped a young girl and left her for dead, way back when he was in law school . . . What makes him take the job of defending a US senator who is charged with a rape and who that same lawyer knows, in his bones, is guilty as homemade sin?'

He stared at me. His eyes were glassy and stunned.

'Good question, huh? Papers ought to have a real good time with that one.'

'There is no court record,' he said, in a quiet, abstracted voice.

'No. You managed to duck it because you'd almost finished law school and were about to take the bar. Seems to me that's all the more reason to hang you by your nuts, but I'm dumb about these things.

'Anyway, I got statements. One from one of your accomplices. A sweetheart of a man. Kind who brings credit to the bar.'

'Wynn?' he said softly.

'Yes.'

'He's a liar.'

'Probably. But his credibility isn't for me to decide. We'll let the public work it out; same way we let the public decide if having an abortion and liking men means you can't be trusted when you say you've been raped.'

'Wynn is in prison.'

'That does diminish his credibility,' I said. 'But I also talked to your victim. She'll be great on *Oprah*.'

He looked at me with his mouth open.

'Like you say, "Sometimes the best defense is a good offense." You'd been taking it to us, in the media. All that old stuff. And, by the way, I got some stuff on the senator, too. You might want to tell him about it. A good lawyer would be able to convince a judge not to allow it as evidence. But reporters have different rules.'

'What kind of *stuff*?' he said, bleakly.

'Other women. In Washington. You could have found them. Sent Longacre up there. If you'd wanted to know.'

'It isn't my job to investigate the allegations. I'm supposed to provide the best...'

'Spare me,' I interrupted.

We sat there, looking at each other, for a few long seconds; him with that bewildered, injured expression you see on someone who has been in a bad wreck that isn't his fault. Lander White couldn't believe this was happening to him. It was monumentally unfair.

'So what are you going to do?'

'Depends.'

'On what?'

'What you do.'

'What do you mean?'

'Play the same kind of offense you've been playing and I'm going to roll you up in a ball and kick your dead ass through the uprights.'

He rallied a little before I left and made some kind of big promise not to be intimidated or blackmailed. I told him that he could still quit the case and he said he wouldn't think of it. But I could see that was just about the only thing he *was* thinking about. All he needed was a story he could sell.

I figured that he would come up with something and that I could hear it at the Monday morning news conference. Between now and then, I wasn't going to think about any of it, anymore.

Twenty-nine

The sun was down when I stepped back outside. The air
had turned cool and was filled with the sounds of frogs
and peepers. Bullbats swooped overhead, feeding on
insects. It was a sweet, melancholy time of day and I
would have enjoyed staying. But I was on Ewell's land
and I didn't feel welcome to walk around and enjoy
myself.

So I climbed behind the wheel of the truck and started
down the long drive back to the highway. I drove slowly,
with the high beams on, since it was the time of day when
the deer were feeding and moving around. I'd made it
about halfway to the black top when I saw another truck
blocking the road. Two men leaned against the truck,
waiting. I didn't see any guns in their hands, but I was sure
they had some close by, probably in the gun rack, where
they could get to them in a hurry.

They could have been a couple of old boys who had
Ewell's permission to run coon dogs on his land, but I didn't
think so. I might have tried to go around them, slammed it
through the ditch and over the pine saplings that were
planted along the side of the road, but I wasn't sure we were
there yet. I didn't have a gun. I stepped on the brake and

opened the door. I felt myself going tense, like slowly twisted rope.

Both men straightened up and took a couple of steps my way. They were both big. Both wore jeans and cowboy hats. They were smirking the way you do when you have the upper hand.

'Mr Ewell told us he had trespassers,' one of them said. He was the shorter one. He had his hands on his hips and his eyes were narrowed down to slits the width of nickels. 'Poacher, roosting turkeys, most likely.'

'Wrong man,' I said. 'I'm coming from the Ewell house.'

'Nope,' the man said, 'I don't think so. We just talked to the man and he didn't say anything about anybody coming from the house.'

'Call him,' I said. 'I've got a phone in the truck.'

'We got our own phone,' the second man said. 'We don't need your fucking phone.'

That way, then.

'What are you boys supposed to do?' I said.

'We're supposed to stop people from trespassing and poaching,' the first one said, closing the distance by another step or two, until we were less than six feet apart. 'That's what Mr Ewell told us to do.'

'You going to hold me here, then,' I said, 'while you call the sheriff? Or the game warden?'

'Sheeeeit,' the second man said. He was the dumb one.

'Mr Ewell didn't say anything about calling the sheriff,' the first one said.

'Maybe he didn't,' I said. 'But the law says that's what you have to do.'

'The law, my ass,' the first one said. He wasn't that much smarter than his partner.

'And,' I said, 'if you do anything stupid you will be interfering with an officer of the court in the lawful pursuit of his duties.' I didn't know if that was true or not but it sounded good. 'That would be one felony charge. Obstruction of justice would be another. That's some serious stuff.'

'It's a bunch of shit, is what it is,' the second man said. He was very close now. Not more than three feet away. In so close that I wanted to do one of two things – back up or strike out.

The other man was moving. Trying to get to my side or behind me. I started to move my head that way, as though I was trying to follow him. That's when the big one took another step toward me and brought up his hands.

But I'd only turned my head slightly, enough to fake him, and I'd never taken my eyes off him. I stepped into him and drove the extended fingers of my right hand straight into his exposed neck. I quickly pulled the hand back, spread the fingers, and drove them into his eyes. Then I used both hands to grab him by both ears and pull his head forward. I raised my leg quickly and the point of my knee caught him right on the nose. I could hear him scream through a wild, roaring sound in my own ears. I don't know, maybe I was doing the screaming. They teach you to scream when you make those moves.

I was turning to take his friend, anticipating, but I was too slow. He had rushed in and caught me on the ear with his fist. It stunned me and I went down, with my legs going watery and my equilibrium gone. Things seemed to be rolling and in the dark, with lights going off in the back of my skull,

I wasn't sure how to get back on my feet. He drove the point of a cowboy boot into my ribs.

I rolled again. I could feel him coming after me. The roaring grew louder in my ears and the lights inside my skull seemed to go dim and then die. I could feel him crowding in on me. Feel the toe of his boot as it landed on my back, then my chest, and then my thigh. There was a sort of heavy, solid sound every time the boot made contact and I could hear it through the roaring in my ears. I could hear it and feel it when he kicked me but it didn't hurt. That's what saves you.

He was going wild kicking me. Like a horse stomping a snake. I covered up and rolled and took the kicks and tried to keep him from landing one on my head and setting off the lights inside my skull. I had my eyes opened and when he drew back to land another kick and I was close enough, I reached out and snatched his other leg just above the ankle. He came down like a sack of mud.

I grabbed the first thing that came close. It was his arm, which I twisted around behind him and then jerked down hard, so it popped out of the shoulder socket with a sound that was like the top coming out of a bottle and something ripping besides. The next sound was him screaming. I put my hand behind his head and pushed his face into the dirt. That muffled his screaming. I could still hear the roaring in my ears and his partner gagging for air and trying to gulp some down through his broken throat.

I stood up. The roaring in my ears dimmed some and then went quiet. They were still making their sounds but that didn't bother me. I'd heard people I cared about make a lot worse. I left them lying there and went over to their truck. I took the guns – a pump shotgun and a bolt-action rifle – out of the rack, unloaded them, and threw them off into the brush on the side of the road. My side felt like someone had stuck a spike into it when I threw those guns. Probably a broken rib. I went back over to their truck, got in and started it. Put it in gear and drove it into the ditch.

I went back and stood between the two men, who were still on the ground and still making their pitiful noises.

'I'm going to get in my truck and drive on up to the black top, boys. If you lie there in my way, I'll run over your sorry asses. So you'd better crawl on over in the ditch. You can moan and suffer and carry on there. You won't be bothering anybody.'

I got in my truck and left them on the side of the road. Before I got to the highway, I stopped long enough to take out the phone and call Ewell's number. He answered himself. Probably expecting a report from the two I'd left behind.

I told him who I was.

'What do you want?' he said. Impatient and imperious. He was the kind of man who, you'd have to hand it to him before he'd know he'd just lost his ass.

'I saw a truck in the ditch on my way out,' I said. 'I expect you might be having a problem with poachers. Better call the sheriff.'

'Now you listen...'

'No. Nothing you say is worth listening to,' I said. 'And if you send anyone else, it will be worse.'

My side was sore and my ear was full of blood and throbbing. But it wasn't bad. My hands were trembling, slightly, but that wasn't bad either. I always shook for a while after I'd gone off like that. Sometimes it lasted for a couple of hours.

I tried to make myself think clearly. If I could get my thoughts organized with a kind of cold clarity, I figured, then that would go a long way to settling me down.

I started by asking myself why Ewell would send those two out to knock me around. What did he expect to get from it?

I turned it over and around and looked at it from every angle and I still couldn't come up with a good answer. It was too late to chase me off; I'd already done the worst damage I was going to do. I couldn't undiscover the evidence. I'd already reported everything I knew to Semmes and he wasn't going to sit on it just because his investigator got his ass whipped on a dark country road.

If it were Lander White trying to scare me out of spreading his story around ... that would have made sense. But there hadn't been time for that.

Or ... maybe there had.

But White had other things on his mind. He wanted me to talk money to Lisa Hutchinson. They wanted to buy her off the case, and breaking my bones wouldn't do that cause any good.

I thought about it all the way back to the interstate and still couldn't come up with any good answers. The best I could manage was this – I'd made Ewell mad and he wanted to hurt me. Since he couldn't do it himself, he got some redneck muscle to do the job.

But that seemed just too low rent and dumb for somebody who lived in a big house like Ewell's. Still, people who lived in bigger, grander houses – even castles and the White House itself – have done dumber things. That may be the greatest mystery of them all. And I sure wasn't going to come up with a solution to it.

So I switched my mind to other things. I stopped at a drug store for some iodine and tape. I picked up a six-pack of cold beer. And I kept a close eye on the Friday evening traffic. I didn't need a collision with some well-oiled college kid. I'd been beat up enough for one night.

I turned off the interstate and headed up the long ramp to the motel. Before I reached the entrance to the parking lot a car that was parked on the shoulder, facing me, flashed its lights twice. The car was a dark Taurus and unfamiliar to me. It could have been a rental carrying some high-priced hitman from out of town. Could have been ... but it didn't seem likely.

Just the same, I didn't know who was behind the wheel of that Taurus, waiting for me, when I pulled off the road and killed my engine. I was hoping, when I opened the door, that I wasn't walking into another brawl. I'd had plenty of that for one night. If I wasn't going to carry a gun around in the truck with me, I thought, then how about a baseball bat. Or a mean-assed dog who loved only me. That would give me someone to talk to, anyway.

I took a couple of steps toward the Taurus, then stopped and waited. In a strange situation, your mind will settle on the worst possibilities. I imagined somebody sitting in that Taurus, holding a shotgun and waiting for me to get closer. At the right moment, the driver would hit the high beams and the shooter would come out of the door on the passenger side shooting buckshot as fast the gun would fire.

My mind did one of those improbable gyrations – it will

go where it wants to go – and I imagined that the killer was holding a cheap Mossberg, like the kind the Menendez brothers out in California had used to grease their parents. They'd bought cheap shotguns as a way of speeding up the inheritance process. Once they got their hands on the money, they spent it on Rolex watches. Me, I'd rather have a cheap watch and a quality shotgun. But, then, I don't live in LA and wouldn't, even if you gave me the place.

My mind was off in that absurd little blind alley and sweat was running down the gully of my spine, and all the old instincts were telling me to go for the ground and get into the weeds for cover, when the driver of the Taurus turned on his inside lights long enough for me to see who he was.

Frank Swearingen.

'Get back in your truck and follow me out of here,' he said. 'We'll talk when we get down the road.'

Thirty

Swearingen led me back across the interstate and down a little side road, through a couple of traffic lights to a parking lot behind a rundown convenience store.

'I could use some coffee,' he said. 'How about you?'

I was still behind the wheel of the truck. He was standing next to it, talking to me through the window.

'What's going on?' I said.

'Let me get the coffee, first. We'll talk here. What do you want?'

'Bring me a beer. Whatever is cold.' The six-pack I bought was warm by now.

He was gone about five minutes.

'Tall Bud,' he said, handing me a small brown bag wrapped tightly around a cylinder. 'I used to drink one for a wake-up first thing every morning.'

He went around to the passenger side and let himself in. He made a production out of getting his coffee out of another brown paper bag and getting the lid off the paper cup. I watched while he took a sip.

'Hope I didn't scare you,' he said. 'You know, flagging you down like that, and all.'

'No,' I said. 'But I am wondering what this is all

about. Eaten up by curiosity, I am.'

'Yeah. Well, I could see how you would be.' He took another sip of his coffee. And they say Southerners are slow to get to the point. Well, I wasn't going to let on that I was eager, so I opened my beer and took a sip. Tasted good after a long day.

'You get that ear fighting with Ewell's guys?'

I looked at him. 'Now how did you know about that?'

He shrugged. 'I don't have some heavy title and I don't swing big, anymore, but I am wired. I know a lot of people and most of them talk to me. Guy in the sheriff's department called me. Said Ewell was raising hell about you. Said you'd been trespassing on his property and beating up on his help. He wants your ass arrested.'

'Like that?' I said.

'Yeah. And you know what?'

'What?'

'That fucking ear looks like shit. If it feels as bad as it looks, you're going to need stronger medicine than Budweiser.'

'I got some stuff at the drugstore. I was going to clean it up when I got back to the room.'

'Not a good idea,' he said. 'The room, I mean ... not cleaning up the ear. You ought to do that. I mean, that fucking thing looks ugly. But they'll have a cruiser watching your room. That's why I stopped you where I did. If you go back there, they'll pick you up and you'll spend the weekend in jail.'

'That bad?' I said.

'Well, the sheriff and his boys will try to keep Ewell

happy. On account of what a big stick he swings. Usual shit. It's Friday night and they could lose you for the weekend. It's a dog shit jail and worse on the weekend. You might as well wait until Monday morning. Go in there and shake your lawyer at them.'

'I appreciate the warning,' I said.

He shrugged again. 'I figured you'd have better things to do with your weekend.'

I was supposed to be at Jessie's house in the morning – well, at lunchtime – and that beat the Leon County Jail.

'How hard will they be looking for me?' I said.

'It's Friday night,' he said. 'And what you are is a case of trespassing and brawling. They'll have told the desk clerk at the motel to give them a call if he sees you and they'll send a cruiser around to check your room every so often. They'll have a BOLO for your truck and license but you know how that is. All you fucking hillbillies drive pickup trucks and there aren't that many cruisers on duty. They aren't going to set up roadblocks.'

He finished his coffee. I finished my beer. He offered to let me stay at his place. I thanked him, politely, and said I thought I'd just try and get on out of town using back roads.

He said he could understand my thinking and offered to call me if anything came up that I ought to know about. I gave him the number for the cellular – I didn't want to be giving out Jessie's number – and we left it at that. He got back in his car and went one way out of the lot. I went the other.

I eased out of town, south to 98, the old east/west road

303

across the Panhandle coast. I drove carefully, holding it right around the posted limit, even though there was hardly any traffic and everybody on the road passed me like I was standing still.

My ear was hot and throbbing. When I touched it, I could feel the swelling and the dried blood. My ribs were tender and when I moved in the seat felt a little surge of pain. I drove with the window down and the cool air felt good across my face.

It was after midnight – even with the time change – when I reached the river house. I parked in a shed down the road then walked to the house and went inside. I usually left one light on when I was away. I didn't turn any others on until I got to the bathroom, where I stripped and took a hot shower, carefully cleaning the ear. It was cut and swollen but I figured it would heal. And, even if it didn't and wound up looking like a cauliflower – like the ears you see on old fighters – *sin loy* and no big deal. I wasn't lined up for any movie parts. I didn't really care that much how my ear looked as long as I could hear out of it.

I stepped out of the shower and felt like I'd been resurrected from the dead. I dried off kind of tentatively, what with the ear and the ribs. I poured iodine all over the ear and cut strips of tape which I wrapped around my trunk as tight as I could. It was a jury-rigged job, doing it myself. I'd get Jessie to retape the ribs in the morning.

I poured a large, medicinal portion of bourbon in a glass and lay down on the bed and drank it in the dark.

I woke up thirsty and sore at dawn. After coffee and breakfast, I walked down to the slough where I keep a canoe. I rolled it over and loaded my pack and my fly rod and eased out in the oily black water. The slough spilled into the river and as the sun came climbing over the tree line I was paddling slowly downstream toward Jessie's house. I could get there in an hour, paddling hard, but I would be taking my time, watching the birds and probably casting to a few fish. I'd been looking forward to a morning like this for the last couple of weeks.

I made a few strokes with the paddle, mostly to test the soreness in my ribs, and watched the mist as it burned slowly off the surface of the river. A couple of wood ducks jumped out of a back eddy, their wings making a furious drumming sound on the still air. A roosting turkey gobbled urgently from a pine tree, a hundred yards inshore. A small alligator slipped away from the bank and swam downstream, leaving a perfect V-shaped wake on the smooth surface of the river.

The morning was hypnotic and I was almost under its spell when the telephone rang. I'd brought the cellular along, in my pack. It sounded obscene.

I fiddled with zippers and it kept ringing. I got it to my good ear on the fourth ring.

'Hello,' I said.

'I thought you'd want to know,' Swearingen said, 'that they found Senator Daniel Vincent dead this morning. He was in bed, in his hotel room.'

'How?'

'Shot with a nine millimeter. Four times. One right through the pump. That rules out suicide.'

A little mordant cop humor.

'He was probably sleeping when he got it. There were burns. Nobody heard the shots. Maid found him. He was in one of those motels where they give you a suite, and he was way around the back. Good quarter of a mile from the front office, which was the only place where anyone was awake.'

'They know who did it?'

'No arrests,' Swearingen said. 'But several suspects. And, listen…'

His voice trailed off and there was a silence long enough for me to imagine how I must have looked, sitting in a canoe on a still, silent, early morning river with a phone stuck to my ear.

'Yeah,' I said.

'You're one of the suspects.'

'Afraid I didn't do it,' I said.

'I didn't think so,' Swearingen said. 'You wouldn't need four shots, for one thing. But they've got somebody who says you told her you'd like to do it. And you did kill somebody once, in a similar sort of case.'

Not that similar, I thought. And it involved my sister. I didn't have a dog in this fight. Just the same…

'I don't suppose you can account for your time, last night, can you? Witnesses who'll say you were in plain sight, all night long.'

'No.'

There was another long silence.

'They've got to be able to come up with a better suspect than me,' I said, sounding defensive, whiny, and scared. Even to myself.

'Most of what they've got, right now, is pretty thin. So a threatening remark from you looks pretty strong.'

'What about Hutchinson's brother?' I said. 'I had to talk him out of killing the senator a couple of weeks ago.'

'He's on their lists. But he's got an alibi that looks pretty good. A girlfriend who says he spent the night.'

I didn't say anything. I was thinking. Nothing was going to happen in a phone conversation between me, paddling the Perdido River, and Swearingen, sitting somewhere in Tallahassee. I needed to think and I needed to come up with a plan. Even if it was a plan for getting out of the country.

'The theory, according to the guy I talked to at the Sheriff's Department,' Swearingen said, 'is that you were kind of a lone-wolf operator on this thing. Semmes sent you over to ask a few questions and you made it into a crusade. Turned it into an obsession. Maybe Lisa Hutchinson reminded you of your sister and you went off the same way. I'm just repeating what they said to me, you understand.'

'I understand,' I said. I looked around at the flat, black river and the lush green woods along its bank. It all looked unreal.

'You went out to see Lander White at Ewell's place last night. You tried to extort money, you made threats, you beat up on two guys who worked for Ewell. You were out of control. A little later, you went all the way around the bend and snuck into Vincent's room and greased him.'

'They have any other scenarios they're working on?'

'Not really. They seem to like that one until something blows a hole in it. You want my advice?'

'Sure.'

'Call that lawyer, Semmes, and do whatever he tells you to do. And whatever you do, don't panic.'

Easy for him to say.

307

* * *

I paddled downstream. Not in a hurry – a few minutes, one way or the other, wouldn't make any difference – but no longer aware of the river's sounds, sights, or smells, either. Ordinarily I would have been totally under the river's spell – that was my reason for being there – but the situation wasn't exactly ordinary.

Think, I told myself. Think clearly, starting with the fundamentals.

All right. First things, then. I wasn't going to go back to jail.

Dead or alive? I didn't know. But I would run, for sure, before I would let myself be locked up again. I would change my name. Get what I had – and it was enough – into an offshore account. Get out of the country. I wasn't doing any more time; not even in the local pound, waiting for trial. Not for something I hadn't done.

Can you beat it? Sure, no sweat. Just find out who really did it. Get the heat off myself by turning it up under somebody else.

Who? We'll have to work on that. No shortage of suspects. Earl Hutchinson. Lisa Hutchinson. They both had their reasons. And maybe Vincent gave Barbara Hanley a reason. Maybe she saw the animal underneath or maybe she caught him while he was practicing his hobby.

Lander White? Maybe. Vincent dead meant no trial. He could keep his secret.

Tim Fulton could have figured that the Senator was the source of all his woes and decided to get even.

And, then, it could have been somebody I'd never heard

of. A woman, for instance, who'd gotten the same treatment that Vincent gave Lisa Hutchinson and the others and had decided that if she wanted justice, the law was just too slow and too unreliable.

What about Swearingen's advice? Do you talk to Semmes? He was Semmes and he would say – 'Turn yourself in. We'll handle it the right way, in court.'

Easy for him to say.

For a few minutes, I enjoyed a little self-pity. I was here in the first place because of Semmes, who had sent me out blind. Put me out there breaking trail so he could take the case with a clean conscience.

Pointless thinking, even if it was true.

And it wasn't.

So what do you do? What's your next move?

I worked on that while I paddled. By the time I'd reached Jessie's house and beached the canoe, I had a plan.

Thirty-one

I left a note for Jessie, telling her something had come up and that she shouldn't believe everything she heard on the radio. I also told her I was borrowing the Chevrolet Suburban she kept parked in the garage and used every now and then to haul things for her gardens. I'd helped her buy the car as junk and had dropped a new engine in it for her.

It might have felt okay taking the Suburban but it seemed a little strange to be standing in Jessie's house. It wasn't just that she wasn't there – I had a key so I could let myself in, and I'd done it before, when she was out of town, to water plants and check on things. But this time, the cops were looking for me because they thought I'd killed someone. And not just anyone, at that. A US senator.

I didn't feel any differently about myself. But I wondered what sort of difference it would make to Jessie. I didn't stay long and I was relieved to get away from her house and back on to the highway.

I stopped at a convenience store when I was a few miles down the road and used the pay phone to call Randolph

Atkins. I didn't want to use the cellular. If things went bad, there would be a record of my calls and I didn't want them going after him with a harboring charge. Atkins might be a computer renegade and outlaw, but that was cyberspace, and right now we were dealing with the old-fashioned, sweat and blood world.

It was still fairly early but Atkins was up.

'Morgan,' he said, 'have you seen the news?'

'No,' I said. 'But I've heard.'

'Who do you think did it?' he said.

'I can tell you who the cops think did it,' I said.

When I told him, there was a long silence from his end. Finally, he said, 'I know you didn't do it, Morgan. You probably wanted to and, under the right circumstances, I'm sure you'd have gone ahead and done it. But I can't see you shooting him while he was in bed. And not *four times*. You might be guilty of lots of things, but bad marksmanship isn't one of them.'

'Thanks,' I said. 'But I'm afraid the cops are going to want a better alibi than that.'

'Do you have one?'

'I was at home, in bed. I don't have any witnesses so you'll have to take my word for it.'

Or not, I thought.

'Well ... *sure*. But what are you going to do? Where are you?'

'I'm right here,' I said. 'And I'm going to ask you to do some work for me. You don't have to and I'll surely understand if you say "no".'

There was a pause. Long enough to tell me he was scared.

'Whatever you want, Morgan.'

I told him what I wanted. And thanked him.

'Hey,' he said, 'I can keep a secret, if you can.'

'Talk to you later.'

He gave me another number to call. And a time.

'Just in case.'

'Absolutely,' I said and hung up.

I drove the speed limit and listened to the radio. The murder of a US senator was big news. Lots of breathless special reports with nothing much to say except that the man was dead. Shot four times. If it had been a .44, somebody might have made a blues tune out of it. But there is no poetry in a nine millimeter.

For the first hour, my name did not come up. The police were 'looking for a suspect', the announcers said in that urgent tone they all use.

'But so far, that's all they'll say. They are looking for a suspect and expect to make an arrest soon. We'll update you as soon as we have something. Now, back to the studio.'

I turned off the radio and imagined the scene in Tallahassee. It had been bad enough before, when the news was a bail hearing for Vincent. Now that he had been murdered, the frenzy would be on. The reporters and photographers would be climbing each other's backs, their eyes bulging and the chords in their necks straining as they tried to get a microphone or a camera into someone's face. A 'no comment' would be news. The bidding for an interview with the maid who'd found the body would be frenzied. Reporters would be flying in from everywhere, willing to sell their mothers to be first on the air with the name of that suspect – my name.

I felt like the prize in a treasure hunt; or the coon in a coon hunt. If I'd needed an excuse to leave the country, the carnival was more than enough. Why stay around for that? In the old days, there might have been some honor in standing up and protesting your innocence; all the way to the gallows, if it came to that. But not for this. Not to pump somebody's TV ratings.

I was in Tallahassee in the early afternoon, wearing a John Deere gimmie hat and a pair of fisherman's sunglasses. It wasn't much of a disguise, but it was the best I could do. Still, I felt naked.

I had my own list of suspects I wanted to talk to, and there was no other way. Anyway, if they were looking for me, they would probably be looking in other places. Not at the little house where Lisa Hutchinson was staying.

I drove by the house twice. Her car was parked out front, by itself. I didn't see anything that looked like an unmarked cruiser or a surveillance van anywhere in the neighborhood. I called her number on the cellular. She answered and I broke the connection.

I parked up the street from her house, thinking that Jessie would have made it home by now and read my note. If the law got in touch with her, she would have to tell them about the Suburban. But they didn't have any reason to think that I'd left the Tallahassee area and been to her house. I still had clothes and things in the chain motel room and I'd never checked out. Nobody had seen me drive home. There was no sign I'd stayed at the river house. If a cop went by to look for me, he wouldn't even find my truck, since I'd parked it in the shed up the road. The last reported sighting of me was at Ewell's place, by the two men I'd left in the ditch.

The Suburban was probably okay for another few hours.

I knocked on Lisa Hutchinson's door and waited. I felt vulnerable standing there, in broad daylight, and almost expected a fleet of cruisers to come at me from both ends of the street. Sirens, flashing lights, drawn guns. The whole show.

But nothing happened for ten or fifteen seconds. Then the door opened and Lisa Hutchinson said, 'God, what happened to your ear? It looks terrible.'

She didn't know.

'May I come in?' I said.

'Sure.'

She'd heard about Vincent that morning, she said, fairly early. She was still sleeping when Dixie Price called to tell her about it.

'I was surprised, I guess,' she said, 'but I wasn't sorry. He deserved it.' We were sitting in her living room. It was cluttered and hadn't been vacuumed or dusted recently. There was a pizza box on the coffee table, along with several empty beer bottles.

'Did you talk to the police?' I said.

'Yes. They thought I might have done it.'

'What did you tell them?'

'I told them I might have thought about it. But if I was going to do it, I would have done it before now. Before his lawyers started saying all those things about me. Or I would have done it later, after the trial ... if he got off. But now ain't the time.'

'What did they say?'

'They wanted to know if I had an alibi.'

'Did you?'

She looked at me. Her eyes had the hard, suspicious country glare.

'Do *you* think I did it?'

I shook my head.

'Okay,' she said. 'I'm glad you don't. And I'll tell you something else, Earl didn't kill him either. The cops asked him. At first, they thought he'd done it.'

'Right now they think I did it,' I said.

'*You*? That's crazy. Why would you do it? He wasn't nothing to you.'

'Maybe not. But I'm a suspect.'

The look in her eyes changed; softened to something like compassion. Or pity.

'Did you have an alibi?' I said. 'When you talked to the cops.'

'Yeah, actually. It was Friday night and I was lonesome. I called a couple of my girlfriends and they came over. We drank beer and watched movies till real late. They didn't want to drive – one of them's already got a DUI – so they stayed over. I'd have had to sneak out and I guess we were all still up, watching videos when they think he was shot.'

She nodded in the direction of the empty pizza box and beer bottles, as though they were her alibi. The physical proof that she had not killed the senator.

'What about you?'

'What about me?'

'Do you have an alibi?'

I shook my head. 'I was a long ways from here. But I don't have any witnesses.'

'What are you going to do?'

'I'm going to ask you to do a favor for me.'

She never hesitated.

'Sure,' she said. 'You done enough for me. Just name it.'

Thirty-two

Lisa Hutchinson listened while I told her what I wanted her to do.

'That's all?' she said, when I'd finished.

'It's a lot.'

'Nothing to it,' she said. 'Why don't you give me a hard one?'

I liked her attitude.

She left to do what I'd asked her to do and while she was gone, I cleared away the empty pizza boxes with the old, uneaten crusts and also the beer bottles, which I rinsed out in the sink. Then I watched the television for a little while. CNN had a report about Vincent's murder, with a line – almost an afterthought – about how the police had a suspect but did not yet have him in custody. The name, according to the reporter, had not been released.

That name would be mine.

I watched the street from the window and had the inevitable moment when I decided that Lisa Hutchinson had not gone out to do what I'd asked her to do but had gone straight to the cops.

You can't help yourself. You feel alone.

I expected to see a whole fleet of police cruisers appear on the street in front of Lisa Hutchinson's house and, then, I realized that she had been gone for an hour and if she wanted to do that, then she would have gone to the cops first thing and they would have been here a long time ago.

Settle down, I told myself. Which was easier said than done.

I sat on the couch and tried to read a magazine. *Cosmopolitan*. It could have been the Chinese edition.

Finally, after she had been gone nearly three hours, Lisa pulled up and parked in front of the house. I was on my feet when she came through the front door.

'It took me a while,' she said. 'She was out and nobody knew where to find her.'

'But you talked to her?'

She nodded. 'I talked to her. What a bitch. Treated me like I was nothing but sorry white trash.'

'She treats everyone that way,' I said. 'Don't worry about it.'

'I'm not worried. She's the one with problems.'

I left Lisa's house and went to the motel where she had rented a room. I didn't like being in her house but I couldn't rent a room myself. Couldn't be seen coming and going. She was taking a chance but it wasn't as bad as it might have been. They still hadn't put my name out as a suspect. But I was sure the motel operators had been told to be on the lookout for me. I tried to slip into the room like a weary, anonymous traveler looking for a little air conditioning, a television, and a few hours of dreamless sleep.

I used the phone to call the number Randolph Atkins had given me. He answered on the second ring. He'd been working and I wrote what he told me in my notebook. I made two more calls; then I waited some more.

A little after dark, Lisa called to say she was on her way.

Ten minutes later, I was outside. Watching. Lisa pulled into the lot, parked, and waited by her car. She was followed, a few minutes later, by a Taurus, probably a rental. Barbara Hanley stepped out of the Taurus and took a minute to study the motel, like a photographer evaluating a set. Then she said something I could not hear to Lisa, who did not bother to say anything back. Then the two of them walked across the lot to the bank of rooms and Lisa opened the door to the one where I had been waiting.

They went inside – Hanley first – and pulled the door behind them. I waited.

I'd give it ten minutes, I thought. If the cops hadn't come by then, they probably wouldn't be coming.

Barbara Hanley probably hadn't told. Why would she? Lisa Hutchinson had promised her a story – that would be me – and it didn't seem likely that she would risk it by telling the law where to find me. She wasn't the kind to give up a story – or even share one. There would have to be a better reason than merely apprehending a fugitive murderer – and that's what she believed I was. But I was also a story.

I checked my watch. Listened to the sounds of traffic on the interstate. Swatted bugs. Ten minutes can take its time about passing. It seemed like an hour. I wanted to get on with it.

Finally, I left my hiding place, walked across the parking lot to the room, and knocked.

Barbara Hanley gave me her withering look. She was sitting on one of the beds. Lisa had opened the door, then gone back to one of the chairs, next to the big window which was covered by a pleated brown curtain.

'I'm surprised you haven't been arrested yet,' Barbara Hanley said. 'But there doesn't seem to be any limit to incompetence down here, does there?'

'You come from Washington,' I said. 'You tell me about incompetence.'

She glared at me.

'Anyway, why should I be arrested?'

'Don't play dumb,' she said. 'That kind of bullshit doesn't work with me. You killed him.'

'I did?'

'Sure you did. And the police know you did. They are looking for you, right now. It might take them a while, but they'll find you. Even these heroes will find you.'

'All right,' I said. 'But since I've got a little time, let's talk.'

'Talk about *what*?'

'Let's talk about who really did it. And why.'

'Waste of time.'

'You know that old joke, don't you? The one with the punch line that goes, "What's time to a hog?"'

'No. And I don't want to. If you've got something to tell me, then tell me. Otherwise, I've got things to do.'

'You want a story, don't you? It seems like you always want a story.'

'Sure. I'd like a story. But it needs to check.'

'Well, what if I tell you everything I found out about Senator Daniel Vincent. All the evidence that I'd given to Semmes to use at Vincent's trial, to prove what kind of creep he was. All the evidence that proved he did what Miss Hutchinson here said he did. Some of that evidence would have been inadmissible at a trial. Some of the strongest stuff.'

'Why?'

'It proves he could have done what Miss Hutchinson said he did because he'd done it before. You can't use that in court, because the law is very fastidious about these things. But common sense tells you, if he'd done it before, then he'd do it again. The dogs that bite people are the dogs that have bitten people.'

'That's country wisdom, I imagine.' She looked distressed. But still tough.

'You're in the news business. I'll give you the names of my sources. You can check them out.'

'I will,' she said. Not very convincingly.

'I'll tell you some other things about Vincent...'

'I knew him, remember,' she said.

'I know. And you believed him when he told you he was innocent and Miss Hutchinson was lying. You might have changed your mind at a trial. Now, there won't be a trial, but you can still look at the evidence. Maybe it will still change your mind.'

'What if it does? That won't do you any good.'

'I know I didn't do it. Maybe, after you've looked at the evidence, you'll decide I didn't do it.'

She shook her head.

'Maybe you already know I didn't do it.'

323

'Why would I know that?' She sneered when she said it.

'Maybe you killed him.'

'*Me?*'

'Sure. Husbands, wives, and lovers are always the first suspects. They've got better reasons for killing than anyone else.'

She shook her head emphatically.

'You told the cops you thought I'd done it because I said I'd like to. Well, I could tell them I think you did it. My reason is the killer didn't have any trouble getting into Vincent's room while he was in bed. The door wasn't forced. So either he let the killer in or the killer had a key. I don't think Vincent would have let me in.'

'You might have had a key.'

'But you almost certainly had one. Right?'

'This is bullshit. Why would I kill him?' She was playing defense, now, but she played it the same way she played offense. Aggressive and very hard.

'Pick a reason. Like I say, lovers kill each other all the time. Maybe you caught him with another woman. Maybe he told you it was over.'

'I wouldn't have killed him over that. I cared about him but not that much. There are other men. You can always find another one.'

'Another senator?'

'Better,' she said defiantly.

You had to hand it to her.

'I'll take your word for it,' I said. 'So, maybe you found out Miss Hutchinson was telling the truth and you knew he'd be convicted. You'd be humiliated.'

I could easily believe she wouldn't kill for love, since love wasn't that important in her scheme. The flip side was – I could just as easily believe she would kill to keep from being humiliated.

She waved that away with her hand, like it was just a fly or some other kind of dirty nuisance.

'You're just speculating. It's all air. No hard facts.'

'How about the gun?'

Something went out of her face. It went limp and for a moment she actually looked vulnerable.

'I saw it, remember. In Washington. I know a little about guns and I know it was a nine millimeter – the fashionable round in the smart set. The thirty-eight and the forty-five are common rounds. Strictly peasant stuff. You told me that the gun was legal. Registered and everything. So I don't suppose it would be hard to prove that you own a gun that shoots the kind of round that killed Senator Daniel Vincent. Would it?'

She shook her head slowly.

'And it won't be any problem to see if bullets that come out of your pistol match up with the four that came out of the senator.'

She didn't say anything.

'So if I tell the law about your gun, you might have to give it to them. Are you ready for that?'

'I can't.'

'Because it is the same gun?'

'No. Because I don't know where it is,' she said helplessly, sounding like she was about to cry.

There was a long silence between us and we just stared at each other.

'Well, well,' Lisa Hutchinson broke in. 'I would of never thought it.'

Thirty-three

The gun had been stolen. From her room. She hadn't reported it.

'Why not?'

'I don't know. Probably because I was embarrassed. I mean, if you're going to have a gun...'

And the thought of going to the local police to report a stolen gun. After the things she had said about those same cops. There was too much humiliation in that; more than she could gag down.

'How long before the killing was it stolen?'

'The same day,' she said, miserably. 'But that doesn't mean...'

'No,' I said. 'Of course not.'

She glared at me. But not with the old conviction. Now it was the look of someone who is cornered.

'Look, dammit,' she said, 'I'm telling you the gun was *stolen*.'

I nodded.

'This is ridiculous. I certainly didn't kill Dan.'

The very idea.

'Neither did I,' I said.

'Well, then,' Lisa Hutchinson said. 'Just who do you suppose *did* kill him?'

* * *

I had an idea but I needed to work it. I couldn't just go to the cops. I told Barbara Hanley that I could keep the information about her gun to myself if she wouldn't go on television with a report naming me as a suspect.

'All right,' she said. She wasn't happy about it.

'What about me?' Lisa Hutchinson said.

She was looking at Barbara Hanley with a kind of cold malice in her eyes.

'You?' Hanley said, in just the wrong tone.

'Yes, goddamnit, *me*. You remember me. I'm the woman who was raped by your big deal boyfriend. And *you* made it sound like it was my fault. You used your television connections to make sure that those stories about me made it onto the air.'

'I thought...' Barbara Hanley said, using a patient, patronizing tone. But Lisa Hutchinson cut her off.

'What you thought is history. I've got to live with what your boyfriend did to me and what you did to me, after that. Now, I know something about you that the television people would love to have. And if it gets out, no matter what you say, some people will think that you killed him; that your story about how your gun was stolen is just bullshit.'

'You don't know...'

'I know more than you knew.'

They sat there, glaring at each other across about four feet of space. I felt like I was in some kind of strange, hateful no-man's-land. If I had to choose, I thought, it would be easy. Lisa Hutchinson was my kind of people.

'I believed what he told me,' Hanley said. 'I didn't have any reason not to believe him.'

'Do you still believe him?'

'I just don't know.'

I had to like that answer.

'Let me ask you something,' Lisa said, boring in like a prosecutor, 'you've gone to a man's house, right. Things went a certain way and you got carried away and it seemed like a good idea at the time and you wound up in bed. That ever happen to you?'

'Yes.'

'Sure it has. And when you left, were you barefooted?'

'Huh?'

'Did you have shoes on your feet?'

'Of course.'

'Well, I didn't have any shoes on when your boyfriend threw me out of that guest house that night. I remembered that. Because the driveway was covered with old oyster shell and I cut my foot. They bandaged it after they took care of everything else at the emergency room.

'I told Hunt, here, about the shoes. That was later, when he was investigating and trying to decide if I was telling the truth or if I was just after a little publicity or, maybe, a little money.'

Hanley looked over at me and I nodded. 'It's part of the evidence I was telling you about.'

'He found my shoes,' Lisa said. 'You know where?'

Hanley shook her head.

'In the dump. Hunt and a couple of other boys opened a couple of hundred plastic bags full of stinking garbage and found my shoes in one of them, along with a bunch of papers and stuff from that plantation where Vincent was staying. There were even some papers of his in there. Stuff he must have brought down from the office, to read on the plane, and thrown away when he got here.'

Hanley looked at me again and I said, 'That's right.'

'He threw my shoes out with the garbage. Now what do you think about that?'

It took a while, but I got Lisa Hutchinson to agree not to say anything about Barbara Hanley's 'stolen' pistol.

'I'll do it,' she said, when we were outside, 'but I'm doing it for you. Not for her.'

'I appreciate it.'

'You were nice to me. You treated me with respect. Enough, anyway, to check my story out and go looking for them shoes.'

I nodded.

'You even took me out for ribs one night when I was feeling low. So I'll do it for you. But I wouldn't piss on that bitch in there, not even if she was on fire.'

Barbara Hanley also agreed not to tell what she knew – namely, that I was a suspect – but she was doing it for herself, not out of any affection for me. I'd never taken her out to eat ribs.

I didn't care about her motives, I just didn't want her out there beating the tomtoms. I might be a suspect but the cops had not put out any alerts. Probably because they didn't have much to go on and were still investigating. A premature arrest can screw things up and they were content to take their time as long as the press wasn't howling for them to arrest somebody in particular – in this case, me. Barbara Hanley could get the howling started.

But she had agreed to hold off.

'You said you think you know who did it,' she said before she left the shabby little motel room.

'Yes.'

'Can you tell?'

I shook my head.

'Was it Lander White?' she said. 'You had something on him that made him not want to try the case. What better way? He doesn't have to try the case and he doesn't have to withdraw. His reputation is saved.'

'No guessing games,' I said, 'but I'll make you a deal.'

'What kind of deal?'

'I'll tell you first. I won't talk to any reporters or producers or whatever about it. But there's a condition. If I find something that proves Lisa Hutchinson was telling the truth, you have to use that too.'

She looked at me with genuine curiosity.

'Why is that important?' she said.

It was a sincere question. That made her my candidate to finish out Vincent's term in the US senate.

Thirty-four

It was that hour in Washington between the end of the working day and the beginning of the working night. The hour when busy people sneak home to bathe and change and, maybe, get in a little quality time with the kids. Then it is back out for a must-attend reception or dinner somewhere.

'Life in the Imperial City,' Stackhouse said through his teeth. 'The worse things get out in the countryside, the better people like it back here. Figure that one.'

I told him I couldn't.

'Who can? Anyway, you've got other things on your mind.'

'Right.'

'We're going to park in the lot outside the office. I can pick you up from there.'

'Okay.'

'You feel pretty confident about her?'

'Pretty confident,' I said.

'Then this ought to be good.'

We bought coffee, in paper cups, and drank it while we waited in the half-empty lot outside the office building. We were in his Corvette and Stackhouse and I were practically touching shoulders.

'Like being strapped down in the ass end of a Huey,' he said. 'Or a one thirty.'

'Quieter, though,' I said. 'I never did get used to the noise.'

'You just go deaf earlier,' Stackhouse said. 'But that's okay. There's a lot of shit you don't need to hear.'

He reached awkwardly behind the seat and brought up a small, black, canvas bag. Unzipped it and took out a radio receiver and a tape recorder. It was small and slightly sinister looking. Not the sort of radio you would use to tune in the ballgame or a little easy listening music.

'My man snuck in and wired the office last night.'

I nodded.

'And you'll be wearing your own wire. I'm a big believer in backup.'

I nodded again. Stackhouse didn't need for me to say anything. He just wanted some kind of sign that I was listening. He liked talking but he didn't like talking to himself.

'I don't *ever* count on equipment anymore. I don't give a shit what it is, it'll break.'

I did my part and nodded.

'You remember the rescue deal in Teheran, when the ragheads had all our guys in the embassy ...'

Stackhouse talked and sipped coffee. I listened and sipped coffee. We'd done it before. Enough that we'd gotten pretty good at it.

Stackhouse had just finished his coffee when the little black receiver came to life. There were no voices. Only the sound of someone moving paper on a desk and then making a few strokes on a computer keyboard. The sounds of someone working alone.

'Time for you to go to work,' Stackhouse said.

I used phony credentials that Stackhouse had given me to get past the guard. When I knocked on the big oak door, an impatient voice said, 'Come in.'

I opened the door and when Anita Lepage saw me, she said, 'What are *you* doing here?'

'I came to talk to you about Vincent,' I said. 'I was outside that night.'

'What?'

'Part of my job,' I said. 'It's called surveillance.'

'Yes . . .' You could hear the confidence go out of Anita Lepage's voice.

'I watched you go into his room. I thought you were one of his ladies. Slipping in for a quickie . . .'

Lepage made a sound. 'I wasn't his type. By about twenty years.'

'I've got a complete log of your movements,' I said and read off the time of her call to change her airline reservation. The time she checked out of the motel. The time she turned in the rental car, and the time of her flight. It sounded, somehow, incriminating. Even though it was just innocent data that Randolph Atkins had pulled out of his computer and passed along to me. But I was able to make it sound like I'd been following her and I knew everything.

'It's been three days,' she said. 'The funeral is tomorrow. And you haven't told anyone.'

'Not yet. Maybe not ever. I didn't care about him,' I said,

pretty much telling the truth, now. 'He was just another cheap politician to me, only worse. I'm not sorry he's dead.'

She was plenty tough but she wasn't an experienced killer. And the strain was too much. She just had to talk.

'I'm not either,' she said, 'I just wish it didn't have to be me.'

She decided to do it, she said, when she listened to him talking about the Hutchinson woman at a meeting with Lander White, after the bail hearing.

'See, I knew he'd done it. He called me that morning. He was always calling me when there was a mess to clean up. He didn't seem to think it made any difference if the mess was some girl he'd hammered.

'Anyway, I knew, and here he was, calling her all sorts of names. Talking about her like *she* was trash. The lawyers were there. And I was there. And he was holding forth. And I *knew* he was guilty. But we were all sitting there listening to the great man and when he finished, we were expected to rise and go out and do battle to preserve his good name and keep his hold on office even though I knew and I'm pretty sure Lander White and his little helpers knew ... he was exactly what the Hutchinson woman said he was. And worse.'

Well, there was a motive. From her own mouth.

She also let it slip that she despised him for the way he went after younger and younger women.

She had a key to his room. She always did when they were on the road together. Not because she ever got into bed with him. As a matter of fact, she sometimes had to go in and roust him. Now and then, he had to take a pill to sleep and when he did, he was impossible to wake up in the morning.

She knew he'd taken a pill that night. 'He never woke up. But I was shaking and it took four shots before I got one where I wanted it.'

'You took the gun from Barbara Hanley's bag?'

She nodded.

'That morning?'

She nodded again.

'And where did you leave it?' I said.

'In the dumpster,' she said, matter of fact about it, 'behind the motel. I didn't care if they found it. I used gloves and it wasn't mine.'

When I left her office, she was sitting behind her desk, mute and motionless. She didn't ask if I was going to tell the law. She didn't seem to care. She seemed, if anything, astonished that it had all happened and she had done it. Telling me had been a way of making sure she was not going crazy.

When I opened the door to Stackhouse's Corvette, he said, 'Got her ass. Got it absolutely cold.'

He held up a cassette for me to see.

'Man, you were perfect.'

'No,' I said. 'She was just ready. It fell into my lap.'

We copied the tape and sent it by Fed Ex to the State's Attorney's office in Tallahassee. Then we went out and did a little drinking.

Thirty-five

Things, as usual, went off at odd angles. Like fragments from some accidental explosion.

The law in Tallahassee found the gun, in the dumpster which still had not been dumped. But the gun had not been registered to anyone. Or, if it had, the police in Washington had lost the paperwork. Incompetence was good to Barbara Hanley. As far as the record showed, she didn't own a gun.

The State's Attorney issued a warrant for the arrest of Anita Lepage, just the same. Which was when things got interesting.

Lepage recovered. Confession may have been good for her soul but doing time was a different thing. She was penitent enough, she must have thought, without that shit. So she called a lawyer. One of the Washington Dobermanns, a man who is supposed to have said, once, that he liked his clients to be both guilty and rich. Anyone, he said, could get an innocent client acquitted. It was the measure of a real lawyer that his guilty clients walked. The other reason he liked them guilty, he said, was that it kept *him* from feeling guilty when he sent the bill.

'I don't mind taking all of it,' he reportedly said, 'because, without me, they wouldn't have any way to spend it.'

When the Bar huffed and puffed over that statement, which appeared in a flattering profile in the *Washington Post*, the lawyer claimed that he'd been misquoted and, furthermore, not only hadn't he said such a thing, he would never even think it. You could almost see him winking.

Anyway, he instantly got his client out on bail and waged pitiless war against extradition, saying, essentially, 'What evidence?'

There was the tape. But it wasn't admissible. It was a confession that his client had been tricked into giving, when she was in dangerous emotional and psychological shape, by a man who worked for a special prosecutor in the state of Florida. Plainly inadmissible. The lawyer wasn't giving an inch and the early guessing was that Anita Lepage would probably never stand trial. I thought that sounded about right.

'How do you feel about it?' Jessie said. We were sitting on her front porch, peeling shrimp and drinking beer. It was late afternoon. The air was cool and the birds were moving.

'Semmes asked me the same question,' I said. I always hate the question. But I didn't say that.

'What did you tell him?'

'I told him that I wasn't going to lose any sleep over it.'

'You think it's justice?'

'No. But what is?'

'She's not even going on trial.'

'I know. But look at it this way – early in the game, it

looked like Vincent was going to get off and he was guilty.
Well, he paid. And, then it looked like I might be charged
with killing him, and I was asleep when the murder was
done. I was never arrested. There is justice in *that*.'

'Yeah, Morgan, but what about her? She killed that
man.'

'I know she did.'

'She's going to get away with it.'

'Like I told Semmes, he deserved killing.'

She didn't say anything for a while.

'You must have been pretty worried,' she said. 'When
you were driving up to Washington, knowing that the cops
suspected you of killing Vincent.'

'Pretty worried,' I said.

'What would you have done if that Lepage woman hadn't
said those things, on that tape?'

'I'm not sure what my next move would have been.'

'But you weren't going to stand around and let them
take you in, were you?'

'No.'

We had finished with the shrimp and the light was dying
over the river. We went inside and added the freshly peeled
shrimp to the pot of gumbo that was simmering in a large
stew pot on top of the stove. The gumbo, so far, was roux
and stock made from the carcass of a wild turkey I had shot.
Also some okra. Lots of cayenne pepper. Tomato. Onion.
Celery. Green pepper. A couple of crabs and a few
crawfish heads. The shrimp were the last of the main
ingredients. Jessie covered the pot. She would let it simmer
for another hour.

Then she would serve it to Nat Semmes and his wife

Bobbie, who had been invited for dinner. The gumbo smelled good.

'That turkey stock, man,' Jessie said, 'it's some kind of rich. It's going to be a righteous gumbo, Morgan. Plain righteous.'

'Smells like it.'

'If you ran away, you probably wouldn't be sitting down to eat gumbo with friends. You'd be hiding out. Eating your supper out of cans and such.'

I nodded.

'I got to go take a bath,' she said. 'Change clothes.'

I went back outside. Watched the last light bleed away, leaving a purple sky which slowly became black. I listened to the deep, constant sounds of the river and the first calls of the night birds. It was a peaceful evening. Nice, if you like that sort of thing.

For most people, though, it just isn't enough. That's where the trouble starts, and has always started.

It just isn't enough.

THE JIGSAW MAN

The compelling thriller from the author of
LOSERS, WEEPERS

DEANIE FRANCIS MILLS

'DEANIE MILLS' WRITING IS SWIFT,
SUSPENSEFUL, INVOLVING AND
UNPREDICTABLE' Dean Koontz

Gypsy Halden is deaf. She's been deaf since the
night the Jigsaw Man killed her mother and
bludgeoned Gypsy into perpetual silence. Now
she is dependent on the signing skills of her
little daughter and the support of her loving
husband. But John Halden has suddenly
disappeared and not even his colleagues in the
Intelligence Division of the Dallas police
department can tell her where he is.

All Gypsy knows is that she is on her own with
a small child to protect and a missing husband
to find. And out there, watching her every
move, is the man who has dogged her through
life, waiting for the kill – the Jigsaw Man . . .

FICTION / THRILLER 0 7472 5095 2

DANGEROUS ATTACHMENTS

A silent watcher in the dark . . .

Sarah Lovett

Psychologist Sylvia Strange is called to New Mexico's male prison to evaluate a convicted murderer seeking parole. But, after deciding that Lucas Watson is seriously disturbed, she cannot recommend his release.

That's where her nightmare begins . . .

Watson is the son of an influential politician, and soon Sylvia finds herself exposed to personal harassment. At first she reckons that Lucas himself is somehow responsible – so when he is dramatically removed from the scene, surely her life will return to normal?

Except it doesn't.

All around her, events spin out of control. Her good friend Rosie, prison investigator, has to cope with a mythical inmate called 'the jackal' who hideously amputates body parts from other human beings – both dead and alive . . . A professional associate is bludgeoned to death in his bath tub . . . And Sylvia finds herself reluctantly attracted to a brash police officer.

As she struggles with her investigations through the bitter cold of a desert winter, a shocking tale of family secrets, obscene murder and diabolic obsession unfolds.

FICTION / THRILLER 0 7472 4616 5

A selection of bestsellers from Headline